THE HALFADAY CREEK SERIES BY
JAMES B. HENDRYX

Skullduggery on Halfaday Creek
The Saga of Halfaday Creek
Badmen on Halfaday Creek
Adventures on Halfaday Creek
Hell's-a-Poppin' on Halfaday Creek

Visit www.jamesbhendryx.com for more information on
forthcoming installments in the Halfaday Creek
uniform matching series.

BADMEN ON HALFADAY CREEK

James B Hendryx

BADMEN ON HALFADAY CREEK

JAMES B. HENDRYX

ILLUSTRATIONS BY
PETE KUHLHOFF

INTRODUCTION BY
GARYN G. ROBERTS, Ph.D.

ALTUS PRESS • 2014

© 2013 Altus Press • First Edition—2014

EDITED AND DESIGNED BY
Matthew Moring

SERIES EXECUTIVE CONSULTANT
Richard Hall

PUBLISHING HISTORY
"Literature of the Great Northwest; or, James B. Hendryx and the Academy" copyright © 2014 by Garyn G. Roberts, Ph.D.
"Black John Pays a Debt" originally appeared in the June 10, 1947 issue of *Short Stories* magazine (vol. 200, no. 5). Reprinted by arrangement with the Estate of James B. Hendryx.
"Justice–and the Law" originally appeared in the December 25, 1947 issue of *Short Stories* magazine (vol. 202, no. 6). Reprinted by arrangement with the Estate of James B. Hendryx.
"Profit on Halfaday" originally appeared in the March 10, 1947 issue of *Short Stories* magazine (vol. 199, no. 5). Reprinted by arrangement with the Estate of James B. Hendryx.
"The Partnership Business" originally appeared in the August 10, 1947 issue of *Short Stories* magazine (vol. 201, no. 3). Reprinted by arrangement with the Estate of James B. Hendryx.
"Slight Misunderstanding on Halfaday" originally appeared in the February 10, 1948 issue of *Short Stories* magazine (vol. 203, no. 3). Reprinted by arrangement with the Estate of James B. Hendryx.
"Conspiracy on Halfaday" originally appeared in the May 25, 1947 issue of *Short Stories* magazine (vol. 200, no. 4). Reprinted by arrangement with the Estate of James B. Hendryx.
"Who Can Write Fiction?" originally appeared in October 1942 issue of *The Writer*. Reprinted by arrangement with the Estate of James B. Hendryx.

THANKS TO
Everard P. Digges LaTouche, Robert Loomis, Richard Moore, Rick Ollerman, Cynthia Whyte, & the Leelanau Historical Society

TABLE OF CONTENTS

LITERATURE OF THE GREAT NORTHWEST; OR, JAMES B. HENDRYX AND THE ACADEMY

GARYN G. ROBERTS, PH.D.

JOHN GRIFFITH "JACK" LONDON (1876 to 1916) has long been considered part of "The Academy"; his work is deemed "canonical" and Literature with an upper case "L." So, too, have been Ernest Miller Hemingway (1899 to 1961) and his writing. In some ways, these labels and categorizations are just; in other cases they are the results of highly subjective value judgments or aesthetics.

Let's be honest. The works of London, and particularly Hemingway, sometimes were and are downright pedestrian. And, if academics are honest with themselves, they have to admit that the adventure and action of these authors' tales and social critiques are what often carry these authors' stories. Never mind the fact that they are very approachable and easily read at a middle school or junior high level.

So, there is a great deal to admire in the works of Jack London and Ernest Hemingway, and there is a percentage of the same with which we need to "get real." Larger-than-life adventurers who drew heavily on autobiography for their story content, and who contributed to the literary schools of "Realism" and Natu-ralism," these two authors were conversely romanticized and lived lives of "Romance." Like William F. "Buffalo Bill" Cody, their reputations became highly fantasized and fictionalized over time.

Having studied the life and works of Jack London for aca-demic purposes for several years—again, because he and they were considered canonical and acceptable for intellectual inquiry and discourse—I have read, studied and written about the majority of works of Jack London. I admire much of the same. *The Iron Heel* (1908), *The Scarlet Plague* (1912), and *The Star Rover* (1915) are political commentary clothed in rather superficial, uninspired Scientific Romance, later in 1929 to be deemed "Science Fiction." Of the three, *The Iron Heel* is the most ambitious and revered. *John Barleycorn* (1913) is a straight, tragic autobiographical account of London's life-long struggle with alcoholism. (This was published near the end of the author's life as a passionate plea against "Demon Rum.") London's novel, *Martin Eden* (1909), a mix of autobiography and metaphor, makes for interesting comparison to Herman Melville's novella, "Billy Budd" (1888, 1924) and to Kate Chopin's *The Awakening* (1899). For my money, London's best work is *The Sea Wolf* (1904).

There were other authors of the early twentieth century who produced realistic, naturalistic and existential literature—and their romantic counterparts—but London and Hemingway are two of the best known and celebrated from this era.

Dramatic, early deaths—both self-inflicted, though London's passing is shrouded in a little more mystery than Hemingway's—defined these guys. And maybe more than a little perversely, some people applauded their respective ends—ends that engendered romantic, exaggerated mythologies and celebrity statuses. London and Hemingway lived hard and fast lives, and their legacies, unfortunately, are often defined by their deaths. Would Jack London and Ernest Hemingway be celebrated as they are yet today in the Academy had they expired in their sleep of old age? Most certainly not. Yet do we then categorically discard the lives and works of these two revered scribes as uninspired fare? No. However, we need to put them into perspective, into a realistic context and understand that they had peers who at times could be as good as, and sometimes even better than, these "masters" at the types and genres of fiction for which they were best known and are remembered.

One such peer was James B(eardsley) Hendryx.

As we read the volumes of Hendryx's work presented, and to be presented, by Altus Press over the next few years—an ambitious project in excellent hands that I personally hope will go on and on—we will note that James B. Hendryx was the most real, the most informed, the most prolific and best Adventure writer of the twentieth century. Controversial statement? Maybe not as much as it first appears—and accurate. Comparisons to the nineteenth century's Jules Gabriel Verne (1828 to 1905, who wrote many more Adventure stories than Scientific Romances) and H(enry) Rider Haggard (1856 to 1925) are not out of line. Of course, the semantics of the term "Adventure" are an important consideration in this evaluation. "Adventure" can be as broadly defined as can "Fantasy" and "Fiction." Here, however, Adventure is defined more narrowly to include rollicking exploits of heroes and villains in exotic, but still real and even historic locales. Extremes in climate and perils of wilderness mark this type of Adventure story. While the genre is not neatly defined by specific parameters, it is characterized by specific settings and character types; lawlessness and laws of nature; makeshift moralities and justices; and life and death struggles.

James Hendryx, best known for rousing tales of the Canadian Northwest and Alaskan frontiers, wrote and published at a time when real-life western frontiers were still very much open. Hendryx's prose was consistently even, and interesting. (London and Hemingway's writing was not consistently even or interesting.) He knew how to develop characters, set vivid atmospheres without overdoing their descriptions (unlike James Fenimore Cooper), and move his storylines along. He was prolific, in a good way, and he was a master of the short story, serial and novel alike. His writing worked very well in hardcover and paperback reprint collections worldwide—collections that have been out of print for decades. His original pulp magazine appearances and book publications command some pretty hefty prices in the collectors' markets. Hendryx's prose usually first appeared in pulps magazines, including *Argosy, Adventure, Short Stories, Dime Western* and *New Western.*

In the first half of the twentieth century—and more specifically the 20s, 30s and 40s—when James Hendryx was busiest as a writer, other authors of Adventure tales had specialized tracts. Some wrote Foreign Legion stories, others of the mysterious Orient, some of the high seas, and still others of darkest Africa. And others wrote, like Hendryx, of the Great Northwest. Perhaps the author with whom Hendryx is most often compared is his fellow Michigan resident, James Oliver Curwood (1878–1927). Hendryx lived from 1880 to 1963. Both were excellent and highly successful storytellers, but there are some marked distinctions between their two styles.[1]

Curwood's writing was Romanticism, Romantic, and Romance in every sense of the terms. He lived in the Curwood Castle—a real castle on the riverbanks of Owosso, Michigan. Today, the Curwood Castle houses the James Oliver Curwood Museum. Curwood, like Hendryx, experienced the great northwest firsthand and wrote about what he knew personally. James Oliver Curwood was a master of rousing adventure, but he also liked to lapse into melodrama—what we would later call "soap opera." Sometimes Curwood would leave the tale of the dramatic dogsled pursuit (good guys chasing bad, or vice versa) and turn to a story of young love (often between two rather

---

1 Pulp magazine fans and scholars have historically created comparisons of authors, main characters, and magazines. Private Eye aficionados have compared the detective fiction of Dashiell Hammett and Raymond Chandler for years; Avenger fans debate the Shadow and the Spider; fantasy fans consider *Weird Tales* and *Unknown Worlds;* science fiction fans wrestle with *Amazing Stories* and *Astounding Stories;* and so on. So, a comparison of Curwood and Hendryx is natural. Such analyses at their best do not discard one for another. Rather they celebrate variant forms and are inclusive as opposed to exclusive. (Hint: Based on this essay, it is obvious that I believe both Curwood and Hendryx were wonderful storytellers, and we should read both. But forced with a choice, I choose JBH.)

helpless people on the frontier for the first time). Curwood wrote wonderful stories of the Canadian Mounted, and two excellent volumes by this author are the novel, *The Valley of the Silent Men* (1920), and the short story collection, *Back to God's Country* (1920). There are others.[2]

James B. Hendryx wrote multiple story series. Characters, settings and storylines of these series often overlap in tales of varying lengths. (There are six Halfaday Creek and at least six Connie Morgan novels alone.) Recurring characters appear in adventures of Corporal Downey, Connie Morgan, and Black John Smith of Halfaday Creek. Corporal Downey is a Mountie, Connie Morgan an adolescent hero. Black John is a rough-sawn rogue who circumvents the law to uphold a higher moral code that may or may not dovetail with the law. He is the mediator of the colorful and varied outlaws of the frontier outpost called Halfaday Creek. Based on photos of Hendryx, existing biographical material and folklore, it is clear that Black John shares more than a few passing character traits with Hendryx. Both Black John and Hendryx were rugged individualists, shrewd frontiersmen, who possessed physical strength, keen intellects, uncommon common sense, a gentle humor and a kind disposition under a grizzled exterior.

James Beardsley Hendryx was born December 9, 1880 in Sauk Centre, Minnesota—about 100 miles northwest of the Twin Cities. His father, Charles, owned *The Sauk Centre Herald;* his mother was a granddaughter of United States President William Henry Harrison. Hendryx enjoyed hunting and fishing from an early age, and his childhood friends were Claude and Red (later Sinclair) Lewis—the famous writer. Hendryx's early years were spent as a newspaper reporter and a hardware salesman; he also sold insurance, worked for a tannery in Kentucky

---

2   An excellent survey and reprint collection of Canadian Mountie stories from the pulps is Don Hutchison's *Scarlet Riders: Pulp Fiction Stories of the Mounties* (1998). Curwood's *Steele of the Royal Mounted* (1911) is also a noteworthy Canadian Mountie saga.

and was a bookkeeper for a sheep-shearing company. He worked as a newspaperman in Cincinnati, and on cattle ranches in Montana and Saskatchewan. In 1898, James and a friend journeyed north to be part of the Gold Rush.

Hendryx's first novel, *The Promise,* was published in 1915. He married Hermione Flagler (1888-1967), of Boston, in Cincinnati on October 27, 1915. Hermoine was a professionally schooled and highly talented musician. They had three children: Hermione (b. 1918), James (1919) and Betty (1921). Betty, the last survivor, died in Fredericksburg, VA in 2009. For many years, Hendryx and his wife split their time between their homes in Canada and northwestern Lower Michigan—specifically the Grand Traverse/Suttons Bay area, populated three and four centuries ago by natives and French missionaries and explorers. James B. Hendryx published some 50 novels in his lifetime, and hundreds of short stories. At least as much as London and Hemingway, Hendryx lived what he wrote. He died on March 1, 1963 in Munson Hospital of Traverse City.[3]

These are the Hendryx family authorized editions. As you read these stories, you will be reading my *all-time* favorite Adventure writer, no small endorsement indeed—James B. Hendryx.[4]

---

3   Personal Note: My wife, Virginia Woods Roberts, was the Director of the Suttons Bay Public Library from 2005 to 2012. Here, she met people who knew and had fond memories of local resident, James B. Hendryx. One gentleman (in his late 80s) often recounted real-life adventures with his friend, JBH, from their joint days working for *The Traverse City Record Eagle.* The pair used to travel back and forth along Highway 22 from Suttons Bay to Traverse City (along a stretch of north/south coast of Lake Michigan). A few signed Hendryx books are available as collectables for sale in the Traverse City area—most notably, Dog Ears Books of Northport.

4   James B. Hendryx letters, manuscripts, and related papers and materials are archived at the James B. Hendryx Collection of the Leelanau Historical Society (Leland, Michigan). Also included in this collection is original black and white interior artwork created for pulp magazine publications of Hendryx's work.

BLACK JOHN PAYS A DEBT

BLACK JOHN SMITH was dimly conscious of a vast discomfort. His head ached, there was a terrific throbbing at his temples, and a continuous thumping against his back. He opened his eyes which smarted so that he closed them again. His chest was heaving and as he coughed and retched a deluge of water cascaded from between his parted lips. The monotonous thumping continued, and again he opened his eyes and blinked in the dim half light that surrounded him. Gradually his brain cleared and his vision penetrated the gloom. He sought to move his legs and succeeded only in wriggling helplessly. His arms hung straight down from his shoulders, and a little stream of water trickled from the fingertips of each hand and sank into wet gravel a foot below. A wall of wet gravel loomed before his face.

The thumping continued. Again he coughed and retched, and more water poured from between his lips. His brain was functioning now, and as he oriented himself he realized that he was hanging suspended by his feet in a shaft. Twisting his head, he could see a pair of feet on the wet floor of the shaft behind him. He was breathing heavily now, sucking air into his tortured lungs in great gasps. Suddenly he realized that someone was standing behind him thumping his back with a pair of fists. But—how could this be? Where was he—and why?

Striving mightily to concentrate, he remembered paddling easily down the Yukon holding close inshore to avoid the floating ice cakes and the numerous floating trees and logs that dotted the surface of the river swollen by the spring flood. The sun was low, he remembered thinking it was time to look for a place to camp. But—damn that everlasting thumping on his back!

"Quit that!" he called, in a voice meant to be a roar, but which sounded in his own ears like a hollow croak. Reaching behind him, he grasped an ankle, and a voice sounded in his ears.

"Leggo! Leggo! So you've come to! Leggo an' I'll let you down an' git you outa here!"

He released his grip on the ankle. There was a scrambling sound behind him, a shower of dislodged gravel, the creak of a windlass, and his hands were lowered to the gravel. As the windlass continued to creak and his face neared the bottom of the shaft he strove to ease himself down, but his arms seemed devoid of strength, his face rooted into the wet gravel, and as the creaking ceased he collapsed in a heap on the floor of the shaft. Another shower of dislodged gravel, and a small man stood beside him, tugging and pulling to help him to his feet.

"Yer all right now. By God, yer all right—jest like I figgered, if I ever got you drug over here. Hold on now—take it easy an' I'll pass this here rope around in under yer arms an' haul you outa here. It ain't no hell of a deep shaft an' when I git you cranked up, I'll chock the win'lass an' git you over to the cabin. Mebbe you kin walk by then. Yer hell to drag—yer that hefty."

The man scrambled up a loose rope, the windlass creaked, the rope tightened about Black John's chest and slowly he was raised to the mouth of the shaft, where by dint of much maneuvering with some loose planks and poles, and no little exertion on his own behalf, he found himself standing on the bank of a small creek a short distance up from its mouth. In the twilight he could see the waters of the mighty Yukon flowing sullenly toward the sea, its surface dotted with cakes of floating ice. "Lay yer arm acrost my shoulders an' I'll help you to the cabin," the little man said, stepping close.

Black John made no move and continued to stare toward the river. "What—what happened?" he asked, coughing, and closing his eyes as the world seemed to spin dizzily.

"What happened! By God, you damn near got drownded! That's what happened! Lucky I was standing there by the spring an' seen it. I seen yer canoe slidin' along nice an' fast like, an' jest when you was passin' the mouth of the crick here, a hell of a big tree, which musta be'n comin' down the crick on the flood an' hit the gravel bar, r'ared up outa the water with its limbs a-thrashin' around, an' I seen a big limb ketch you right plumb on the top of the head—an' then fer a minute I didn't see nothin'. I dropped my pail, which I'd went to the spring fer some water, an' I run along the shore, an' yer paddle was floatin' alongside the tree, an' yer canoe come up all smashed to hell, an' then you come up an' I jumped in an' swum out there an' got holt of yer shirt collar an' swum to shore. You'd drifted quite a piece down-river by then. I hauled you out on that there gravel strip down by them three spruce trees. If I hadn't of got you out there, by God, we'd of both got drownded, 'cause it's only high rocks an' nowheres to land fer a couple of mile downriver."

THE BIG man's eyes rested on the narrow strip of shingle that terminated abruptly a short distance below in a high rock wall, and shifted to the little man's face. "How come you'd take a chanct of haulin' me ashore when you know'd damn well if you got swept past that strip of gravel you wouldn't have a chanct? Hell—I wasn't nothin' to you."

"No," the little man replied, "you wasn't nothin' to me—an' you ain't, now. But by God, *I'm* somethin' to me!"

"What?"

"Like this here—s'pose I run along the gravel there, like I done, an' seen you come up, an' I look ahead an' see them rocks, an' seen how if I hurried an' was lucky mebbe I could haul you out—an' then I didn't do it. Tonight when I'd got to bed an' the light blow'd out an' I'd got to thinkin' about it, I'd have to say, 'Damn you, Emory, you mighta saved that man—an' you never even tried it!' An' in the mornin' when I woke up it would be the same thing, 'Damn you, Emory, you never tried to save him!' An' the next night—an' every night, an' every mornin', an' lots of times in the daytime. I'd know I was a damn coward. An' I hate a coward. What kinda way is that fer a man to live all the rest of his life—layin' there hatin' hisself?"

Black John's gaze met the upturned blue eyes squarely. "I guess you've got somethin' there, Emory," he said. "But go on—what's the rest of it?"

"The rest of it? Hell—there ain't no rest of it. I done it—an' I made the gravel, jest like I figgered I might."

"Yeah—but that don't put me hangin' by my feet in that shaft."

"Oh—that! Well you see, when I'd got you drug up on the gravel, I seen how you was practically drownded if I couldn't git the water outa you. I heard about rollin' drownded folks over a bar'l—but I didn't have no bar'l. An' I've heard how a man kin git holt of a man's ankles an' bend his knees over yer shoulders an' then trot up an' down with the man hangin' head down along yer back, an' jolt the water outa him that way. But cripes, the man that's doin' it has got to be bigger than the drownded man, er it wouldn't work. Like if I'd tried it on you, yer head would of drug an' bumped along on the rocks an' the gravel, an' likely wore all yer hair off, er busted yer skull, er somethin'. But I had to figger some way to git the water outa you, an' I happen to think of this here shaft an' win'lass, so I drug you over here, an' tied the rope around yer ankles, an' chocked the win'lass, an' shoved you in the shaft. Then I lowered you fer enough down so's I could stand on the bottom an' thump on yer back an' knock the water outa you—an' by God, she worked! Good thing that shaft an' win'lass was here, an' the rope hadn't rotted, ain't it?"

BLACK JOHN nodded. "Yeah," he agreed, "a mighty good thing fer me. But you say it's a good thing the windlass was here, an' the rope hadn't rotted—ain't this your layout, your windlass, an' your rope?"

"Well, it's kinda mine—an' then agin, it ain't. I ain't no pros-

pector. I'm a trapper. But come on over to the cabin. I'll cook supper, an' you better git them wet clothes off an' dried out. You might ketch cold."

In the cabin Black John's clothing was hung up to dry and he sat Indian fashion, wrapped in a blanket. After supper, the little man produced tobacco, and both filled their pipes. "You say this place is kinda yours, an' then again it ain't," Black John reminded him. "What do you mean by that? An' you say your name's Emory—Emory what?"

"Emory Twiddle. I come from Walker, Minnesoty. It's on Leach Lake. I usta trap in the winter, an' in the summer I worked fer Sam Clark, which he's got some cabins on a little bay, an' he rents 'em out, an' he rents boats to folks that comes up to go fishin'. An' in the fall he rents the cabins to duck hunters an' deer hunters.

"They's Injuns up there—Pillagers, mostly—an' seems like city folks likes to come some place where they's Injuns, so's they kin look at 'em, an' buy baskets an' stuff off'n 'em.

"Sam, he was doin' all right, till couple year ago the Injuns upriz an' killed some solgers on Sugar P'int. I know'd most of the Injuns on the reservation—stopped with 'em when I'd be trappin', along the shore an' over on Bear Island. And, they was good folks. If you'd come along there hungry, an' even if they didn't have nothin' but a rabbit, er a owl, er mebbe a couple of little pups to throw in the stew, you was welcome to your share, same as the rest.

"Flat Mouth an' Moose Dung, they was the chiefs, an' they was fine men. An' if I'd of be'n them I'd of upriz, too. It's on account of them contractors an' a crooked Injun agent—the contractors payin' the Gov'ment fer to cut dead an' down timber on the reservation, an' then goin' in there an' slashin' into the standin' timber.

"**FLAT MOUTH** an' Moose Dung kicked to the agent, but he wouldn't do nothin' about it on account them damn contractors was payin' him not to. So the Injuns upriz, an' the Gov'ment sent some solgers up there—which they wasn't nothin' but some parade solgers from Boston—an' they hired a tug name of *The Chief*, to take 'em up the lake to Sugar P'int where the Injuns was camped near. They landed on the p'int, which it was a long p'int that stuck out in the lake without no trees on it, an' started marchin' up the p'int to the woods where the Injuns was camped in. An' the Injuns took some shots at 'em an' killed five, six solgers, an' the rest got scairt an' dug little ditches in the sand an' laid down in 'em, an' kep' a-shootin' into the woods till they wasted all their shells, an' never seen a damn Injun—an' never hit none, neither. They laid there fer two days, afraid to git out of their trenches—even to eat their grub. But there wasn't no Injun within ten mile of 'em after that first shootin'—they all snuck away in the woods.

"Then *The Chief* come an' took the solgers back to Walker—an' that's all they was to the Pillager War, because the Gov'ment sent a man up there name of General Scott, which he savvied Injuns, an' he went out an' talked to Flat Mouth an' Moose Dung an' found out what the trouble was, an' he fired that crooked agent off'n the reservation, an' put one on there that was claimed to be honest—an' they ain't be'n no trouble sense.

"But Sam Clark, he didn't savvy the Injuns, an' when the trouble started he got scairt an' moved into Walker till it was over. He'd come from St. Paul, an' he was still scairt an' tried to sell out his land an' cabins an' boats, but no one wanted to buy 'em but me—an' I didn't have no money. Sam, he wanted six thousan' dollars fer the layout, an' I seen where it would be worth more'n that in a few years, so I tried to borry the money from the bank, but they wouldn't loan it to me on account they claimed that what with the Injun scare folks would stay away from Leach Lake fer years. But I scraped up five hundred dollars an' give it to Sam an' a lawyer draw'd up an option—which it give me two years to pay the other five thousan' five hundred.

"If trappin' had of be'n good that winter I could of paid damn near all of it, an' the rest the next winter—but it worn't. I'd heard about this Klondike, so when I seen how I couldn't never trap enough in the time I had, I come up here to try an' dig me some gold. I tried it a while on some cricks, but I couldn't find none to speak of, so I worked fer a while fer the British-American outfit on Bonanza. But I seen where I'd never save up enough outa my wages, so I quit an' went to trappin'. I got till this fall to pay Sam off—but I ain't goin' to make it. This here ain't a bad trappin' crick. I got a couple of trap camps up the crick an' I seen this cabin was empty, so I ask Mr. Gaudet down to Ogilvie if anyone lived here, an' if not, could I move in? An' he says a fella name of Curley built it an' worked the claim here till he found it worn't no good, an' was jest about to move out an' hunt some other location, when he got ketched in a ice jam early this spring an' got squorshed in the ice. So I moved in. It's a good cabin—better than them trap camps I got up the crick— so I stay here, an' make my rounds about onct in ten days."

"You say you ain't goin' to make it? Ain't goin' to have enough, come fall, to pay this Sam Clark? How much you short?"

"I'll be about three thousan' short, I figger. But even if I had the three thousan', I'd need damn nigh that much agin to fix the place up right. Them cabins an' boats has be'n layin' idle fer a couple of years, an' they're goin' to need overhaulin', an' over- haulin' costs money. Then I figgered on puttin' up some more cabins. Folks'll fergit about them uprisin' Injuns by now, an' they'll be goin' back there 'cause there's damn good fishin' an' huntin', too. I could of made money if I could of swung it. If I could git hold of about ten thousan', I'd be rich in ten year."

"You got a canoe I can rent to go to Dawson in?" Black John asked.

"I wouldn't charge a man no rent fer a canoe when he had bad luck," the other said. "I'd loan you my canoe, but I need it to go up the crick. Tell you what I'll do, I'll paddle you down to Dawson, an' that way I kin fetch the canoe back."

"But hell, man—it's twenty mile to Dawson! Look at the

time you'll waste—besides the hard work."

"I won't be wastin' much time. It wouldn't make no difference nohow. I ain't goin' to make enough to pay Sam—so there ain't no hurry about the traps." He rose and put on his cap. "I'm a-goin' out now an' cut some wood fer the mornin' so's we kin git an early start."

AS THE man talked Black John noticed a section of puncheon in the floor next the wall that showed evidence of having been removed. The lamplight slanted across it just at the right angle to show that the crack between it and the next puncheon was free, while all the others were packed with dirt. Picking up his knife, he pried the puncheon loose and peered into a small aperture. It was empty. He replaced the puncheon and grinned. "Thought mebbe this Curley might of left some dust in his cache when he got killed," he said, and slipped between the blankets.

The two got an early start the following morning and toward the middle of the afternoon drew the canoe ashore near the wharf in Dawson.

"Come on up to the Tivoli an' I'll buy a drink," Black John invited.

"Well, I ain't no hand to drink," the little man replied, "but I guess one wouldn't hurt none."

"Prob'ly not," the big man grinned, and led the way to the saloon. When the glasses were drained, he shoved the bottle toward the other. "A man can't walk on one leg," he said. "Have another."

But the little man declined. "No. One's enough fer me. I don't like it much. It feels kinda hottish goin' down—an' after it gits there, too. A man might burn his guts out."

Black John nodded solemnly. "Yeah, he might, at that. There's be'n times when I fancied I heard mine sizzle. Come on—let's step over to the bank a minute."

Stepping to the window Black John busied himself for a few

minutes, then turned to the little man who waited near the door. Stepping up to him he extended a hand in which was a neat packet of bills. "Here you are," he said, with a smile. "Here's that ten thousan' that'll set you up in that boat an' cabin business back there in Minnesota."

The little man's face flushed slightly, and he backed away. "What do you mean—ten thousan'?" he asked.

"Why that's what you said you needed, ain't it? Here it is. I'm givin' it to you. I figger my life is worth a damn sight more'n that."

"You mean—yer tryin' to *pay me?* Pay me fer savin' yer life?"

"Why, shore. Take it, an' welcome."

The flush deepened. "You go to hell!"

Black John stared at the man in surprise. "Do you know who I am?" he asked.

"No. An' I don't give a damn! If the shoe'd be'n on the other foot—if you'd saved me from drownin' would you of took pay fer it?"

"Why—"

"Not no why, or but, or if," the little man interrupted. "Would you?"

"Well—no. But—"

"Well—I'm jest as good a man as you be—no matter who you be! An' to hell with yer money!" With which dictum, he turned on his heel, and disappeared out the door, leaving Black

John standing there in the bank holding the ten thousand dollars in his hand. "Well—I'll be damned," he muttered, when he had recovered from his surprise. Shoving the money into his pocket he returned to the Tivoli. "Mebbe them damn sourdoughs can take this away from me playin' stud."

II

OLD CUSH, PROPRIETOR of Cushing's Fort, the combined trading post and saloon that served the little community of outlawed men that had grown up on Halfaday Creek, hard against the Yukon-Alaska border, folded the month-old newspaper he had been reading, placed it carefully on the back bar, shoved the square-framed, steel-rimmed spectacles from nose to forehead, and set out two glasses, a bottle, and a leather dice box as Black John stepped into the room and crossed to the bar. The big man picked up the box and cast the dice, failing to get better than a pair of sixes in three shakes. Cush promptly beat them, and threw four fives in one, which Black John failed to beat. Cush made an entry in his day book as the big man filled his glass.

"What's the news down along the river?"

"Not much. Downey's off on some patrol, an' most of the sourdoughs is busy on the cricks."

Cush filled his own glass and jerked a thumb toward the folded newspaper. "Well, I see by the paper where the British has got them damn Boers licked, at last. Looks like it took 'em a hell of a while to do it. Cripes, accordin' to what the papers has be'n printin' them Boers wasn't nothin' but a bunch of farmers, nowhow."

"Yeah—but you got to remember, them farmers was fightin' on their own home ground. Hell, that's all the Americans was in the Revolutionary war—an' the British never did lick us."

"Looks like them British would have better luck if they done their fightin' closter to home. What was they fightin' them Boers fer, anyhow—way down there in Afriky?"

"Gold, diamonds, good farmin' land—three damn good reasons fer startin' a war."

"How come them Boers is down there in Afriky? Accordin' to the papers they're some kind of Dutchmens, like. But accordin' to what we learnt in g'og'fy, this here Afriky is nigger country."

"Yeah, the Boers are Dutchmen. They went down there an' run the niggers out, an' took over that good farmin' land."

"They ain't got no kick comin', then, if the British runs them out. That's a hell of a way to do, though, when you stop to think about it—one country startin' a war to grab off what some other country's got. By God, you wouldn't ketch the U.S. doin' no sech dirty trick."

Black John grinned broadly. "This here geography you claim to have learnt wasn't mixed in with no hell of a lot of hist'ry, was it?"

"How do you mean?"

"Well—who was the original inhabitants of the United States?"

"Why—Siwashes was."

"An' how did we git it from the Siwashes?"

"Dickered with 'em, an' then made treaties, an' bought it off'n 'em—that's what the hist'ry claims."

"Oh shore—but they forgot to put in that the Government never give the Siwashes more'n a cent for every hundred dollars worth of land they bargained for—an' then broke damn near every treaty, at that. An' when they couldn't get it by treaty—they sent the army out an' took the land away from 'em. An' what's the United States doin' in the Philippines, right now?"

"Hell—they're kind of niggers like, an' we're civilizin' 'em!"

"Yeah—with Krags, an' whiskey, an' Bibles. An' when we've got 'em civilized, we'll be importin' their sugar, an' hemp, an' cocoanuts an' whatever else they got that we want, duty free—

and' shippin''em soap, an' baseballs, an' toothbrushes at a damn good profit to pay for these items. It kind of amuses me to hear Americans criticizin' the British fer fightin' the Boers when we done the same damn thing to the Siwashes, an' are doin' the same thing to the Philippinos, right now."

"Somehow, it don't look right," Cush opined.

"Ethically—usin' the word as applied to individuals—it wouldn't be right. But in the concept of nations, the word 'might' has be'n substituted fer the word 'right'—so you see, that makes it all might."

"'Tain't right, nohow," Cush affirmed, with conviction. "Lookit—if some big guy jumps onto some little guy an' robs him—what happens? He goes to jail, if they kin ketch him—that's what happens. What makes it any righter if some country does that, instead of some guy?"

The big man's grin broadened. "I've often wondered," he said and glanced out through the open doorway. "Drink up—here comes someone."

STEPPING THROUGH the doorway, a man crossed the floor as Cush set out another glass and shoved the bottle toward him. "Fill up," he invited. "This un's on the house."

As the stranger stood a rifle against the bar and elevated a foot to the brass rail his glance shifted from the speaker to the big man who stood beside him.

"This here is Cushing's Fort, an' you must be Black John Smith, ain't you?" he asked.

"It is. An' I must," the big man replied, his shrewd gray eyes taking in the unkempt red mustache, the stubble of red beard, and the mop of red hair that showed beneath the visor of the battered plush cap.

"That's what I figgered," the man said, as he grasped the bottle in a hand mottled with huge brown freckles and filled his glass to the brim. "Hell of a place to git to, ain't it?"

"From where?"

"Why—from the river—the Yukon. Where the hell would a man be comin' from? Feller in Dawson told me how to git here. Claimed he know'd you."

"Yeah?"

"Yeah. Cuter Malone, his name is. Runs the Klondike Palace. Cuter, he figgered he was doin' you a favor, 'cause if I like it here, I aim to jine up with yer gang."

Reaching for the bottle Black John filled his own glass. "Sech favors as Cuter has heretofore conferred on us ain't always be'n onmixed blessin's, as the Good Book says. What's yer qualifications?"

"What's my which?"

"Oh—professor of English, eh?"

"Hell, no! I ain't no professor, no more'n what I ain't no Englishman, neither. My name's Conway—Pete Conway. You prob'ly heard about me."

Black John shook his head. "No, the name has an onfamiliar ring to it. I'm afraid, Pete, yer fame ain't penetrated to these parts."

"You talk like some kind of a lawyer, er somethin'—not that lawyers ain't all right. It was a lawyer, an' a damn good one, that got me off, down there in Dawson! I figgered I was a goner when old John Law laid the finger on me—an' I would of be'n, too, hadn't be'n fer my mouthpiece findin' where some clerk in the prosecutor's office made some kind of mistake makin' out the papers. Boy, was that cop burnt up when my case was throw'd out an' I walk out past him an' give him the grin! He's a kind of a smart cop, at that—Downey, his name is. He's a Mounted, you've prob'ly heard tell of him."

"Yeah," Black John replied, "seems to me I've heard the name mentioned down along the river. I take it you're more or less a stranger in these parts."

"That's right. I come from the States—Chicago an' St. Louie, mostly. I'm a kind of an all around guy—heister, gum shoe worker, peterman—an' I'm doin' all right till this spring when a young punk I'm breakin' in gets picked up an' instead of clammin' it, he opens up an' spills his guts. Not only he names off enough jobs I've pulled to keep me in the can fer the long stretch—but he belches all my hideouts an' spots, so when a flattie I'm greasin' plenty slips me the word about this song the punk sung, there ain't nothin' fer me to do but blow. I hits fer the coast an' hears about all the gold they're diggin' up here, in the Klondike, so I come on up, figgerin' to git in on some of it."

"Has the venture met with success?"

"You mean have I had any luck at it? Well, I pulls this here job on Bonanza. I hang around Malone's an' hear how they're takin' out plenty of gold on this here Bonanza Crick, so I hits up there an' moves in on a claim which a couple of guys has abandoned on account they figgered it had petered out. I done a little work there fer a blind whilst I was lookin' around. There's a guy a couple of claims below me that's doin' all right, an' I gits acquainted with him, an' hangs around till I finds out where he's cachin' his dust at, an' then, one day he tells me he's goin' to Dawson the next day an' bank his dust. So I lays fer him along the trail.

"He ain't a bad guy, an' I figgers to conk him with a blackjack from behind, an' cop off his dust. I know jest how hard to tap a guy to put him out so's he'll come to in a little while without nothin' worst than a headache.

"Well, I slips up behind him, an' jest when I was goin' to let him have it, he trips on a rock an' looks around. 'Course, after he seen me, there wasn't nothin' to do but croak him, which I done, an' drug him off'n the trail an' rolled him in a holler. An' that's where I slipped up on account it was kinda wet in there an' I steps in some mud an' left my tracks in it. Like in a city, where I always worked before, you don't have to figger on leavin' no tracks in no mud. I goes back to my claim an' shoveled around in the gravel fer a few days, an' then this here Downey, he comes along an' asks me if I know this guy, which someone had found his body there in the holler. I says sure I know him, an' he went to Dawson couple days ago. Downey he tells me about the guy gittin' knocked off, an' he sort of walks around smokin' his pipe, an' lookin' here an' there an' he asks me if I be'n workin' the shaft that's on the claim? I tells him I ain't even bothered to go down in it, on account the guys that moved off'n it, claimed there wasn't no more gold in there.

"Well—next thing I know'd he was snappin' the bracelets on me. He chains me to the sluice an' goes down the shaft, an' digs up the guy's sacks of dust which I'd planted down there. Then he walks me down to the holler where I'd rolled the guy, an' another cop's down there pourin' plaster in some of them foot-tracks in the mud. Downey, he yanks off my shoes an' fits 'em in the tracks, an' when the plaster drys they takes the moulds, an' we hit fer Dawson.

"'Course I claim I didn't have nothin' to do with it, but I figger the jig's up on account of them tracks, an' the guy's gold bein' in my shaft, an' all. Then, like I said, my mouthpiece found this here mistake the clerk made—an' I'm in the clear. An' what I mean—that's luck!"

"Yeah," Black John agreed, "it shore is."

"DRINK UP," the man invited, tossing a limp moosehide sack onto the bar. "An' have one on me."

The big man eyed the sack as Cush shook some dust onto the scale. "I see you managed to save out some of the dust," he said. "That looks like a sourdough's poke."

"Hell, no! This here dust is what a guy paid me in wages. I lammed out of Chi with a couple thousan' in bills, but my mouthpiece there in Dawson took every damn cent I had left to git me off. So when I got turned loose I went to work fer a guy on Shorty Crick, an' he paid me an ounce a day. I figgered on workin' there till I got a chanct to look around, but after I'd worked fer him a few days he went down to Dawson, an' when he come back he paid me off an' fired me, on account he heard about what happened over on Bonanza. There was a bunch of them empty gold sacks layin' around there an' I grabbed off a dozen of 'em, figgerin' they'd come in handy later. I ain't broke yet. I got some more dust cached down along the river. I'll pick it up one of these days. I didn't dast to go back to Bonanza on account I was afraid some of them boys that know'd the guy I cooled might take a shot at me. So I went back to Dawson, an' it was then Cuter Malone told me about you boys up here, an' how it might be better to throw in with you than try to go it alone. How about it? You got a place fer me?"

The big man's eyes strayed from the man's face to the open window where the wooden slabs of the little graveyard showed stark against the background of green spruce. He nodded slowly. "Yeah," he said, at length. "I think if you stick around, we can make a place for you."

"Okay. I figgered you could use a good man. I throw'd my stuff in a cabin three, four mile down the crick. Seen a one-armed guy fishin' down there, an' he claimed there wasn't no one livin' there—claimed the place was unlucky. But hell—with luck like mine, no place is unlucky!" He purchased some supplies and departed down the creek, after assuring Black John that he was ready to get on the job any time he was called on.

When the two were alone again Cush scowled across the bar at Black John. "What the hell d'you mean—you kin make a place fer a damn murderin', robbin' coot like him! Cripes—knockin' off that pore fella goin' to Dawson to bank his dust!" The big man made no reply, his eyes still centered on the little wooden slabs. Cush followed his gaze, and an idea dawned on him. "Oh—you mean like that, eh? What you goin' to do, John—call a miners' meetin' an' hang him? He sure won't git off up here on account of some clerk makin' a mistake! That's one good thing about miners' meetin's—we don't need no clerks. A man either done it, er he didn't—an' if he did, we hang him."

Black John nodded. "That's right, Cush. But we can't go ahead an' hang Pete fer that murder on Bonanza. The crime was committed outside our jurisdiction."

"You an' yer damn jewishdiction! Yer allus talkin' about con-tiggerous territory, an' subtenderin' cricks an' mountains, an' all it means is if you want to hang some guy, you just call a miners' meetin' an' go ahead an' hang him—no matter where he done it!"

The big man grinned. "It wouldn't be ethical. We mustn't bog down on our ethics, Cush."

"Ethics! What the hell's a ethic, anyhow? I never seen one—an' neither did you! It's like ghosts—folks talks about 'em, but no one ever seen one!"

"I have a hunch that, given time, our friend Pete, will reap a just reward."

"He ain't no friend of mine," Cush growled. "An' that reminds me—the safe's gittin' so damn full I can't hardly git nothin' more into it. How about you hittin' down to Dawson with a batch of dust? If I'd know'd you was goin' t'other day, I'd of sent it then, an' saved you a trip."

"Oh, I don't mind an extra trip now an' then—sort of breaks the monotony. Might's well start now as later. You make the dust up in a pack, an' I'll go over to the cabin an' throw my stuff together."

A half-hour later Cush stood at the landing as Black John stepped into his canoe. "You might," he suggested, with elaborate sarcasm, "show yer friend Pete the dust when you go past Olson's, an' tell him where yer goin' with it. He claims he kin tap you with his blackjack light enough so you won't have nothin' worst than a headache when you come to."

Black John grinned. "Guess I won't take a chance. Pete, he's learnt not to make tracks in the mud. An' them old shafts of Olson's are half full of seepage. Downey might not feel like divin' down to recover the dust. Besides I don't like headaches."

III

ARRIVING IN DAWSON Black John banked the dust and proceeded to the Tivoli Saloon to find Old Bettles, Swiftwater Bill, and Moosehide Charlie ranged before the bar. Bettles downed his liquor as the big man approached the group. "Speak of the devil, an' up he pops," he grinned. "We was jest talkin' about that run of luck you had in the stud game the last time you was down. Yer jest in time to buy a drink—an' how about a little game tonight?"

Black John smiled, drew a roll from his pocket and held it up. "Here's that ten thousan' I drew out of the bank the last time I was down. I don't mind givin' you boys another chanct to put a nick in it." Peeling off a bill he tossed it onto the bar, and the glasses were filled. "What's the news along the cricks? Any new strikes?"

Bettles shook his head. "No—nothin' to write home about. Chechako stampede up on some feeder somewheres up the Klondike where a couple of fellas hit a pocket. It didn't amount to nothin', outside of the one location."

"Had a murder trial sence you was here," Moosehide said. "Some guy name of Pete Conway lays fer Joe Baxter an' caves in his head with a blackjack an' robs him of the dust he was takin' down to the bank. Downey, he comes up to Bonanza where this here Conway's squattin' on an abandoned location, an' he seen where this guy's boots fit some tracks where he'd drug Joe through the mud, so he arrests him, an' finds Joe's dust down in the shaft on the location this Conway's squatted on. Downey, he's got him dead to rights—but when the trial come off, damn if Conway's lawyer didn't git him off!"

"Proved he was innocent, eh?"

"Innocent—hell!" Bettles exclaimed. "He done it, an' everyone knows he done it—the Crown prosecutor, the jedge, the jury, an' even his own lawyer knows it, an' Downey had the evidence to convict him. But he gets turned loose fer some damn pifflin' reason like his name wasn't spelt right, er his necktie was on crooked, er he had a hole in his sock, er somethin'."

"The law's a damn fool," Swiftwater Bill opined. "If that's the way it works, we'd sure ort to go back to miners' meetin's! Hell, a miners' meetin' would have had him convicted an' strung up quicker'n the law could pick a jury."

"He went to work fer old Bill Jackson on Shorty Crick. But when Bill heard about the murder he fired him. An' he better not show up on Bonanza agin, if he knows what's good fer him," Moosehide stated ominously. "The boys is all riled up, an' someone'll take a shot at him shore as hell."

AFTER A few more drinks, Black John sauntered over to detachment headquarters, tilted his chair against the wall, elevated his heels to the edge of the flat top desk, filled his pipe, and grinned at Corporal Downey. "Jest stopped in the Tivoli an' the boys was tellin' me you had a murder trial sence I was down."

The officer scowled. "Call it a murder trial, if you want to! I work up an iron clad case an' get throw'd out of court because some damn clerk makes a mistake in the papers! An' the murderer walks out past me grinnin' like a chessy cat. I sure could have socked him one on the jaw—come damn near doin' it, too. But I'll get that guy yet! He got away with murder once, an' he'll think he can do it again. There's a couple of things I'd like to question him about, right now—but he seems to have disappeared. He'll be showin' up on some crick before long, an' next time I'll have better luck—I hope. Anyhow, the prosecutor fired his clerk. Got another murder on my hands, right now."

"Same fella prob'ly pulled it, eh?"

"No. The bird that pulled this one's a trapper. I've got him locked in a cell. He shot a British-American Company messenger a couple of miles up the Bonanza trail, an' got away with six hundred an' twenty-five ounces of dust the messenger was bringin' in to the bank."

"Funny kind of a stunt for a trapper to pull," Black John opined. "What is he—a Siwash?"

"No. He's a chechako. Says his name's Emory Twiddle. Claims he was trappin' down in Minnesota an' come up here when he heard about the gold rush. He's trappin' a crick that runs into the river about twenty mile above here. He was livin' in a cabin a fellow name of Curley built on a claim that petered out on him. This Curley was drowned this spring when the ice went out. We reported it at the time. Don't do much good to record an accident like that, when you don't know any name but Curley. Hell, there's a hundred Curley's along the river—an' chances is, back where he come from they didn't call him Curley, nohow."

"This Emory Twiddle—did he confess to killin' an' robbin' this messenger?"

"No. He claims he had nothin' to do with it. But I found the dust cached under the floor of his cabin—noticed where a puncheon had be'n lifted, an' pried it up. There was the dust— every damn ounce of it in eight moosehide sacks."

"What did he say to that?"

"Says he don't know nothin' about it. Claims he didn't even know the puncheon would lift up. Says it must be dust that Curley had cached there when he died."

"H-u-u-m," Black John said. "How come you suspected this Twiddle in the first place?"

"He'd be'n here in town the day before the murder, an' several people swore they saw him talkin' to this messenger. Twiddle don't deny that. He admits he talked to the messenger here on the street. Says he knew him because he worked for a while for the British-American outfit after he found he couldn't make a go of prospectin'. But he sticks to his story that he didn't kill him, an' that he don't know how the dust got under his floor."

"This dust you found there—you said it was in eight moose-hide sacks. Does the British-American sack their dust in moose-hide? Most of the outfits use canvas."

"The British-American does, too. Mrs. Lowe makes the sacks for 'em. I figger Twiddle changed the dust into those sacks, an' did away with the canvas ones."

"Kind of funny a trapper would have dust sacks," Black John said. "Do you figger he made 'em himself?"

"No. They're sourdough sacks, all right." Reaching into a drawer, he drew out a sack and tossed it onto the table. "That's one of 'em," he said. "I'm holdin' 'em for evidence."

"This messenger—what was he shot with? Did you get the bullet?"

"No. The bullet went on through him. It's hard to tell the exact calibre of the bullet when you've got nothin' but the wound to go by. But in this case I've got more than the wound. I found where the murderer stood while he waited for the messenger to come along, and I found an empty shell right where it should have lit when he ejected it from his rifle, after firin' the shot. It's a 30-40 shell. An' Twiddle's rifle is a 30-40. Here's the shell. Take a look at it."

Black John picked up the empty cartridge case that Downey tossed onto the desk top, and examined it. "What's all these scratches along the side of the shell? Looks like it had be'n scraped with a knife."

Downey nodded. "Prob'ly was. I figger somethin' got stuck to it in his pocket, er somewhere, an' he scraped it off."

"Did Twiddle have any shells for his rifle when you picked him up?"

"Yeah, there was five in the magazine, an' a dozen more in a box in the cabin."

"Was any of the rest of 'em scraped?"

"No—that's the only one. Prob'ly had that one in his pocket an' it got stuck up with somethin'."

"Did you look in his pockets an' find anything sticky in 'em?"

"Yes, I looked—but I didn't find anything."

"Did you fire one of his shells out of his gun, an' compare

the firin'-pin dent with the dent in this cap?"

Downey's brow drew into a frown. "Yes, I did—an' the dents don't quite jibe. You'll notice the dent in that shell ain't quite round—there's a sort of a nick in one side of it. Here's the shell I fired from Twiddle's rifle, an' the dent's perfectly round—his firin'-pin don't show no irregularity, either. I examined it with a magnifyin' glass. I figger there must have be'n a grain of sand stuck either to the cap of the shell, or the pin—an' that's what made that irregular nick."

"Could have be'n, I s'pose," Black John admitted. With the point of his knife blade, he scraped a few dark colored crumbs from the groove about the dented cap. Applying one of the crumbs to his tongue he tasted it. "Chocolate," he said. "This cartridge was carried in a pocket with some chocolate. I better leave the rest of it in there. It might come handy fer evidence."

Downey grinned. "Guess I've got all the evidence I need to get a conviction. Look at the facts—Twiddle was seen with this messenger the day before the man was knocked off. The man was undoubtedly shot with a 30-40 rifle. I've got the empty 30-40 shell I found right where it should have be'n. Twiddle's rifle is a 30-40. An' I found the dust the British-American lost in Twiddle's possession. It's an open an' shut case. Any jury would convict a man on that evidence."

Black John nodded slowly. "Yeah, Downey, I reckon you're right—any jury would. The law's hell fer evidence, ain't it?"

"Why, of course! How else could it conduct a trial?"

"Might run one like a miners' meetin'—hang 'em if they're guilty, an' turn 'em loose if they ain't. You wouldn't catch a miners' meetin' turnin' no blackjack murderer loose because some damn fool clerk made a mistake in his spellin'. An' I'll bet you can't name one man we ever hung on Halfaday that didn't have it comin'."

"I guess this Twiddle's got it comin', all right," Downey said.

"Mebbe. But this dust you figger was stole off that messenger—you say you found it in Twiddle's possession?"

"Sure I did! Hell, it was cached right there in his cabin!"

"Well, jest s'pose, fer the sake of argument, that this British-American dust should be found elsewhere—that you'd pick up some other party with stronger evidence agin him than you've got agin Twiddle—evidence so strong that no one could doubt he murdered that messenger, an' this guy should be convicted. Then what would become of the dust that Twiddle had in his possession—the dust you've got here in them moosehide sacks? You'd have to return it to Twiddle, wouldn't you?"

DOWNEY PONDERED the question. "He claimed he didn't know anything about it—how it got there in the cabin."

"But," persisted Black John, "it was in his possession. A man don't have to explain where he got his dust. If the law can't prove he got it dishonestly he'd be allowed to keep it, wouldn't he?"

"Why—yes, of course."

"Then, in case someone else was convicted of this robbery, you'd return this dust to Twiddle?"

Corporal Downey grinned. "Yes—sure I would. If it turns out that someone else killed the messenger, and we get the dust back, I can promise to return this dust to Twiddle, all right. But—he's got a fat chance of gettin' it—with the evidence we've got against him! What the hell are you drivin' at, anyway. What are you so interested in Twiddle for?"

"These here moot questions always interest me, an' I like to get 'em ironed out," Black John replied. "But aside from that, I'm interested in Twiddle because he saved my life. Hauled me out of the river when a rollin' tree smashed my canoe an' knocked me out, an' drug me to that shaft there by his cabin, an' hung me by the heels till he got the water pounded out of me. So naturally I'm sorry to see the little cuss in trouble. He was tellin' me about havin' a chanct to buy some kind of a resort proposition down in Minnesota but he didn't have the cash to swing it. I offered him ten thousan' in cash when we got to Dawson an' he refused to touch it—claimed he wouldn't take a cent fer savin' a man's life." Rising from his chair, he pocketed his pipe. "Well, so long, Downey. By the way, there's a character showed up on Halfaday an' located in Olson's old shack that looks to me like he might turn out to be ontrustworthy. Mind you, Downey, you know damn well, that on Halfaday we don't never either help nor hinder the police, an' I ain't claimin' that this here Pete Conway is—"

"Pete Conway!" Downey exclaimed. "Why, he's the damn cuss that murdered Joe Baxter, up on Bonanza! The guy that got turned loose on account of that clerk's mistake!"

"Oh, so that's who he is, eh? I didn't figger I was goin' to like him the first time I laid eyes on him—an' now I knowed I ain't. I'm shore sorry he settled on Halfaday."

"He won't bother you long," Downey said. "I'll come up and get him. There's several things I want to question him about— an' he's goin' to have to think pretty fast to find the answers. When you goin' back?"

"I'm startin' in the mornin'."

"I can't leave here for a couple of days. Lay over an' I'll go with you."

The big man shook his head. "Nope," he replied with a grin. "I don't care to be seen travellin' in no sech company. S'pose some of the boys should see us goin' up there together, an' then you was to arrest this Conway—they'd jump to the conclusion that I steered you up there—an' that's a reputation I can't afford to get. I'll set in the stud game tonight, an' pull out in the mornin'."

Making his way down a side street, Black John knocked at a slab shack above the door of which was a sign:

MRS. G. I. LOWE'S, LAUNDRY.
MENDING FREE OF CHARGE. FORTUNES TOLD.

The door opened and the proprietress greeted the big man

with a smile. "Land sakes, John—you don't expect me to tell your fortune, do you?"

White teeth flashed behind the black beard. "No, no, Mrs. Lowe. If anything's going to happen that would disturb my humdrum existence I wouldn't want to know about it till it gets here. Fact is, I've got a little job of sewin' for you."

"What did you do—rip yer pants tryin' to keep about four jumps ahead of the Mounted?"

"No, Downey don't bother us sterling characters. He's got his hands full tryin' to sort out the sinful from amongst the onslaught of chechakos that's infestin' the Yukon."

"Ain't it awful the way the chechakos is pilin' in on us! A body could wish the police would run the whole kit an' kaboodle of 'em back where they come from. Time they get through messin' up the cricks there won't be no dust left in the country except what the big outfits can scoop out with their dredges."

"You spoke a true word, there," Black John agreed. "An' that time ain't so far off, neither. But speakin' of big outfits, I understand you make the canvas sacks they keep their dust in?"

"Yes, I make quite a few of 'em."

"Make 'em all alike, do you?"

"Yes. Dust's heavy, you know, an' if you make 'em too big it's hard on the seams. A little leak in a gold sack can run into money."

"That's jest the p'int. Most of the boys up on Halfaday banks their dust in Cush's safe, an' every once in so often the safe gets filled up, an' I've got to fetch a batch of dust down here to the bank. I've be'n dependin' on moosehide sacks that Cush's klooch has be'n makin', but lately she's got kind of lax with her sewin' 'cause I noticed when I got down here this trip some of them sacks was leakin' a little at the seams—so I wish you'd make me up a dozen or so good stout canvas ones—same as you make fer the big outfits. I'm pullin' out in the mornin'. Can I have 'em by then?"

"Sure. I'll get 'em out tonight—an' I'll guarantee that none of 'em'll leak dust, too. The way I sew 'em they'll hold water!"

IV

WHEN THE STUD game broke up well into the wee sma' hours, Black John turned in for a few hours sleep. After breakfast he picked up his sacks at Mrs. Lowe's and proceeded to the bank. Drawing a roll of bills from his pocket he thrust them beneath the wicket. "Here's that ten thousan' I draw'd out, last time I was down," he said. Figgered the boys might take it off me in the stud game—but hell, they never put a nick in it."

The teller smiled. "Want to deposit it?"

"No," Black John paused and shoved eight canvas sacks toward the man, "I've got a deal on that calls for dust—so jest slip six hundred an' twenty-five ounces in them sacks—an' don't bother to mark 'em. I'll have to weigh out the stuff anyway so the party I'm dealin' with can be shore I didn't slip out a few ounces on him."

Proceeding to the wharf he loaded his canoe onto the *Sarah* and a few hours later was set ashore at the mouth of the White River. That evening as he smoked beside his campfire, his brow drew into a frown, and he muttered to himself as the little flames licked at the dry spruce. "With all the evidence Downey's got, things shore looks bad for Twiddle. An' I guess he's guilty, all right. Downey found that dust cached under that loose puncheon, an' Twiddle claimed it must have be'n there all the time—that Curley must have left it there. But I know damn well it wasn't there, 'cause I lifted that puncheon when Twiddle went out to chop wood, that evenin'—an' the cache was empty. But he's sech a sort of meek little cuss—an' the way he turned down that ten thousan' that I offered him there in the bank— it's shore hard to believe he'd pull off a cold-blooded murder an' robbery. It jest goes to show a man can't never tell. But guilty er not, the fact is he saved my life, an' I owe him plenty. As the

Good Book says, he cast his bread upon the waters, an' it's up to me to see that he gets it back. It's shore lucky I happened to notice that Pete Conway's rifle's a 30-40 that day he stood it against Cush's bar. An' when Downey finds that out—an' finds the six hundred an' twenty-five ounces the British-American lost in the original sacks in Conway's cache he's shore goin' to have to revize his 'open an' shut case' agin Twiddle. Of course, as an abstract proposition, a moralist might possibly cavil at the ethics of my proceedure—but hell, this ain't no abstract case! It's a concrete one—an' damned important, from Twiddle's angle. I ain't got no compunctions about framin' that damn Pete Conway—the blackjackin' scum! He'd ort to be'n hung for that Bonanza murder. He shore had his nerve, comin' up to Cush's an' braggin' about a dirty play like that—an' braggin' about his luck in gettin' out of it! Well, Downey'll be along a couple of days after I get to Halfaday, an' I don't have to look in Mrs. Lowe's teacup to predict that Conway's luck is goin' to run out on him."

UPON REACHING Halfaday Creek, a few days later, Black John beached his canoe some distance below Olson's old shack, and after ascertaining that Conway was nowhere about, he carried the gold sacks to the foot of the rimwall opposite the cabin, slipped them into an aperture in the rocks, and carefully fitted a flat stone into place completely concealing the cache—a cache that he himself had devised some time before for the convenience of such transients as elected to settle in Olson's old shack. It was a cache that also was well known to Corporal Downey, who had had occasion to visit it on numerous occasions in search of the evidence that would convict certain criminals not wanted on Halfaday.

Returning to his canoe, he proceeded on up the creek. A mile or more above Olson's the sound of a shot broke the stillness, then another, and another. Beaching the canoe, he proceeded toward the foot of a high ridge a short distance back from the creek, and came upon Conway standing beside the carcass of a dead moose. The man greeted him jovially: "I got him! First damn moose I ever shot! I sure didn't know they was big as they be! There's enough meat to last a man all summer, if it wouldn't sp'ile on him."

"Ain't you bled him?" the big man asked.

"What d'you mean—bled him? I ain't done nothin' to him. Hell, I jest shot him a couple minutes ago."

Stepping to the animal Black John drew his belt knife and severed the great artery low in the animal's throat, stepping back as a torrent of blood gushed out. "The meat ain't fit to eat onless you let the blood out," he explained.

"Cripes, it's goin' to be a hell of a job to git that hide off'n him, so a man kin git to the meat. I ain't never skun no moose—nor nothin' else, fer that matter. Tell you what I'll do—you help me git him skun an' cut up, an' we'll go fifty-fifty on the meat. There's a damn sight more of it than I want."

Black John agreed and the two set to work. When the task was finished, they sat down and filled their pipes. Picking up his rifle, the man ejected an empty shell from the barrel, reached into his pocket, drew out several cartridges, and scowled at them. Then, with his knife, he began to scrape at the brass jackets. "Got 'em all gummed up with chocolate," he grumbled.

Black John started, then as the other glanced at him he coughed violently. "Damn the black flies!" he said in a choking voice. "I breathed one in, an' it damn near strangled me!" He glanced with seeming indifference at the cartridge the man was scraping. "Chocolate, did you say? You got 'em gummed up with chocolate?"

"Yeah, it's a month er so ago, down on Bonanza, I stuck a couple of chocolate bars in my pocket along with my shells an' went huntin'. It was a hot day, an' I didn't find nothin' to shoot, an' the damn chocolate het up in my pocket an' run out onto my shells an' then dried onto 'em, so every time I stick one in my rifle I got to stop an' scrape the chocolate off'n it."

"H-u-u-m," Black John said, idly picking up the empty shell the man had ejected from the rifle, noting the knife scratches on the case, and also, that the firing-pin dent in the cap was not quite round. "Interestin', I'm shore."

The other grunted. "I don't see nothin' so damn interestin' if some guy gits his shells stuck up with chocolate. What I claim— it's tough luck, havin' to scrape all them shells."

"That's right, Conway," the big man agreed, as, unnoticed, he slipped the empty shell into his pocket. "It shore is tough luck. But you had good luck bringin' down this moose with three shots. How clost was you to him when you shot?"

For answer the man got up and led the way to a spot some thirty yards away. "I stud there behind that tree when I heard him comin', an' when he showed up I let him have it, see—there's the two empty shells I throw'd out of my gun."

Black John glanced at the shells and nodded. "Pretty good shootin'," he said. "Well, so long, Pete. I'll pack my meat to the canoe an' pull out."

ON THE second day thereafter, carrying a light pack, he slipped down and camped at the mouth of Halfaday. About noon of the following day he stepped to the bank and hailed Corporal Downey, who had nosed his canoe into the creek. The officer beached his canoe, and glanced into the big man's face. "What you doin' down here?" he asked.

"Waitin' fer you to show up. Be'n here sence yesterday. Come on over to the fire. I've got a b'ilin' of tea on. Got somethin' I figger you'll be interested in seein' before you get to Conway's." Squatting beside the little fire, with the teacups filled, Black John drew an empty cartridge case from his pocket and handed it to Downey.

"Ever see one like that before?" he asked, with a grin.

The corporal glanced at the shell, drew a magnifying glass from his pocket and examined it minutely, then from another pocket he produced another shell—the one he had found at the spot where the British-American messenger had been shot. Finally he returned the glass to his pocket and, holding the two shells in the palm of his hand, stared at them. "They're jest alike," he said. "Both be'n scraped with a knife, both have got chocolate stickin' in the rim around the caps—an' the firin' pins shows they was both fired from the same gun. Where'd you get this shell?"

"I picked it up a couple of days ago when Conway ejected it from the barrel of his rifle after shootin' a moose. I can show you two more of 'em right where he ejected 'em. He took three shots to bring down the moose. He didn't eject this last shell till we'd finished skinnin' out the moose. I come along in my canoe on my way back from Dawson an' heard the shots, so I went over to see what it was all about an' found Conway standin' there lookin' down at this moose he'd shot. He'd never killed a moose before, an' didn't know nothin' about skinnin' it—didn't even know enough to bleed it—so he offered me half the meat if I'd help him. When we finished we set down there, an' he ejected this shell, an' started to slip some more loads in his gun, but he had to stop an' scrape 'em first. He claimed he'd carried 'em in his pocket along with a couple of chocolate bars a couple of months ago down on Bonanza, an' the chocolate melted an' gummed up the shells. You'll find more of them shells in his pocket, an' ondoubtless you'll find the linin' of the pocket is messed up where that melted chocolate has hardened."

"Well!" Downey exclaimed. "Then—it was Conway, an' not Twiddle that murdered that messenger!"

"That's the way it looks from here," Black John agreed.

"But—hell, John—Twiddle had the dust!"

"What dust?"

"Why—the six hundred an' twenty-five ounces the British-American lost, of course!"

"That," replied Black John, "is merely a matter of opinion. Mebbe it was the dust the British-American lost—an' then agin, mebbe it wasn't."

Downey eyed the big man sharply. "Have you looked in Conway's cache—that one covered with that flat rock that damn near everyone that camps in Olson's shack finds an' uses?"

Black John grinned. "Well, yes. You see, Downey, after seein' that empty shell, an' seein' him scrapin' chocolate off'n the loaded ones he took from his pocket, I sort of mistrusted he was the bird that knocked off that messenger, so yesterday when I come down here to head you off, I slipped over an' lifted that rock an' peeked into the hole."

"Was there any dust in it?"

Black John shrugged. "That's for you to say. I did see some new canvas sacks in there—an' they ain't empty. What they contain I figgered, was a matter for the police to find out. I put the rock back without investigatin' 'em."

"Where was it he shot this moose?" Downey asked, as he drained his cup. "I want to pick up them other two empty shells."

Black John finished his tea, and doused his fire. "It's about a mile above the shack. We'll circle around to the place, then we can slip down along the rimwall to the cache, an' you can investigate them sacks, an' then we can go to the shack."

Conway emerged from the cabin, an empty water pail in his hand, as Downey, closely followed by Black John, stepped into the clearing. He halted abruptly, stared at the officer, then threw back his head and laughed insolently. "Well, damned if it ain't Corporal Downey! Caught any murderers lately?"

"Yeah—one," Downey replied, halting directly before the man.

"That so? Who was he?"

"You."

"Oh, yeah—sure," the man sneered. "Hell, I'd most fergot that! If I was you I'd tell that there Crown prosecutor to fire that clerk an' git one that kin spell."

"He's fired," Downey replied evenly, as he drew the handcuffs from his pocket. "Drop that pail an' stick 'em out, Conway. You ain't gettin' off this time."

"You can't try a man but onct fer the same crime!" Conway exclaimed. "That's the law."

"This ain't the same crime," the officer replied, as he slipped the cuffs on the man's wrists. "I'm arrestin' you for the murder of a British-American messenger on the Bonanza trail, an' the robbery of six hundred an' twenty-five ounces of dust. An' it's my duty to warn you that anything you say may be used against you."

"It's a damn lie! Use that agin me, if you kin!"

Shoving the man ahead of him, Downey entered the cabin, picked up the rifle from a corner, and ejected the cartridges, each of which showed scratch marks on the case. Taking the man's coat from a nail, he drew several loaded cartridges from the pocket—cartridges to which adhered a coating of crusted chocolate. Turning the pocket inside out he pointed to the dried chocolate sticking to the lining. Then reaching into his own pocket he produced an empty shell, and held it up for Conway's inspection. "This shell, with these scrape marks on it was found where the man who shot that messenger ejected it from his rifle. Notice the scrape marks on it, Conway—the same as on these shells of yours. Notice, also, that there's dry chocolate stickin' in the groove around the caps of both shells."

The man stared at the shell, then blustered. "That don't prove a damn thing except mebbe that some other guy got his shells gummed up with chocolate, too! Hell, I ain't the only one that could carry chocolate in his pocket, am I?"

"No—but you're the only guy that could have shot that messenger. Look at the firin'-pin dents in the two caps. Your firin'-pin ain't quite round, Conway. Both of those shells show the same irregularity." The man's face suddenly paled, as he stared at the dented cap, and also at the dented cap of another shell that Downey showed him. "This shell is one of the three that you ejected from your rifle when you shot that moose. An' if that ain't enough evidence, here's the dust you took off that messenger after you shot him—right in the original sacks."

The man's face flamed suddenly red, and his eyes seemed to bulge from their sockets as they fastened on the canvas sacks of gold that Downey laid on the table. "It's a damn lie! It's a frame-up! It's a damn lie! Them sacks—I— it's a lie, I tell you!" His glance shifted from Downey to Black John, who stood framed in the doorway. "By God, this is your doin's! How could Downey of got them empty shells if you hadn't showed 'em to him?" He turned to Downey. "Where'd you git them sacks?" he demanded.

"Right where you cached 'em, in a hole in the rocks that damn near every crook that camps in this shack uses fer a cache."

"I never seen no hole in no rocks! I never cached them sacks! I say Black John cached them sacks so's you'd find 'em there! I mistrusted he didn't like me the first time I seen him there in Cush's bar!"

"Yer right in that surmise, at least, Conway," Black John said. "I didn't like the way you bragged about blackjackin' that pore devil on Bonanza. But does it look reasonable that I'd cache ten thousan' dollars worth of dust jest to frame you, when I'd know damn well I'd never see the dust agin? Hell, if you're convicted—which you damn well will be, that dust goes back to the British-American Company—an' I ain't the sap that would contribute ten thousan' dollars to any big outfit."

THE MAN'S eyes rested on the shells Downey had placed on the table beside the sacks of dust. "I'll git convicted, all right," he said in a dull voice. "Them shells will do it. I shot the messenger, all right, an' I got the dust. But it ain't that dust. I took the dust out of canvas sacks, an' put it in moosehide sacks, an' then filled the canvas sacks with rocks an' throw'd 'em in the river. I was in a canoe above Dawson, right at the mouth of a crick, an' I seen a canoe comin' down river with two police in it, so I headed into this crick an' found an empty cabin there, so I went in, an' was huntin' a place to hide the dust when I seen a loose puncheon, an' pried it up an' shoved the dust in the hole, an' put the puncheon back. I stayed in the shack overnight, an' in the mornin' I was afraid to take the dust along, so I hit out fer here, figgerin' to git the dust later. That's the God's truth—an' I don't know nothin' about this here dust, nor no cache, neither."

Black John yawned and stretched. "Well, I guess I'll be goin' on up to Cush's," he said. "So long, Downey. I s'pose you'll be headin' back to Dawson."

Downey nodded, and stepping outside, closed the door behind him. He eyed the big man sharply. "What about this dust?" he asked.

"What about it? Why—take it along an' use it fer evidence an' then turn it over to its rightful owner—the British-American outfit, of course."

"How about the dust I found in Twiddle's shack—the dust Conway claims he cached there?"

Black John grinned. "Cripes, Downey—the British-American didn't lose but the one batch of dust! You know damn well, Downey, that Conway's a thoroughly onreliable citizen—an' if I was you I wouldn't believe a damn word he says. Turn this dust back to the British-American, an' let Twiddle keep the dust you found in his shack. Wherever Twiddle got that dust, he got it honest—he ain't no criminal—he never shot that messenger—an' you know it."

Downey nodded. "Yeah, I know that, now. An' I'm damn glad to know that it was Conway pulled that job, instead of Twiddle. But there's several things I don't know. One of 'em is, how that dust got in the cache there? I've got my own good guess, though."

The grin on Black John's face widened. "What the law wants is evidence—not guessin', Downey. You've got yer man, an' the evidence that'll convict him—if some clerk don't make another spellin' mistake. So you ort to be satisfied. There's an old sayin' that seems to fit this case, Downey. It goes somethin' like this. 'God moves in a mysterious way his wonders to perform.' So long. Next time I see you I'll buy you a drink."

JUSTICE–AND THE LAW

CORPORAL DOWNEY, OF the Northwest Mounted Police, drew his canoe from the water at the landing, ascended the steep bank, and crossed the little clearing in front of Cushing's Fort, the combined trading post and saloon that served the little community of outlawed men that had sprung up on Halfaday Creek, close against the Yukon-Alaska boundary, as two pack-laden men emerged from the building and headed for the landing. Both nodded to the officer as they passed, and Downey nodded in return.

Stepping into the saloon he was greeted by Black John Smith who stood at the bar, leather dice box poised in his hand. "Well, damned if here ain't Downey!" He set the dice box down and grinned as the officer stepped to the bar. "Yer arrival at the psychological moment is nothin' short of providential in pre-cludin' the necessity of my endeavoring to beat the four fours Cush jest shook in one. Because, accordin' to immemorial custom, the house sets 'em up upon the advent of a newcomer."

Behind the bar Old Cush scowled. "Downey ain't no new-comer, an' all the big words you kin think up won't make him none. So you go ahead an' beat them four fours, er by heck, you go dry!"

"The issue," argued Black John, "seems to hang upon the definition of the word 'newcomer.' Now, accordin' to—"

"Accordin' to me havin' the bottle, you don't git no drink till you beat them four fours," Cush cut in.

Black John shook his head in resignation. "The onpresidented penuriousness of the prolitariat is nothin' less than astoundin'."

Abruptly Cush turned, made an entry in the day book on the back bar, and shoved the bottle across the bar. "Fill up," he invited. "An' drink hearty, 'cause the drinks is already charged agin John, whether he beats them four fours, er not. Damn if I'm goin' to stand here an' listen to all them big words fer nothin'." He turned to the officer who chuckled as he poured his drink. "You up here huntin' someone, er jest passin' through?"

"Jest passin' through, this time," Downey replied. "I've be'n up to Father Cassatt's mission. Ottawa figgers we ain't got enough to do up here, so they want us to take a census of the Siwashes. I jest passed Abbott an' Boyle as I come in. Are they located up here, now?"

Pot Gutted John, and Short John, drifted in and joined the two at the bar. Black John nodded. "Yeah, they come along a couple of months ago an' located on a feeder to hell an' gone up the crick. Accordin' to Abbott, they're doin' all right up there."

Pot Gutted John filled the glass Cush slid across the bar. "Abbott, he ain't so bad," he opined, "but that there Boyle—I wouldn't want him fer no pardner, by a damn sight."

Short John concurred. "Me neither. He's a grouchy cuss. Abbott allus has a hell of a time gittin' him back to the claim. Sometime I'll bet he'll knock Abbott off, the way they're allus scrappin'."

"Oh, I don't know," Cush said. "Trouble is Boyle he likes a longer drunk than what Abbott likes. They show up every two, three weeks fer a drunk, like any reasonable men would, an' after a day er so Abbott's ready to go back to the claim. But Boyle, he'd string his drunk out fer a week, if Abbott would let him. Men's different, that-a-way—some likes a long drunk, an' some likes a short one."

"Long drunks is hard on the stummick," Short John opined. "I told Abbott yesterday when he was tryin' to git Boyle to go

back up the crick an' Boyle wouldn't go. 'Abbott,' I says, 'by God' I says, 'if I was you I wouldn't have no truck with that ornery buzzard. Sometime he's goin' to git you.' But Abbott he jest laughs an' says how Boyle's all right, onct he sobers up. He claims Boyle's a good hard worker, an' says how they're doin' all right up on that feeder."

"They're doin' all right as fer as the work goes," Pot Gutted John said. "I stopped in there couple weeks back whilst I was huntin' moose, an' they've got a good dump piled up fer the time they've be'n at it. Good stuff, Abbott claims, accordin' to the test pannin's. But I'm like Short John, I wouldn't trust that damn Boyle none. They wasn't quarrelin' none, up there, like they do down here, but Boyle, he don't say nothin' much, an' he's got a mean look in his eye. I wouldn't want no pardner of mine eyein' me like I seen Boyle eyein' Abbott whilst him an' I was talkin'—not by a damn sight, I wouldn't."

"They worked a claim together down on Squaw Crick," Downey said, "an' it was the same way in Dawson as it is here—they'd go to town an' get soused, an' then Abbott would have a hell of a time gettin' Boyle off'n it an' back to the claim. The sourdoughs down there figger about like you do—that one of these times Boyle will knock Abbott off. The claim on Squaw Crick petered out, an' Boyle an' Abbott faded out of the picture." He turned to Black John. "How do you figger 'em, John?"

THE BIG MAN swallowed his liquor and refilled his glass. "W-e-e-l-l, takin' 'em by an' large, as the Good Book says, I don't know's there's a hell of a lot to choose between 'em. Boyle is surly an' onsociable, an' like Pot Gut says, he's got a bad look in his eye. Abbott seems to be a genial cuss, but one day whilst I was huntin' up the crick, I come on him maulin' hell out of a Siwash who, he claimed, was snoopin' around tryin' to locate their cache. I made him lay off the Siwash—Maktab, his name is, an' he's a good lad, who jest happened to be passin' along the rim of the feeder when Abbott spotted him. Maktab tried to tell Abbott that, but either he didn't understand him, or didn't believe him, an' beat him up anyhow. What I claim, any guy that would beat up a Siwash without no more reason than Abbott had, ain't no one to write home about. So, if Boyle should knock Abbott off an' we'd call a miners' meetin' an' hang him, in my opinion the scale of jestice wouldn't tilt no hell of a ways, one way or the other."

"Better let the law handle the matter, if a murder comes off," Downey remarked. "I'll promise to get on the job the minute I hear of it, an' take the murderer down to Dawson."

"Oh shore, Downey, we ain't doubtin' but what you'd be on the job, all right, nor that you'd take Boyle down to Dawson onct you'd caught him. But how about promisin' what the jury would do with the murderer after you'd got him there?"

Downey shrugged. "No one can promise what a jury will do."

"That's why I claim a miners' meetin's got the law beat all to hell," Black John said. "Take this here case—if Boyle should knock Abbott off some day, we'd fetch him down here an' call a miners' meetin'. Exhibit A—that's Abbott's corpse—would be layin' here on the bar for everyone to see, an' I'd go ahead an' outline the evidence we'd be'n able to collect, an' if sech evidence p'inted to Boyle, the boys would vote him guilty, an' he'd be strung up to that rafter over your head there, an' left hangin' fer a couple of rounds of drinks, an' then took out back an' planted under a slab. containin' his name, an' the check letter H."

"What do you mean—the check letter H?" Downey asked.

"Jest a device me an' Cush evolved fer the convenience of sech parties as finds enjoyment in whilin' away an idle hour perusin' the slabs in a graveyard. It also serves the purpose of preservin' a historical record of the progress of Halfaday Crick. An H on a slab indicates that its owner was hung. An M indicates that the occupant of that particular grave was murdered. There's a few Ds scattered around in there too, fer them that died natural—but not many. Halfaday is a healthy community, providin' a man's willin' to eschew murder, robbery, larceny, an' all other forms of skullduggery.

"So you see, Downey, if a man commits a crime on Halfaday he gets hung, which is reducin' jestice to its lowest terms—no ifs, ands, nor buts, about it—no nolle prosses, demurers, appeals, or other form of legal quibblin' that the defense lawyers has figured out to defeat the ends of jestice."

The officer nodded. "I shore wish court procedure was as simple as all that. I ain't sayin' that a prisoner shouldn't have all the breaks that's comin' to him—but after I've spent time an' good hard work on a case, an' know to a certainty that some damn cuss is guilty, it shore burns me up to see him walk out of the courtroom scot-free because of a legal technicality, or because a jury can't agree." Tossing off his drink, he turned from the bar. "Well, so long. I've got to be shovin' along. Jest stopped in to say hello. Be seein' you."

II

ONE EVENING, A month later, in the little pole and mud cabin on a feeder far up Halfaday Creek, Abbott pushed his plate aside, filled his pipe, and eyed his partner across the table. "Accordin' to the tally we've got a little better than three hundred ounces in the cache."

Boyle mopped the last of the stew from his plate with a piece of bannock, and eyed the other surlily. "Yeah? What of it?"

"That's right around five thousan' dollars—too damn much money to leave layin' around loose."

"Hell—it's cached, ain't it!"

"It's cached, all right," Abbott admitted. "But s'pose someone was to locate the cache?"

"He'd git hung, then. Accordin' to Black John, they hang cache robbers on Halfaday."

"They'd hang him if they caught him. But s'pose they didn't ketch him? I ain't felt easy about that cache ever sence I caught that Injun snoopin' around here. I was knockin' hell out of him when Black John come along an' made me quit. He claimed the Injun jest happened to be passin' by. But I ain't so sure. Black John don't know everything. Most of the boys on the crick banks their dust in Cush's safe. I figger we'd ort to take ourn down there an' bank it, too."

UNNOTICED BY Abbott, Boyle's eyes narrowed slightly in the deepening twilight. "Yeah, mebbe yer right," he admitted. "But there ain't no hurry about it. Hell, it's laid here this long, it won't hurt to leave it a little longer. Wait till we git the dump sluiced out, an' then take it down. By then we'd ort to have damn clost to three hundred ounces more. I ain't worryin' none about that Injun. Black John says he's an honest guy."

"It ain't only the Injun that might rob the cache. There's

Crandal. His claim ain't only a quarter of a mile below here on this same feeder. How the hell do we know he ain't snooped around an' located our cache?"

"Cripes, you don't need to be afraid of a hard workin' guy that minds his own business. I figger we'd ort to wait till we sluice the dump out. If we go down to Cush's with the dust now, it would mean another drunk. Then when we sluiced out we'd have to make another trip—an' another drunk. What I claim—too many drunks is a waste of time."

"It's you that wastes time on a drunk," Abbott retorted. "Couple of days of it's enough fer me. But you'd string it along fer a week, if I'd let you."

"Couple of day's drunk don't git a man nowheres," Boyle retorted. "Cripes, I was on a drunk one time fer six weeks solid. Was a kind of a waste of time, at that," he admitted, as an afterthought. "It took me another week to git over it. I damn near died—an' I was broke, to boot. Back in Sauk Centre, Minnesoty, it was. I was workin' in the harvest fields. Had right around five hundred dollars on me when I hit town—an' not a damn cent when I left."

"Must of made damn good wages, workin' in the harvest fields, to have five hundred dollars on you," Abbott said.

The other leered and winked. "Workin' in the harvest fields ain't no bad grift, what with them hick elevator guys keepin' plenty of dough in their boxes overnight to pay the farmers fer their wheat. A hand drill, an' a horse blanket, an' a little bottle of soup, an' them old cans opens out like they was made of tin.

"The last time I cracked one though, the guy lives right next to the elevator, an' he hears the noise, an' shows up with a shotgun, so I has to cool him. Hell, it was the guy's own fault. But I got to hell outa the country, on account a couple of bindle stiffs seen me hangin' around there, an' I was afraid they'd spill their guts." The man paused and eyed the other. "By the way, you never did tell me what your trouble was."

"What do you mean—trouble? I ain't never be'n in no trouble

with the law."

Boyle sneered. "Don't try to kid me. Don't never think I wasn't hep down there in Dawson to you eyin' every uniform you seen, an' sort of cuttin' wide circles around 'em. Then, when the Squaw Crick claim petered out, an' I says how about tryin' our luck on Halfaday Crick, you grabs the idee pronto. You'd heard the talk around Dawson about the boys up here all bein' outlaws, same as I did, an' how the police didn't dast to show up here. If you wasn't on the run, you wouldn't of be'n so hell-bent to come up here."

Abbott shrugged. "Yeah, I'm on the run. But I never knocked no one off. I was drivin' an express wagon—an' a package got lost. It was s'posed to have ten thousan' dollars in it. How the hell did I know they'd rigged a dummy? I never got nothin' but some pieces of newspaper cut the size of a bill."

"Tough luck," Boyle grinned. "But, cheer up. Looks like we've got somethin' here."

"Accordin' to the talk in Dawson," Abbott said, "the police don't dast to show up on Halfaday. But I damn near swallowed my cud when we come out of Cush's that time, an' run right plumb into Corporal Downey. What the hell was he doin', up here?"

Boyle frowned. "I be'n studyin' about that, myself. Anyways, it ain't us he's after. He's saw us both in Dawson plenty of times, an' there in front of Cush's, he meets us, face to face, an' gives us the nod. Chances is he was jest passin' through, er somethin'. Looks like we're in the clear, fer's Downey's concerned. But we've got to eat, an' we ain't got only one more feed of meat on hand. I heard Black John sayin' he seen plenty fresh moose sign below them rapids over on the White. It ain't only a little ways acrost from here to where we've got that canoe cached, in case we had to pull out in a hurry. We better slip over there tomorrow an' try to git us a moose. We kin drop down to the head of the rapids an' walk around 'em, shoot us a moose an' pack the meat up to the canoe."

Abbott nodded. "Okay. We'll clean up these dishes an' git to bed, so's we kin git an early start. Some fresh moose meat would go good."

III

SQUATTING CLOSE BESIDE a rock on a hillside that slanted upward from the head of a quarter mile turbulent rapid, shortly after daylight, Black John scanned the moose trail that skirted the fast water. Upriver a blur of motion caught his eye as a canoe swept around a bend and headed straight for the head of the rapid. As it neared the whitewater an exclamation escaped him: "Good grief, can't them damn fools see that no canoe ever made can run them rapids!"

Even as he spoke, the man in the stern reached far out, placed the blade of his paddle flat of the surface of the water, and leaned on it. The paddle snapped like a match stick. The canoe overturned in a flash, and swept down toward the rapid with the bow paddler clinging desperately to a thwart. The man in the stern, thrown free of the canoe was swimming toward the rock-studded bank with powerful strokes. He reached it just as the canoe, with the man still clinging to it, disappeared in the welter of whitewater at the head of the rapid.

Making his way down the hillside, Black John approached the swimmer who had crawled out onto a flat rock and sat staring at the spot where the canoe had disappeared. "Hello, Boyle," he said, "kind of a close call you had, eh?"

The man whirled at the sound of the voice, and stared at the speaker, wide-eyed. "Did you see it—?" he cried. "Pore Abbott— gone down through them rapids—an' he can't swim a lick! I was in the hind end, an' I was jest goin' to swing her ashore when my damn paddle broke an' the next thing I know'd I was in the water. I seen Abbott grab the canoe, an' then I struck out fer shore. Jest made her, too. Another hundred foot an' I'd of be'n in the rapids, too!"

Black John nodded slowly, his eyes on the man's feet. "Lucky you had your shoes off," he said, "or you might not have made it."

"Yeah," the man replied. "I pulled 'em off when I got in the canoe on account my corns was hurtin' me. We come acrost early to try to git us a moose. I heard you tellin' in Cush's the other day, about seein' some down here below the rapids, an' bein' as we was out of meat, we figgered on gittin' one." He paused, and his eyes again sought the whitewater. "Pore Abbott," he said, "goin' down through them rapids, he wouldn't have a chanct."

"Not much of a one," Black John agreed. "We'll foller the moose trail down. There's a big eddy at the foot of the rapids. We might find Abbott's body, an' what's left of the canoe floatin' around in it. Be tough walkin' without no shoes on. But it ain't only a quarter of a mile er so."

"Oh, I'll make it, all right," Boyle replied. "The walkin' ain't so bad. The rocks is mostly flat-like."

MAKING THEIR way down the moose trail, the two reached the foot of the rapid to see Abbott sitting on a strip of gravel beach beside the wreck of the canoe. He scowled at Boyle.

"What the hell happened?" he asked. "How'd you come to tip us over?"

"My paddle busted when I tried to swing her ashore," Boyle replied, and pointed to a flat piece of wood floating around and around in the eddy. "Look, there's the blade—broke off short where she narrows down to the handle. My God, I'm glad you come through, all right! When I seen the canoe hit them rapids, an' knowin' you can't swim a lick, I figgered you'd git drownded sure as hell. You ain't hurt, be you?"

"No, not to amount to nothin'. One leg hurts a little where it whammed agin a rock, an' my shoulder's a little sore where I hit another one. It's a damn good thing I hung onto the canoe er I'd of be'n smashed all to hell. The canoe floated fast an' I sort of drug along behind, so it sort of whammed into the rocks first an' bounced off. I sure was glad when she swung in agin this gravel. By Cripes!" he added, his eyes on the foaming whitewater that spewed from the mouth of the rapid. "I wouldn't come down through there agin fer no money!"

Black John grinned. "Who the hell would?" Reaching down, he loosened a knot, and tossed Boyle his shoes. "I see you had 'em tied to a thwart. The rifles is lashed fast, too."

Boyle nodded as he drained the water from his shoes. "Yeah, I figgered we better tie the stuff in—jest in case."

"Sech foresight is commendable," the big man replied, dryly. He turned to Abbott. "You able to walk?" he asked.

The man stood up and took a few steps. "Yeah, I can make it, all right. Leg's a little sore, but it don't 'mount to nothin'. I'm lucky as hell to git out of it the way I did."

"You shore are," Black John agreed. "Yes sir, you shore are. It sort of sets a man wonderin' how long luck like that can hold."

IV

AS THE TWO made their way back to their feeder, they jumped an old cow moose in a spruce thicket, shot it, and spent the remainder of the day packing the meat to their shack.

Awakened during the night by a snarling commotion, the two leaped from their bunks, fumbled in the dark for their rifles, and took a couple of futile shots at several wolves that had succeeded in tearing down one side of the meat cache.

Packing the undamaged meat into the shack, they went back to sleep. In the morning Boyle sliced off a quantity of neck and flank meat, chopped it fine, and taking a strychnine bottle from the clock shelf, proceeded to make up a dozen or more poison balls. "That's the second time them damn wolves has be'n at our meat cache," he growled. "I fetched this strychnine up after they done it the last time, an' by God, I'll git 'em this time. I'll string these balls around where they can't help but git 'em."

"Better not string 'em below, er one of Crandal's dogs might git one. Crandal he thinks a heap of them dogs."

"To hell with his dogs! Let him keep 'em to home if he don't want 'em pizened." Placing the balls in an empty flour sack, Boyle stepped from the shack and proceeded up the feeder.

A half hour later, he tossed the empty sack away, and stared for a long time at the single meat ball that remained in his hand. "It's got to be pretty quick," he muttered. "Abbott, he's hell-bent to git the dust in Cush's safe, on account he's scairt someone'll rob the cache. I can't stand him off much longer, an' onct it's in there, I'd only git the half of it. An' it's got to look like an accident. Who'd ever a thought a man could go down through them rapids—an' him not able to swim!" Wrapping the meatball in his handkerchief, the man placed it in his pocket, and returned to the shack.

At noon the two knocked off work, and Abbott fried a couple of moose steaks. "Cripes!" he exclaimed, as they sat at the table and sawed away at the meat with their knives. "This is the toughest damn meat I ever seen! That there cow musta be'n a hundred years old!"

Boyle nodded. "Tough is right," he agreed. "The only way a man kin eat it is chop it up fine before we fry it. Takes a little longer to start out with but, by God, a man kin chaw it when he gits it cooked. I'll knock off a little early tonight, an' chop up a batch of it."

"Listen," Abbott said, "I can't help worryin' about the cache. You claimed we'd bank the dust down to Cush's after we'd sluiced out the dump. But we can't sluice it out till we fix the slats in the riffles, an' patch up the flume where the wind blow'd that tree down acrost it a ways up the crick. What I claim, we'd ort to fix up the sluice an' flume an' sluice out the dump before some damn cuss comes along an' knocks off our cache."

Boyle frowned impatiently. "Oh, all right, all right! If yer so worried about that cache, we'll patch up the sluice an' flume an' take the dust down to Cush's. We'll work in the shaft today, an' tomorrow mornin' I'll go up an' fix the flume while you work on the sluice."

V

OLD CUSH CLOSED the Bible he had been reading, placed it carefully on the back bar, set out a bottle, two glasses, and the inevitable leather dice box, as Black John Smith entered the room and stepped to the bar.

The big man picked up the box and cast the dice. "Beat them three fives in one," he said.

Cush failed to beat them, took three shakes to make three treys on the next horse, which Black John beat with three sixes. As they filled their glasses Cush shoved the square-framed steel-rimmed spectacles from nose to forehead. "I jest be'n readin' in the Good Book, there, where it tells about some fella name of Joshuary, which he was a colonel er a general er somethin' of the army they had back there in them days, an' they was fightin' another army which had holed up in a town name of Jellico. There's a Jellico down in Kentucky er Tenneessee, er one of them states. My second wife come from there—she claimed. But chances is it ain't the same town, on account I don't believe this here Jellico is that old. They was a hell of a ways back—them things you read about in the Book. An' besides this here town had a stone wall built around it, an' I never heard my wife say nothin' about no stone wall bein' around this here Jellico. Chances is them mountain folks jest copied the name fer their town out of the Book.

"Anyways, this here Joshuary strung his army around this town an' hollers fer the army inside to give up. But their general, figgerin' they was safe behind the wall, tells Joshuary to go to hell. An' not havin' no cannons, like they didn't have them days, Joshuary figgered he was up agin it, but along comes a angel, er someone like that, an' slips Joshuary the word that if they'd march around the town every day fer a week an' toot their horns an' then all give a big yell, the walls would fall down. So they done it that way, an' damned if the walls didn't, an' Joshuary's army went in an' cleaned up on 'em.

"What I can't figger—why in hell would a stone wall fall down if some army walked around it fer a week tootin' horns an' hollerin'? You claim you went to one of these here Bible schools where they learn you to be a preacher, so I figgered mebbe you'd know how they worked it."

The big man downed his drink and refilled his glass. "The celestial technique annent the machinations of miracle workin' are unfortunately so involved in the fog of deep mystery that the human mind is totally unable to grasp the significance of its underlyin' principles."

Cush frowned. "Oh—he worked it like that, eh? Well, I don't mind tellin' you that I don't know no more about it than I did before, an' I don't believe you do neither in spite of what you said. Fer's I kin see, all the good that there school done you was learn you a lot of big words fer the confusal of someone yer talkin' to. It shore botched the job when it tried to make a preacher out of you!"

Further discussion was interrupted by the entrance of Pot Gutted John, and Red John, who took their places at the bar.

"We run outa meat," Pot Gutted John said, as he filled the glass Cush slid toward him, "so me an' Red John went up the crick to see if we couldn't knock us over a moose. But we never seen none."

"We stopped in to Abbott an' Boyle's claim," Red John added, filling his glass. "They was jest about to eat supper when we come along an' Abbott ask us to jine 'em. Boyle had went to the crick fer a pail of water, an' Abbott was fryin' up a batch of meatballs which Boyle had made up before he went fer the water. Abbott, he had part of 'em fried settin' there in a plate on the edge of the table, an' Boyle come back with the water.

"I was waitin' till Pot Gut got through worshin' up, an' I seen Boyle look damn sharp at them meat balls on the plate, an' then he went over an' set the water pail on the bench, an' when he turned around he knocked the plate off 'n the table an' spilt the meat balls on the floor. It was a damn clumsy move—almost like he done it a-purpose—an' Abbott bawled him out fer it, an' then he picks the meat balls up off 'n the floor an' throw'd 'em out the door.

"You know Crandal's got a claim a little ways down the crick an' one of his dogs was hangin' around there, on account Abbott says, he eats up the bones an' stuff that's throw'd out. Well sir, he swallers them meat balls, an' a few minutes later he's layin' there on the ground, frothin' at the mouth an' twitchin' somethin' fierce, an' ten minutes later he was dead.

"Boyle started in givin' Abbott hell fer throwin' out them meat balls, an' Abbott come back at him twice as hard, claimin' it was Boyle's fault, on account of that mornin' he'd made up a batch of meat balls an' pizened 'em with strychnine fer to pizen some wolves which had tore into their meat cache. He claimed Boyle got one of them pizened balls mixed in with these ones they was goin' to have fer supper. 'By God,' he hollers at Boyle, 'what if one of us had et that there ball! We'd be dead—an' it would be your fault!'

"Boyle, he can't think of nothin' much to say, so he shuts up, an' Abbott, he takes a bottle off 'n the shelf, an' dumps it in the stove. 'No more wolf pizen around this camp,' he says, 'if the wolves gits all our meat!'"

POT GUTTED JOHN grinned and tossed off his drink. "After seein' that, me an' Red John kinda lost our appetite. How the hell did we know that Boyle didn't have another one of them pizen balls mixed in with the ones Abbott was goin' to fry? So we come away without eatin'." He turned to Black John. "By God, what I claim—a man as careless as what Boyle is hadn't ort to be let run around loose! Hell, he's liable to kill someone!"

The big man nodded. "That's right," he replied dryly. "Damn liable."

"Who's liable to kill who?" The men at the bar turned at the sound of the voice to see Corporal Downey standing in the doorway.

Black John grinned. "Come on over, Downey, an' wet your whistle. Barrin' a slight grammatical error, your question seems a fair one. We was referrin' to Boyle. An' in my humble opinion the one he's liable to knock off is Abbott—not that Abbott would be no hell of a loss, any way you take him. I rec'lect that we discussed this very eventuality the last time you was up here—me advocatin' dealin' with Boyle by means of a miners' meetin', an' you holdin out for a strictly legal procedure."

Downey nodded. "Yeah, I remember. But you boys won't need to worry about Boyle knocking Abbott off. Fact is, I come up here to arrest Boyle. I'll be takin' him back with me."

"Ondoubtless some infringement of the law?"

"I'm arrestin' him fer the American authorities. He's wanted for a murder an' robbery back in Minnesota."

Several drinks were had, and Pot Gutted John and Red John took their departure. "Goin' down to my place," Pot Gutted John explained, "an' cook us up some supper. We're hungrier'n hell. Cripes, after I seen what that there pizen meat ball done to that dog of Crandal's, I shore couldn't of took no delight in eatin' some of 'em."

Red John grinned. "Me neither. I didn't breathe easy till we got to hell outa there."

When the three were alone in the room Downey ordered a round of drinks. "The last time I was here you said somethin' about Abbott an' Boyle workin' a claim on some feeder way up the crick. Could you tell me how to find 'em? There's a lot of feeders along Halfaday."

"I could. But, I'll be damned if I will. You know, Downey, on Halfaday we neither help nor hinder the police," the big man replied.

Cush mopped at a splash of liquor on the bar. "Take it like when it wasn't only a question of would Boyle knock Abbott off it was all right with us, 'cause if he done so, we'd of called a miners' meetin' an' hung him. But if Boyle's gittin' loose with his wolf pizen, that's somethin' else agin. Cripes, he's liable to pizen anyone that stopped in there. Like John says, we won't neither help nor hinder the police. But the fact is, we're runnin' damn short of meat, so if John was to go up the crick a piece huntin' a moose, an' you was to go with him, there couldn't no one stop you. An' if John couldn't find no moose by the time he got to the mouth of that there feeder where Abbott an' Boyle's got their claim on, an' he turned around there an' come back here, you could go on up that feeder an' git Boyle—an' there won't no one neither help nor hinder yer doin' it."

Black John grinned. "There's a thread of intelligence runnin' somewheres through that maze of misapplied words, if a man could follow it."

"Yeah. Well, whatever Miss supplied you with words shore got aholt the heavy end of the book when she done it! 'Cause there ain't no intelligence to none of 'em."

Corporal Downey laughed. "How about it, John—goin' up the crick to hunt a moose? It would be too bad if Cush should run out of meat."

The big man downed his drink. "Yeah, I'll go. Come to think of it, our meat is gettin' a trifle high."

"Guess I'll go 'long, if you don't mind," the officer said. "It's be'n quite a while sence I've had a moose hunt."

VI

AS THE TWO partners were eating breakfast, on the morning following the poisoning of the dog, Boyle glanced through the doorway, made a dive for his rifle, and dashed out of the cabin. A yearling moose, some forty yards down the feeder, turned his head at the sound, paused for a moment and eyed the cabin with ears acock, then stepped into the bush. Slipping to the bank of the creek Boyle peered into the thick scrub for a few moments, then, leaning his rifle against the sluice, returned to the cabin. "Damn the luck!" he growled. "That there was a young moose, an' if I could of got him we'd had good tender meat instid of this tough stuff we're eatin'. No use follerin' him, though. Dry as it is, he could hear me comin' a mile."

"We'd ort to git the flume an' sluice fixed up by night," Abbott opined, "an' then we'll sluice out the dump, an' take the dust down to Cush's. Then we'll take us a damn good moose hunt."

Boyle shrugged. "Okay," he agreed. "Like we said yesterday, I'll go up an' work on the flume, an' you stay here an' fix up the sluice."

Half an hour later, armed with ax, hammer, and spikes, he headed up the feeder. For a couple of hours he worked, chopping the fallen tree and shoring up the damaged flume. Seating himself on a rock, he filled and lighted his pipe. "It won't be long, now," he muttered to himself. "We've got three hundred ounces in the cache, an' there's prob'ly another three hundred in the dump, that's six hundred ounces—around ten thousan' dollars—an' with him outa the way, it'll all be mine. But I gotta be careful. I gotta figger on knockin' him off with his own gun, an' it'll be accordin' to the way he drops whether I tell 'em it was suicide er accident. Either way, I'll lay his gun right there beside him. If it's like somewheres he could of tripped an' fell, I'll tell 'em he done it like that. But if it ain't, I'll tell 'em how Abbott was low-minded, allus talkin' about killin' hisself. They'll believe me, all right. Hell, they'll have to! There ain't no one to tell 'em any different. I'll wait till we git the dump sluiced out, then I'll let him have it."

And that same morning, on his claim a quarter of a mile below the Abbott and Boyle location, Jack Crandal mixed up a mess of dog food, stepped out of his cabin, and whistled for his dogs. Four big huskies responded to the call and stood, ears acock in eager anticipation. Crandal's eyes swept the tiny clearing, and the edge of the surrounding bush. "Here Skookum! Here Skookum!" he called, and when the dog failed to appear he tossed the others their portion, and turned to the Indian he had hired the day before to help with his sluicing. "That damn Skookum—best lead dog on Halfaday—smarter'n the others—gets plenty to eat, right here, but on top of that he slips up to Abbott an' Boyle's. They ain't got no dogs, an' they feed him their leavin's. I seen him head up that way last evenin', an' I reckon he ain't come back. By God, I'll chain him up! First thing you know they'll be makin' a kind of pet of him, an' then he won't be worth a damn for a leader. What was it you said your name is?"

"Nem Maktab."

"Well, Maktab, you slip up there to Abbott an' Boyle's an' fetch that dog back."

The Indian hesitated. "Me, I'm no lak Abbott. One tam I'm com' down de crick an' Abbott, she see me an' she say I'm sneak 'roun' hont hee's cache, an' she jomp on me an' poun' me wit' de fists, an' she say nex' tam she see me on de crick she shoot me, an' Black John com' 'long an' mak' heem queet. I'm t'ink, ba gos, I'm go oop dere Abbott she poun' me som' mor'—mebbe-so shoot me."

"To hell with Abbott! Tell him you're workin' for me. Tell him I sent you up after my dog, an' he won't bother you none."

Rather reluctantly the Indian slipped into the bush and headed up the feeder. He stepped from the edge of the bush to see Abbott dragging Crandal's huge lead dog across the tiny clearing by the tail. "Hey," he called. "You keel Crandal dog! Heem git mad, lak' hell!"

Letting go the dead animal's tail, Abbott whirled at the sound of the voice and faced the Indian who had advanced to the sluice.

"What the hell you doin' back here? Still sneakin' around tryin' to locate our cache? An' now you'll kick up a hell of a stink tellin' Crandal I killed his dog! I told you I'd shoot you if you ever showed up here agin—an' now, by God, I'll do it!" Dashing for the cabin, he had almost reached it, when Maktab snatched up the rifle Boyle had left leaning against the sluice, sighted it on Abbott's back just as he reached the doorway, and pressed the trigger. Abbott fell sprawling across the sill. And beside the sluice, Maktab stared for a few moments at the twitching form, then stood the gun against the sluice and slipped silently into the bush.

Down on his claim, Crandal paused, shovel in hand, at the sound of the shot. "I wonder if Abbott did shoot the Siwash! Maybe I ortn't to sent him! By God, if he did shoot him it's murder!" he cried. "A miners' meetin' will 'tend to his case jest as quick as I can get down to Cush's an' tell 'em."

Tossing the shovel onto the dump, Crandal struck into the bush at a run, and a short time later burst into the Abbott and Boyle clearing. For several moments he stood, his glance shifting from the dead man sprawled in the doorway, to the body of his lead dog, and then to the rifle leaning against the sluice. "I don't know what killed Skookum," he muttered, as he surveyed the scene. "But it's a cinch Maktab shot Abbott—shot him through the back just as he reached the door. There's only one answer—Abbott made for the cabin to get his gun, and Maktab grabbed up this gun here, an' shot him. By God, that's self-defense! Abbott threatened to shoot him if he ever showed up here again, an' when he went for his gun, Maktab beat him to it." His glance rested on the rifle, then his eyes narrowed and he emitted a long, low whistle. "That's Boyle's rifle—the only .32 in the country. The boys all know it—I've heard 'em kiddin' about Boyle's pop-gun. An' what's more, there's plenty of 'em figure that some day Boyle will kill Abbott. An' when they see that Abbott was shot from behind with Boyle's rifle, it wouldn't take a miners' meetin' five minutes to string Boyle up! I sure don't like the guy—but I can't stand back an' see him hung for a murder he didn't commit. None of the boys know about the Siwash. I'm the only one that stands between Boyle an' a hangin'! I've got to get down to Cush's—an' get there before anyone comes along an' sees what I'm lookin' at, right now!"

Turning on his heel, he crossed the clearing at a run and

disappeared into the bush—just as Boyle, who had also heard the shot, paused on the opposite edge of the clearing and eyed the fleeing man in astonishment.

Advancing toward the cabin, Boyle glanced at the body of Crandal's lead dog where Abbott had left it. Stepping around the corner of the cabin, he halted abruptly and stared wide-eyed at the dead man lying sprawled, half in, half out the doorway. "Good God!" he cried, "Crandal figgered Abbot killed his dog, an' shot him! Looks like Abbott was draggin' the dog off when Crandal ketched him at it, an' when Abbott seen him, he run fer his gun, an' Crandal plugged him before he could git it."

His glance strayed to the sluice with his own rifle leaning against it, and as a sudden thought struck him, he crossed to the sluice, picked up the rifle, and working the lever, threw out an empty shell. Then suddenly his eyes narrowed and his jaw tightened. "Why—the damn bum!" he bellowed. "He shot Abbott, all right—an' he shot him with my rifle! He knows damn well it's the only .32 in the country—an' he knows me an' Abbott quarrels frequent amongst ourselves—an' plenty others knows it, too. The dirty skunk! He figgers when they find Abbott shot in the back with my rifle, I'll git blamed fer it! An' I will—'cause everyone else'll figger the same! They'll call a miners' meetin' an' string me up, sure as hell!

"Like's not, he'll tell 'em he seen me shoot him! But by God—he won't git away with it! I ain't be'n asleep on this here feeder! I know where his cache is! Figgered on robbin' it when I seen a good chanct. By God, I'll knock him off 'fore he has a chanct to talk—an' I'll take what dust's in his cache an' ourn, an' get to hell outa here 'fore anyone comes along an' finds Abbott!"

Turning, he plunged into the bush and reached the Crandal clearing just as Crandal stepped from his doorway, rifle in hand, and headed down the creek. Dropping to one knee, Boyle took deliberate aim on the middle of the man's back, and fired. Crandal whirled halfway around, staggered a few steps, and crashed face downward onto the gravel.

Making sure that the man was dead, Boyle walked to the foot of the rimwall, jerked a loose stone from the mouth of an aperture and removed several small heavy moosehide sacks. "Just about what we've got," he gloated, eyeing the little sacks, and fingering the cardboard tabs, on which Crandal had noted the exact weight in ounces of each sack.

CURSING THE heat, he dashed the sweat from his brow with his hand, picked up the sacks and his rifle, and returned to the cabin. Tossing the little sacks into Crandal's pack sack, he secured Crandal's rifle and returned to his own claim. Removing the dust from the cache there, he entered the cabin, added food for a two-weeks trail, and a pair of blankets to his pack, and kneeling, examined Abbott's body, ascertaining that the bullet that killed him had gone on through. "Crandal's gun is a .30-30," he muttered, "an' they can't tell whether it was his gun er mine that killed him. If anyone should happen along before I git outa the country, I'll tell 'em Crandal shot Abbott an' robbed our cache, an' then I took out after Crandal an' got him."

Placing Crandal's rifle near the sluice, he shouldered his pack, and struck out down the feeder.

VII

AS BLACK JOHN and Corporal Downey proceeded up Half-aday Creek several miles above Cushing's Fort, the sound of a shot reached their ears, and as they neared the mouth of a feeder, another shot sounded. "Moose huntin' most likely," Black John said. "Crandal, prob'bly—or it might be Abbott or Boyle. We shore ain't seen no fresh moose sign, so I guess I'll be headin' back. You goin' with me—or you got somethin' else on your mind?"

Corporal Downey grinned. "So long, John—an' much obliged. Guess I'll head up this feeder an' look around a bit."

A couple of miles down Halfaday on his return to the Fort, Black John was accosted by a young Indian who slipped silently from the bush and barred his way. "Me, I'm see you go oop de crick wit' p'lice, I'm t'ing you com' for git me."

The big man grinned. "Git you? Hell, no, Maktab! Why should the police want to get you?"

"For keel Abbott."

"Kill Abbott!" Black John exclaimed. "You mean you killed Abbott?"

"Yes, I'm shoot heem leetle w'ile 'go. She goin' shoot me, so I'm shoot heem firs'. I'm work for Crandal. Crandal lead dog no com' for git feed. Crandal say go oop to Abbott an' Boyle place an' git dat Skookum dog—mebbe-so heem up dere. I'm no want to go, 'cause Abbott she say she goin' shoot me nex' tam she fin' me 'round dere, but Crandal say he no shoot me w'en I'm tell heem I'm work for Crandal. So I'm go oop dere an' Abbott she haf' keel dat Skookum dog an' drag heem off by de tail. So, me, I'm holler at heem an' say Crandal git mad lak hell you keel he's beeg lead dog, an' Abbott, she drop de tail an' den she git mad on me an' yell I'm hont hee's cache, an' now I'm tell Crandal 'bout heem keel de dog, so he goin' to shoot me. So she ron to de cabin to git de gon, an' I grab up gon w'at stan' by de sluice, an' I'm shoot heem w'en she git to de cabin, an' she fall down rat een de door. So ba gos, I'm ron 'way lak hell, an' I'm see you an' p'lice go by, an' I'm foller t'rough de bush. Den you com' back, so I'm foller 'long till p'lice ain' here, an' I'm come tell you 'bout dat."

Black John nodded gravely. "You done right, Maktab, to tell me about what come off up there. I believe you've told the truth, 'cause when I made Abbott quit workin' you over, that time, I rec'lect he threatened to shoot you if you ever showed up there again. An he'd ondoubtless of done it if you hadn't got him first. You better go home now, an' keep your mouth shet. Don't say a damn word to no one about what come off up there—don't even let no one know you was on that feeder. I was headin' fer

Cush's, but I guess I'll turn around an' go back up there. If I find out that things worked out like you said, there won't no one bother you. But if you've lied to me we'll take you down to Cush's an' hang you shore as hell."

"Me, I'm ain' lie 'bout dat—I'm tell de troot."

TURNING ON his heel, Black John hastened back up the creek. A short distance up the feeder, he overtook Corporal Downey, who had paused to boil a pail of tea. The officer greeted him with a smile. "Thought you headed back to Cush's," he said. "I got a little hungry an' stopped fer lunch."

"I did head back," the big man replied, "but then I got to thinkin' about them shots we heard, an' I thinks, cripes, if there's moose up that feeder I'd be a damn fool not to get one, as long as I've come this far."

Heavy footsteps sounded on the trail up the feeder and a moment later Boyle, carrying his rifle and a heavy pack, rounded a bend and halted abruptly within twenty feet of the two seated beside the little fire. Sweat glistened on the man's face as he stood staring into the two upturned faces. His Adam's-apple worked convulsively, and he found his voice. "By God," he blustered, his eyes on Black John's face, "I'm lucky! Here I'm hittin' out fer Cush's to tell you what come off, up here, an' damn if I don't run plumb onto you—an' the law, too!"

Black John's eyes met the other's squarely as he nodded slowly. "Sech luck is astoundin'," he agreed. "Was you aimin' to tell me you'd shot a moose?"

"Moose—hell! There's be'n shootin' up here—but not no moose! Crandal, he shot Abbott an' robbed our cache! I was up the feeder a ways, workin' on our sluice, an' I heerd the shot, an' run back an found Abbott layin' halfways in the door of the cabin, deader'n hell, an' I seen Crandal throw down his rifle an' run into the bresh. Then I seen our cache had be'n robbed, so I grabs up my rifle an' took off down to his place, an' ketched him hittin' out with his pack, so I took a shot at him before he could git to the bush, an' I got him. Then I seen where he'd took the dust outa his own cache, so I know'd he was makin' a gitaway with his dust an' ourn, too. So I picks up his pack, an' headed fer Cush's fast as God would let me, when I runs onto you boys here."

"Yer zeal is commendable, Boyd," Black John said, "but didn't it occur to you that God would let you make better time if you'd cached that pack an' rifle somewheres?"

The other scowled. "Cache it—hell! There's goin' on ten thousan' dollars in dust in this pack! I ain't cachin' no ten thousan' dollars where the first damn cuss that comes along kin find it!"

"That's right," Black John agreed. "You should have cached it where they couldn't find it. You say you picked up Crandal's pack from where it lit when you shot him? Is that it—the one you've got there?"

"Shore it is! There's his 'nitials he got stamped onto it—J C—Jack Crandal. An' like I says, I grabbed it up right where it lit when he dropped it."

"You didn't, perchanct, onpack it before you hit out—sort of rearrange the load, did you?"

"Hell—no! Tellin' you about me, I was in a hurry."

"That I believe," Black John replied. "How much was it Crandal lifted out of your cache?"

"Three hundred ounces—right around five thousan' dollars."

"You claimed there was clost to ten thousan' in the pack there. How do you know what Crandal had in his own cache—if you didn't onpack his pack sack?"

Boyle hesitated only a secend. "Why—he told us that's what he had in his cache. He was talkin' jest the other night, an' he says he's got right around three hundred ounces cached, and me an' Abbott, we told him we had about the same. That's prob'ly what put it into his head to rob us—figgered to double his money an' beat it."

"Did he tell you where his cache was?"

"Hell, no! A man would be a damn fool to tell that to anyone!"

"So, you didn't know where it was, eh?"

"No. It wasn't none of my business where his cache was."

"Then, how do you know he'd took his dust out of it, an' put it in the pack there? You say you didn't onpack it?"

Boyle's eyes shifted from one face to the other, and he floundered among his words.

"Well—hell—'course he'd take the dust outa his cache. He was gittin' out the country after killin' Abbott an' robbin' us, wasn't he? He'd be a damn fool to go off an' leave his own dust."

CORPORAL DOWNEY smiled grimly. "Guess I'll take over from here," he said. "Fetch the pack along, Boyle. We're headin' up to Crandal's. After that we'll go on up to your place an' look around a little."

Reaching the Crandal location, Downey examined the body as Black John and Boyle looked on. Then picking up the pack from where Boyle had set it, he proceeded to the cabin. Removing the blankets, he proceeded to remove the contents, placing a slab of salt pork and various tins of food on the table, being careful to grip them close to the ends. When all were removed, he peered into the pack and glanced up at Boyle. "You an' Abbott was methodical, the way you wrote out the ounces on tickets an' tied 'em to the sacks," he remarked casually.

"We never done it like that," Boyle replied surlily. "If there's any sacks with tickets tied onto 'em, they're Crandal's sacks. An' that proves I was right—he'd of took his own dust along when he skipped out."

Downey nodded. "That's so," he agreed. "But about this grub he had in the pack. These here tins is all a different brand from the ones yonder on the shelf. Those brands is all ones Al Scougale carries, down to Dawson. Cush don't carry no sech brands, does he, John?"

The big man shook his head. "No. His stuff comes up from Seattle. These is Canadian brands."

"What's that got to do with it?" Boyle growled.

"Mebbe nothin'—mebbe quite a bit," Downey replied. "These tins from the pack sack come from Cush's. You an' Abbott trade there, don't you?"

"Sure we do. It's handier'n goin' clean down to Dawson."

Downey nodded. "I happen to know that Crandal was down to Dawson, not long ago, an' fetched back a lot of tinned stuff Al Scougale sold him cheap on account of a good turn Crandal done him a while back."

"What if he did?" Boyle growled. "He could of had some of Cush's stuff, too, couldn't he?"

"Oh, shore," Downey replied. "Seems funny, though, he'd take jest the one kind, when there's plenty of the other there on the shelf, right handy to lift off." Carefully he replaced the tins in the pack sack. "We'll bury Crandal, now," he said, "an' then go on up to your place. But first I'll take his fingerprints."

"Fingerprints!" Boyle scoffed. "I've heard about these here new-fangled fingerprints. What the hell have they got to do with who shot Abbott?"

"They might have a hell of a lot to do with it," Downey replied, "as you'll damn well find out."

Reaching the clearing, Boyle pointed to some tracks in the fine gravel. "Them's Crandal's tracks," he said. "They ain't mine, nor Abbott's neither. We both got bigger feet than them tracks."

Downey glanced at the tracks and nodded agreement. "That's right. Crandal was here recently, all right."

"Yer damn right he was, er elst how could he of shot Abbott?" Boyle said. "An' besides that, there lays his gun—by the sluice there—right where he throw'd it when he run away after killin' him."

Downey glanced at the rifle. ".30-30, eh? Don't touch it. I'll want to look it over. First, though, let's look at Abbott." The three proceeded to the doorway and gazed down intently. "Shot in the back as he was about to go in the cabin," Downey concluded.

Boyle assented. "That's the way it looks to me. The way I figger it, he prob'ly ketched Crandal robbin' the cache, an' run in to git his rifle, an' Crandal shot him. Ain't that the way it looks to you, Corp'ral?"

"Well, not quite. Let's see—Crandal's gun was a .30-30. What's that rifle of yours, Boyle?"

"It's a .32. But, what's that got to do with it? Hell, you don't think I shot Abbott, do you?"

"What I think don't cut no figure," Downey replied. "But what I'll know, when I get through lookin' things over, will cut a hell of a lot of figure."

"The bullet that killed Abbott went clean on through him," Boyle said. "No one could tell if it was a .30-30, er a .32. They're damn near alike."

"That's so," Downey agreed. "The main difference is that the .30-30 bullets are jacketed with steel or copper, an' that old .32 of yours shoots a lead bullet."

"An' I s'pose you figger if I did shoot him some of the lead might rub off on Abbott when it went through him, eh?" Boyle asked, a half-sneer on his lips.

"No," Downey replied evenly, "but I do figure that after it went through him it would stick in one of the cabin logs acrost the room, there. When I find that hole an' dig the bullet out, I'll know damn well which gun shot him."

"The same thought occurred to me," Black John said, "so I hunted along them logs till I found the hole. I struck a broom straw in it, there. The bullet's goin' to be easy to dig out. It didn't go in far. A jacketed bullet would have gone farther."

A look of sudden fear flashed into Boyle's eyes. He leaped forward and laid a hand on Downey's arm. "Look-a-here!" he cried. "If Abbott was shot with my rifle, it was Crandal shot him! I left my rifle standin' there agin the sluice when I went up to work on the flume! When I heard that shot an' come back, it was still there. So I grabs it up an' took out after Crandal. I rec'lect, now, that I did pump an empty shell out of it—but I thought Abbott had prob'ly took a shot at somethin'.'"

It was but the work of a few minutes for Downey to recover the misshapen lead slug from the log. Tossing it onto the table, he walked over and snapped the handcuffs onto Boyle's wrists.

"By God," the man cried, "you can't never prove Crandal didn't shoot him! Jest 'cause he was shot with my gun ain't no reason I shot him. Hell—the gun stood there agin the sluice—anyone that come along could of shot him—an' the tracks shows that man was Crandal."

As the man talked, Downey removed a carefully wrapped kit from his own pack. Pressing Boyle's fingers onto an ink pad, he took the impression of his fingerprints on a sheet of writing paper. Then he carefully dusted the tins he removed from Boyle's pack with a grayish black powder. Also he dusted the two rifles. And lastly, the little cardboard tabs on Crandal's gold sacks. Then he produced his camera and took a number of shots. Closing the cabin door and hanging a blanket over the single window of the cabin, he developed his films while Black John stood guard on Boyle outside.

AT THE end of an hour he stepped from the cabin. "The jig's up, Boyle," he said. "It's your prints that shows on your rifle. There's a dim set of other prints—but they ain't Crandal's. You was sweatin' most of the time, Boyle, so your prints stands out good an' plain—not only on your own rifle, but on Crandal's, when you laid it there by the sluice. That gun was carefully placed there. If it had been throw'd, like you said, it would have left marks in the gravel.

"Then agin, the prints on these tins are yours—not Crandal's. An' look' at the shelf, yonder, the tins that's left are like these—and you can see the place you took 'em from when you made up your pack. Crandal's tins were in even rows on his shelf.

"But your worst mistake, Boyle, was in fingerin' them little tabs on Crandal's dust sacks. Your prints is on them too—an' you claimed you'd never opened his pack. Fact is, Boyle, you've told so many lies, an' made so many mistakes, that any jury in the world would convict you on the evidence."

Beside himself with terror Boyle raved like a madman. "I shot Crandal, 'cause he shot Abbott! But, by God, I never shot Abbott! He was dead, when I come back after hearin' the shot that killed him! He was dead, I tell you! I never shot him!"

"You can tell that to the jury," Downey said, and turned to Black John who was eyeing the terrified man from between narrowed lids.

"An' you didn't drown him nor pi'zen him, neither—but you shore tried like hell, didn't you, Boyle?" the big man asked.

"So you see, John," the officer said, "it's best to let the law take its course. A man can stand up an' lie like hell. But evidence don't lie. It don't make any difference now what the Minnesota law would have done to Boyle. He'll be tried for Abbott's murder right here in Dawson—an' he'll be convicted, too. Like I've often told you, John—in the long run, the law works out justice."

A CURIOUS smile twisted the corners of the lips behind the heavy black beard, so the big man nodded, slowly. "Yeah, Downey, I guess I'll have to admit that sometimes the law does work out jestice—in a bumblin' sort of a way."

PROFIT ON HALFADAY

WHITE TEETH FLASHED behind the heavy black beard as Black John Smith stepped from the canoe he had beached before the door of a cabin on Sixtymile, to be greeted by a girl who stood in the doorway. "Well, if it isn't Uncle John! Whatever are you doing on Sixtymile—and Dominion Day only three days off?"

The smile widened as the big man's eyes took in the trim, overall-clad figure, the mass of dark hair above a face whose sparkling blue eyes smiled back at him—a face that fairly radiated the keen joy of living. The checked flannel shirt, open at the throat, revealed arms tanned a rich brown below sleeves rolled to the elbow. "Well, dog my cats, it's Margy Benton! Browned up the way you be, I thought for a minute Steve had got him a klooch! An' at his age, too!"

"What do you mean—at my age?" cried a man who emerged from the cabin as the girl stepped aside. He was a tall man—lean, with the sinewy leanness of physical strength. Strong, too, was the smooth-shaven face, whose lantern jaw, and weather-lined features might well have been rough-chiseled from a solid block of copper. "Why, damn your hide, I don't feel a day older than you—if as old!"

"Well—so what? If I could find a klooch as good lookin' as Margy I might even be tempted myself."

"Why—Uncle John!" laughed the girl, shaking a finger in mock admonition.

"I jest said 'maybe'. Fact is, I tempt hard. By gosh, but you've grow'd! Cripes, it don't seem no time at all since you were a little kid down there on Birch Crick. Let's see—that was quite a while back. Why, you must be crowdin' twenty!"

"Nineteen the tenth of January. Daddy says I brought on a spell of the strong cold."

"You tellin' me! Cripes, it was me an' Bettles that made the dogsled run to Forty Mile to fetch Father Judge. There wasn't a doctor in the country then. But believe me, Father Judge is as good as any doctor."

Steve Benton, the girl's father, nodded. "You spoke a mouthful there, John. If I was ailin', right now, I'd sooner have Father Judge than any doctor. By God, there's a man! Us old sourdoughs, we know!"

Black John winked at the girl. "There he goes again—tryin' to make out I'm as old as he is. I might be, at that. Maybe he jest looks older. But you ain't helpin' out any. If you go 'unclein' me before folks, they might get to thinkin' I am as old as Steve. When you were a little kid it was fine, but when a grow'd up woman 'uncles' a man—it kind of makes him feel old, himself."

"Yer headin' fer Dawson, ain't you?" Steve Benton asked.

"Oh shore. Got a kind of a late start, so I cut acrost by way of Miller Creek. It saves a couple of days, an' I figure I ort to hit the big river in time to sort of practice up on my drinkin' an' stud playin' before the festivities begin."

STEVE GRINNED. "From what I hear, you boys up on Halfaday don't git none rusty, on either drinkin' or stud."

"Ondoubtless mere hearsay," the big man replied. "Why, we're the moralist crick in the Yukon. I'll leave it to Downey."

"So when we get to Dawson, I'm not to call you Uncle John? Okay. If I meet you on the street I'll say 'Good evening, Mr. Smith'."

The big man scowled ferociously. "Listen, brat! One 'Mr. Smith' out of you, an' I'll take you accost my knee, if it's right

there on Front Street—an' the parade goin' by!"

"Lay over with us tonight, an' we'll pull out in the mornin'," Benton invited. "We'll stop in an' pick up Tommy Dean, an' all go down together. You an' me'll team up, an' Margy kin paddle the front end of Tommy's canoe. We kin fetch Dawson day after tomorrow night easy."

"I can paddle the front end of your canoe, or Uncle John's just as easy as I could paddle the front end of Tommy Dean's," the girl said, with a toss of her head.

"Who's Tommy Dean?" Black John asked.

"He's a young fella that's located on a dry gulch couple miles below here. Seems like a likely lad. Takin' out a little better'n wages. I offered to let him work a lay fer me on a good proposition I bought above here. But he's got faith in his own location. Says he'd rather be on his own. Figgers, I reckon, that I was sort of favorin' him on account of Margy."

"You don't need to favor him on my account," the girl cut in.

"He's nothing but a chechako, and he's stubborn as a—a mule! No one but a dumb chechako would locate in a dry gulch. Suppose he is taking out better than wages out of the top gravel? When winter comes he's going to have to burn in and sink a shaft the same as anyone else. Then in the spring how is he going to sluice out his dump? When the break-up comes the snow water will come roaring down the gulch so fast it would rip out a sluice if he had one—and then in three or four days the gulch would be dry again."

"Gold's where you find it," Black John reminded her. "It wasn't so long ago everyone was laughin' at Side Hill Frank Berry over on Eldorado. But they ain't laughin' at him now. Fact is, Frank could buy out most of the ones that laughed."

"That's right," Steve agreed. "An' there's be'n plenty more in the same boat. By God, I've got respect fer a man that's got the guts to stick by a proposition he's got faith in. Us sourdoughs don't know it all."

The girl sniffed. "We know enough not to stake a location on a dry gulch without a chance of any water for more than four or five days in a year."

"He kin git water, when he gits around to it," Steve replied. "He found a little spring lake half a mile above his location that'll give him all the water he could use—an' more, too. It lays clost to the top of the rimwall with nothin' but a rock dike between. Onct he taps that lake he kin git all the water he wants—an' control it, too."

"Yes," the girl replied, "but when will he ever be able to tap it? Pipe and valves cost money. And it'll cost money to cut through that rock dike—plenty of money. At the rate he's going it will take him years to save up enough to tap that lake—and you know it."

"He could borrow the money," Steve said.

"He could. But he won't. He's too stubborn. You know what he said when you offered to lend him enough to finance the job. He turned it down flat. Said his father lost a mighty good farm by borrowing money on it and running into a couple of crop failures, and he wasn't going to take any chances. He's got a horror of going in debt."

Black John grinned. "It ain't a bad horror to have," he opined. "If he's got a good proposition he'll be better off, in the long run, if he handles it himself."

Steve Benton grinned and winked. "That's the hell of it. You see, Tommy an' Margy be'n pretty thick—an' he's asked her to marry him. But she figgers, the way he's goin' the long run will be too damn long. Tommy's a likely lad. Like I told her, she could go a damn sight further, an' do a damn sight worst."

"I won't marry a man that's content to work a location that only pays a little better than wages, and I won't marry one that's willing to wait maybe ten or twenty years to develop it, and I won't marry one that's so stubborn he'll stick to a proposition like that instead of ditching it and taking on a better one. Daddy offered him a lay that would pay good money right from the start. I don't have to marry Tommy Dean. There's someone else I can marry the minute I say the word—and he's got plenty of money, too!"

Steve Benton's rugged face clouded slightly, as he glanced at Black John. "Yeah," he said. "Clyde Barto's be'n pesterin' Margy to marry him fer the past year."

The big man nodded. "Oh. Him, eh?"

The girl flushed and the blue eyes snapped defiantly. "Yes— him! He's got plenty of money in the bank, and he's got good propositions on a dozen cricks."

"Yeah, that's what the talk is," Black John admitted. "But you got to remember, Sis—it ain't always what a man's got, but how he got it, that counts."

"What do you mean by that?"

"It's true, ain't it?"

"Sure it's true! But what's that got to do with Clyde Barto?"

The big man smiled. "If it's true, it's got jest as much to do with Barto as it has with anyone else. Jest think that over, Sis. I ain't got any more to say."

II

SUPPER OVER, STEVE BENTON and Black John seated themselves on a bench beside the door, filled their pipes and talked over old times on Birch Creek and Forty Mile while the girl busied herself with the dishes. Knocking the dottle from his pipe, Steve stood up and glanced at the sun well above the western rim. "It's early yet," he said, "Tommy Dean's got a pretty good foot trail wore acrost to his gulch. 'Spose we walk over an' tell him we'll be gittin' an early start in the mornin', so he kin be waitin' fer us at the mouth of the gulch."

Margy appeared in the doorway, dish towel in hand. "Wait

a few minutes and I'll go too," she said. "I'd just like to see what Uncle John thinks of a chump that will turn down a good proposition to fool away his time on a dry gulch. Web Foot Hartz and Howard Franklin have seen his location, and so have Gene La Porte and Bob Henderson, and they all told him he was fooling away his time there. They're all sourdoughs—and they know. But he wouldn't listen to them. They told it around, and the last time Tommy was in Dawson everybody was kidding him about it."

Black John nodded. "Yeah. They would. But—like I told you a while back, Sis—gold's where you find it. I rec'lect that both Web Foot Hartz an' Bob Henderson was amongst the ones that laughed the loudest when Frank Berry staked his location on that hillside. There's an old sayin' about him laughin' best who laughs last, or some sech wordin'."

"I think those old sayings are dumb," the girl scoffed. "'Gold's where you find it.' Of course gold's where you find it! So is everything else. But the place to look for it is where it's most apt to be. You don't see the sourdoughs wasting their time on dry gulches when there are plenty of cricks left to prospect. How many times would Frank Berry have made a strike staking out on a sidehill?"

The big man grinned. "A man wouldn't have to strike it but once—the way he did. An' I rec'lect that a good many sourdoughs passed up that moose pasture before George Carmack made his strike on Bonanza. Yup—plenty of sourdoughs tromped acrost that flat without botherin' to scratch it—too wide, or too flat, or the crick run too slow, or the willers bent the wrong way. All of 'em had good reasons for passin' it up—all except Carmack, him bein' a squawman, he wasn't s'posed to know nothin'—so one day he begun shovellin' around amongst the grass roots—an' turned up the biggest strike that ever hit the Yukon.

"An' down to Forty Mile we all laughed an' kidded hell out of him when he showed up in Bergman's with his first poke of dust. You see—we was sourdoughs. We was the wise ones. We know'd it all. We know'd that Larue was in the upper country, an' we figured it all out—he'd staked out a townsite, an' slipped Carmack that poke of dust to flash around Bergman's, claimin' he got it on Bonanza to start a stampede so he could sell off his buildin' lots. An' if I remember right," he added, "Carmack done a little laughin' on his own hook—later."

"Just the same," the girl retorted, with a toss of the head, "you know as well as I do that a good many more strikes have been made on likely locations than on unlikely ones."

"Oh shore. But, at that, a man ain't necessarily a fool because he stakes one of them onlikely claims. Tellin' you about me, Sis—I'd rather be a rich fool than a poor wise man."

The girl smiled in spite of herself. "You make me tired, Uncle John! I guess nobody can accuse you of being a fool, or a poor man either—from what I've heard."

"Ondoubtless mere hearsay," Black John returned the smile. "Up on Halfaday we work hard for what we get—but we're happy."

Steve Benton laughed. "Well, if you two've got through scrappin' let's get goin'. An' talk about workin' hard, John—I'll bet some nights yer right arm's damn near wore out shakin' dice with Cush fer the drinks!"

THE THREE crossed the divide, following a well worn foot trail, and descended into a narrow gulch, running parallel to the Sixtymile, whose opposite rimwall was a high perpendicular rock cliff. A quarter of a mile below, the gulch made a sharp right angle turn toward the river, and on a narrow gravel flat at the foot of the slope in the crook of this elbow Tommy Dean had built his cabin.

"Hi, Tommy!" Steve greeted the young man who stepped from the doorway. "I want you should meet up with my friend Black John Smith, prob'ly the orneriest son of a gun that ever hit the Yukon."

The younger man smiled. "That's not the way I heard it," he

said as he shook the big man's hand. "The Broncho Kid told me all about how you saved him from being hanged for a murder he didn't commit. And later how you made it possible for him and his sister to develop their claims by cutting her in on some kind of a deal you had with Cuter Malone and a fellow by the name of Morocco."

White teeth showed beneath the black beard as the big man returned the other's smile. "My benefactions has ondoubtless be'n greatly exaggerated," he said. "It ain't no particular credit to a man if he saves an innocent man from gettin' hung. An' as for cuttin' the kid's sister in on that deal—hell, it was the least I could do, seein' she was the one that slipped me the information that made the deal possible. As I rec'lect the incident, it netted us a profit of fifty thousan' apiece, or some sech matter. Nice little layout you've got here," he added, glancing at the neat log cabin. "How's she pannin' out?"

"I'm taking better than wages out of the top gravel," the young man replied. "And I'm cutting wood to burn in with this winter. I'm going to sink a shaft or two and maybe I can figure some way in the spring to hold back snow water enough to sluice out my dumps with. When I get going I'll have all the water I want—and have it steady. There's a little lake up the crick a piece that lays on high ground just back of the rim. When I tap that I'll have all the water I need."

Black John nodded. "Yeah, Steve was tellin' me about it."

"And I told him I think you're a fool to stick here on this dry gulch when daddy has offered you a lay on a good location!" the girl exclaimed.

Young Dean smiled. "Sure, I know how you feel about it, Margy. And I'm sorry you can't see it my way. I've got faith in this location. I believe it's going to pay out big. And it's mine. I'm going to develop it myself. I'm not asking odds from anyone—not even Steve. Nor Clyde Barto either. When I get water in here, I'll show you I'm right."

The girl shrugged. "By the time you get water in here I won't care whether you're right or not," she retorted.

Black John filled his pipe. "I'd like to take a look at this lake," he said. "I ain't a minin' engineer, but I've be'n around some."

The young man's eyes lighted. "I'll show it to you. It's only half a mile." He turned to the Bentons. "You coming along?"

Margy, who was peering into the cabin, shook her head. "No, I'm going to stay here and wash out your dishtowels, and shake out your blankets, and sweep out. You men go ahead."

"I've saw the lake," Steve said. "I'll jest set here an' take a smoke. I knocked my right knee agin a rock yesterday, an' it's botherin' me a little. We'll wait here till you git back."

Ascending the rimwall, some half mile above the cabin, the two reached the shore of a spring fed pond some half dozen acres in extent, and separated from the gulch by a rock dike of varying width. Young Dean led the way to a point where this dike was only about five feet in thickness. "I figure if I could drill through the rock here, I could put in pipe and a valve that would give me all the water I'll need—and I'd be able to control the flow."

The big man nodded. "Yeah. But outside of some of the big outfits, I don't know of a diamond drill rig in the country. An' it would be a hell of a chore to drill a pipe hole through that rock by hand."

"That's right," the other admitted, "but I've been wondering whether I couldn't drill in from the top and then shoot off a face—maybe a foot or so thick—and keep on doing that till finally I could drill through?"

BLACK JOHN shook his head. "Any one of them shots might blow the wall out, an' you'd have the whole damn lake down onto you all to onct! I saw a proposition of this kind worked with a siphon onct. But the pipe an' valves would run into money."

"I believe it would be worth it, though," the other replied. "I believe I've got a good proposition there in the gulch." Reaching into his pocket he withdrew his hand and extended it, palm upward. Black John's eyes widened at sight of the half dozen big yellow nuggets.

"Where in hell did you get them?" he asked.

"Down on my location just below the cabin. I happened to be in the Tivoli Saloon one day where some of the sourdoughs were talking, and a fellow by the name of Moosehide Charlie showed some nuggets that he'd found on a location he'd recorded. He said he dug them out just above a rock dike that ran crosswise to this little crick he was prospecting. The top of the dike didn't show above ground, nor above the surface of the water, and these nuggets lay close against the dike right in the crick bed. You see, they'd washed down and the dike held them there. All the other sourdoughs agreed that he has a swell location—and several of them named other strikes that had been located behind transverse dikes.

"Well, in digging around in my gulch, I located just such a dike—and I got these nuggets, just as Moosehide Charlie did, right up against the dike, and almost on the surface. I've never mentioned this to a soul—not even to Margy or Steve. They think I'm foolish for sticking to my location—and I'll let 'em think so till I can prove beyond any doubt that I'm right."

The big man nodded. "You stick to your proposition, son," he advised. "Don't let no one talk you out of it. Fact is, I happen to have a few thousan' that ain't workin'. I could let you have enough to finance the siphon proposition."

The other shook his head. "Thanks," he said, "but I want to work it out alone. Steve offered to lend me the money to drill with, and Clyde Barto offered me a loan, too."

"Barto! Does he know about your proposition?"

"Not about the dike down at the cabin. He was through here about a month ago, and he saw the lake, and offered me a loan. But he wanted fifteen percent interest, and a partnership. I told him to go to the devil."

"You done right," the big man approved. "Barto's a man whose ethics is open to question."

"He's smart, and he seems to have plenty of money."

"Yeah, he's well heeled—in an onderhanded sort of way. I wouldn't know how smart he is. Maybe sometime I'll find out."

The younger man's face clouded. "The hell of it is," he said, "he's making a play for Margy Benton. I—er—Margy's the finest girl I ever knew. We—that is—I—I want to marry her. I think she would marry me if I'd take Steve up on a partnership proposition he offered me. She thinks I'm a fool to stick to this location. She hasn't got faith in it, like I have."

"Why don't you show her them nuggets, an' tell her about that cross dike?"

"No." There was a stubborn, almost a defiant note in the other's voice. "If she hasn't got faith enough in me to marry me, I'll be damned if I'll bribe her to with a handful of nuggets! I want to know she's marryin' me—not a gold mine. She'll have the gold mine, all right. We'll have it together. She'll know I'm right about this location, but she'll find that out later."

"Yeah—but s'pose she finds it out too late? She might get tired waitin', an' marry Barto!"

Tommy Dean shrugged. "That would be my hard luck," he said, "and hers, too."

Black John shook his head in resignation. "The ways of young folks in love is too devious fer my limited comprehension. By God, if ever I wanted a woman bad enough to marry her, I'd get her—an' I wouldn't give a damn how. We'd better be movin' along. Steve's knee's kind of botherin' him, an' he'll be wantin' to get back to his place before dark."

Back at the cabin Black John seated himself beside Steve. Tommy glanced in as the girl was returning the broom to its place behind the door. "Gee, that looks swell, Margy," he said, his eyes sweeping the smoothly made bunk, and the clean floor. "That's the way it would look if—if you'd—if you'd marry me and move in—everything nice and clean—and just us two. We'll be hitting out for Dawson in the morning and we could get Father Judge to marry us. It would be the biggest Dominion Day celebration we'd ever have."

"I'll marry you, Tommy," the girl said, "if you'll quit this location, and take up that proposition of dad's."

"I can't do it, Margy. This is my location, and I've got to stick with it. And some day you'll know I'm right."

Steve rose from the log where he and Black John were seated and knocked the dottle from his pipe. "We better be gittin' along," he said. "We'll be pullin' out, come daylight, Tommy. We'll pick you up at the mouth of the gulch. Better throw a couple of clean shirts in yer pack. What with the Fourth of July crowdin' Dominion Day like it does, we won't be hittin' back fer a week er ten days."

III

TOMMY DEAN WAS waiting as the two canoes swept around a bend of the Sixtymile shortly after daylight the following morning. The girl waved to him from her father's canoe as Black John swerved to the bank. Tossing his light pack amidship, Tommy took his place in the bow and the two light craft slipped smoothly downriver.

Toward noon they beached, boiled a pail of tea, and devoured the sandwiches the girl had prepared.

"There'll be a hell of a crowd in town this year, what with the way the damn chechakos has be'n crowdin' in on us," Steve opined, between huge mouthfuls of his moosemeat sandwich.

Black John nodded. "Yeah, an' every damn one of 'em'll be tryin' to get drunker'n the next one."

"The hotels is goin' to be full up," Benton said. "I stopped in to the Northern the last time I was down an' ordered a couple of rooms fer a week, startin' today."

The big man grinned. "They always save me a room. They figure I'd take their damn hotel apart if they didn't."

"Guess I'll have to sleep standing up," Tommy said ruefully. "I haven't engaged any room."

"You'll make out all right," Black John said. "Me an' Steve won't be usin' our beds much at night. We'll be too busy tryin' to figure out the relative merits of two pairs an' three of a kind."

AS STEVE had predicted Dawson was a madhouse of milling chechakos. Hotels were turning them away, and every saloon in the big camp was crowded to capacity, with extra bartenders on all three shifts.

When Margy Benton stepped into the room that had been engaged for her she uttered a gasp of surprise. "Oh look, Daddy! A huge bouquet of flowers! And a box of bon bons! Why—who could have sent them?"

Steve Benton, who had tossed his pack into the adjoining room, glanced over her shoulder from the doorway. "There's a paper sticking out from in under that vase," he said. "Mebbe it'll say."

Withdrawing the folded note, the girl opened it and read aloud:

"Welcome to Dawson! May I have the pleasure of your company at the grand ball tonight? Will see you, I hope, at dinner.
"Devotedly
Clyde Barto"

Steve grunted. "Huh. Wants you to go to the dance, eh?"

The girl nodded, her eyes on the vase of flowers. "Yes, that's what he says."

"You goin' with him?"

After a moment of hesitation she nodded slowly. "Yes," she answered. "He's asked me, and I'm going." Then with a toss of her head and a hint of defiance in her tone she added, "Why shouldn't I?"

Steve shrugged. "Suit yourself," he replied. "I sort of figgered mebbe Tommy would be wantin' you to go with him."

"Why didn't he ask me, then?"

"We jest hit town. Chances is, he ain't heard about no dance."

"I've known Tommy for quite a while, and he's never yet sent me any flowers, nor given me any candy."

Steve gave a snort of disgust. "Flowers an' candy—hell! Tommy knows the hills is full of flowers you kin pick fer yerself, if you wanted 'em. An' where would he git any candy—there in his gulch?"

"That's just it—there in his gulch!" the girl cried. "And if I'd marry him that's where I'd spend the rest of my life—right there in his gulch!"

"Not if she pans out like Tommy thinks she will," her father retorted. "Not if I know Tommy Dean, you wouldn't."

"His location, never will pan out like he thinks it will—and you know it! He's just a—a stubborn fool to stick with it! You don't see Clyde Barto holing up in some gulch fooling away his time on a worthless location. He's made money, and he keeps on making money because he's got sense enough to look around and buy in on good propositions. And he's got sense enough to live here in Dawson where there are people—and things to do, and see. And he's got sense enough to know that a woman likes little things like flowers and bon bons—not because they're flowers and bon bons—but, they're sort of—of symbols—"

Steve interrupted her with a snort of disgust. "Well, if you know what yer talkin' about, it's more'n I do!" Turning on his heel, he called over his shoulder. "I'm goin' down an' hunt me a drink. I shore as hell need one after listenin' to that line of guff. Flowers an' candy an' symbols—cripes!"

Downstairs he encountered Tommy Dean and Black John, who had returned to the lobby after depositing their packs in the latter's room. Together they stepped out onto the street and made their way to the Tivoli Saloon to be vociferously greeted by Swiftwater Bill, Bettles, Moosehide Charlie, and several old sourdoughs. Tommy Dean was introduced, and a round of drinks downed.

"Fill 'em up agin!" Bettles ordered. "It'll take half a dozen er more to steam John up fer the dance."

Black John grinned, and winked at Swiftwater Bill. "Bettles is no damn fool. He figures if he can get enough licker down me to get me dance minded, I wouldn't be settin' in the stud game tonight—figures what he put out for the drinks would be a damn good investment."

"Contrary as you be," Bettles chuckled, "the shorest way to toll you into the stud game, is fer me to try to steer you to the dance. Tellin' you about me—I don't know no better investment than gettin' you in a stud game—after what we done to you last time you was here. Remember them three kings you draw'd to yer pair of aces, an' then tried to make me lay down my four feeble little treys? I don't want no better investment than that. Cripes, I ain't got that pot spent yet—an' it was a good three months ago!"

As the bottle reached Tommy Dean he shoved it along. Black John glanced at him in surprise. "What's the matter, kid? Don't you like our brand of firewater?"

The younger man smiled. "One's plenty for me, thanks. I guess I'm not much of a drinker."

"If you're quittin' at one drink, I'd say you made a damn good guess," the big man laughed. "What I claim, one drink ain't worth a damn. Two or three is what you might call an appetizer. From three on a man's conscience has got to be his guide."

"Yeah," grinned Swiftwater Bill, "an' yore conscience, backed up by yore capacity, is what keeps the distilleries runnin' three shifts."

A couple of drinks later Steve Benton shoved back his glass and glanced at Black John and pointed to the clock. "Ten minutes to six," he said. "We better git back to the hotel. The clerk said they throw'd open the dinin' room at six, an' what with the crowd they've got, if we ain't there on the dot we ain't goin' to git no table. I'm hungry as a wolf, an' damn if I want to wait around fer an hour an' then fill up on leavin's!"

"That's right," the big man agreed, and turned to the others. "We'll be seein' you later. An' I'm warnin' you, Bettles, that play I give you on them four treys was only a come-on. Sometime durin' the evenin', I'm hopin' to get you in a real pot."

As they entered the hotel lobby Tommy Dean saw Margy talking with Clyde Barto, who turned to greet the three as they stepped through the door. "Hello, Steve! Hello, John! And you, too, Dean! Wait just a minute—I've got an idea!" And turning, he wormed his way through the crowd to the desk.

Tommy stepped close to the girl. "There's a dance tonight, Margy," he said. "Will you go with me?"

She shook her head. "Can't do it, Tommy. Sorry—but I've already promised to go with Clyde Barto."

Barto rejoined them rubbing his hands with satisfaction. "It's all set," he announced. "Money sure talks in this man's town. I slipped the clerk a twenty, and he's reserved a table for the five of us. The supper's on me. Fact is, I feel kind of flush today—just cinched a good proposition on Hunker Crick."

"An' the other fellow?" Black John asked dryly. "Is it a good proposition for him, too?"

Barto grinned and winked. "He thinks it is. When he wakes up and finds out different, he's going to be sick. It's every man for himself in this world—and the devil take the hindmost."

The big man nodded. "Ondoubtless a comfortin' philosophy," he admitted.

Barto laughed and nudged him in the ribs with his thumb. "It's a philosophy that you're a past master of, if some of the things I've heard are true."

Black John smiled. "Prob'ly like most rumors—half lies an'

half truths scrambled up together. Fact is, though, if a man's got it comin', I ain't in nowise loath to see that he gets it."

"That's the idea! If a man isn't smart enough to hang onto what he's got, he ought to lose it."

"If a *crooked* man ain't smart enough to hang onto what he's got, he ought to lose it," the big man amended with a laugh. "An' once in a while, he does."

Toward the close of the meal Barto glanced at Tommy across the table. "How about it, Dean? You remember I looked your location over a while back. You've got a good proposition there, if you'd put a little money in it. The way you're going, though—just a little better than wages, there's nothing ahead of you but a lot of hard work, and damn small profit. I'll put up enough money so you can tap that lake and clean up the whole gulch in a couple of years at a good profit for both of us."

Tommy shook his head. "No, I'll keep on the way I am, Barto. I'm making a living there, and if I should strike it lucky, it'll be all mine."

The other shrugged. "Suit yourself. You're one of these birds that have to learn the hard way that stubbornness never gets a man anything,"

IV

THE MEAL OVER, Black John and Steve Benton rejoined the sourdoughs in the Tivoli.

Tommy Dean avoided the dance. For an hour or more he roamed about mingling with the drunken rowdy chechakos, his heart heavy within him. Finally in disgust he returned to the hotel. To hell with it all! To hell with Dawson, and Dominion Day, and Fourth of July, and the drunken chechakos! Making his way to Black John's room where he had left his pack, he pulled off his shoes and threw himself on the bed. He'd get a few hours sleep, and when the big man returned from the stud game, he'd get up, throw his pack and a load of supplies into a canoe, and hit back to his gulch on the Sixtymile. If Marjory Benton wanted Clyde Barto she could have him. If they all thought he was a stubborn fool—let 'em think so. He slipped a hand into his pocket and fingered his half-dozen nuggets. They didn't know about those nuggets—Margy, and Barto and Steve. Only Black John knew—and he had approved his determination to stick by the claim.

For a long time he lay there staring straight up into the dark. Idly his attention riveted on a faint play of light on the ceiling. Pale and scarcely noticeable, at first, it increased in brightness, writhing curlicues of light that formed ever changing patterns. Swinging his feet to the floor, he crossed to the window and glanced out. At first he could see nothing. Then a flicker of light caught his attention. It came from a window of a two-story house on a side street a short distance back from the hotel. The whole window glowed a dull ominous red, and he could see little tongues of bright flame reaching out from its upper corner and licking up the outside wall.

Fumbling for his shoes in the darkness, he hastily drew them on and rushed from the room and down the stairs. "Fire!" he yelled, "Fire! Fire! Fire!" The lobby was deserted save for three or four obviously drunken chechakos asleep in chairs, and the night clerk, who dashed past him and ascended the stairs to look for the fire, as Tommy catapulted into the street and around the corner, still yelling "Fire" at the top of his lungs. Many men were on the street, most of whom glanced at him and grinned— just another drunk trying to start something. A few followed, however, and these were joined by others as the flames that licked up the wall of the doomed house leaped momentarily higher and brighter. Men were swarming about the building, now, milling about and yelling senseless orders. Someone kicked the door in, and the crowd fell back as a blast of flame burst outward and shot up the wall to the eaves. Close beside Tommy a woman, who had dashed out of a house across the street, started shrieking: "Oh, the baby! The little kid! My God—they went to the dance and left him alone in there! I told 'em—"

Tommy grasped her by the shoulder and shook her roughly. "In where?" he demanded. "Where is the kid—what room?" The woman pointed hysterically to an upstairs window at the gable end, over a lean-to that was evidently the kitchen. "Up there!" she screamed. "And he's all alone!"

Two men appeared, dragging a short ladder. Jerking it away from them, Tommy raised it against the lean-to, and scrambled to the roof. Dragging the ladder after him, he raised it to the upper window. Loud yells reached his ears as he ascended the ladder. "Look out! Come down! You can't make it! The front wall's bulgin' already!"

Reaching the window, Tommy smashed in the lower frame with a blow of his fist. Smoke billowed out, stinging his eyes, and half choking him. Could he make it? Could anyone make his way through that smoke and find a bed in that room—a bed with a little kid in it. Below him the yelling was redoubled. Tommy hesitated. Then distinctly to his ears came the words. "Come back down—you damn stubborn fool!" There it was again—stubborn fool. All right, if he was a stubborn fool he'd play his string out. Drawing a deep breath, he crawled over the sill. Thrusting his head far out the window for a lungful of fresh air, he saw a man scramble onto the roof of the lean-to by means of a plank. Turning, he groped across the smoke-filled room, holding his breath, water streaming from his eyes. His knees struck an obstruction, and reaching downward with both hands he felt bed clothing, and the next instant his fingers closed about the shoulders of a tiny form. Raising the infant in his arms, he grabbed up a blanket and wrapped it around the baby, and staggered across the floor to the window. Below him he could see two men on the roof of the lean-to. "Catch the kid!" he cried, in a voice that was a choking croak. He tossed the infant into their upraised arms—and the next instant there was a dull roar, a blast of intense heat, and the world went black.

V

A SHORT DISTANCE down the street from the hotel the dance was in full swing when a man dashed through the doorway. "Fire! Fire!" he yelled in a voice that penetrated to the farthest corner of the hall. The music stopped abruptly as dancers and orchestra stared at the man in a moment of hushed suspense.

"Where's it at?" someone cried.

"It's Joe Saunders's house, an' when the walls went down the sparks ketched the roof of the next house afire, an' they want help to keep it from spreadin'."

At the words a young woman uttered a piercing shriek: "Oh, my baby! My baby!" Her husband, who had been dancing with her, plunged through the crowd, knocking people right and left and, with wide staring eyes and set lips disappeared through the doorway. Her face paper white, the woman sought to follow, but was held back by the rush of men who were already crowding the doorway. The man who had sounded the alarm, reached the side of the sobbing woman and shook her roughly by the shoulder. "Shet up, mom—an' listen! Yer kid's all right—nary a scratch on him! Yer house is gone—but yer kid is safe. A guy drug a ladder up on the shed roof, an' clumb up it an' smashed in the winder an' crawled in the room through smoke so thick you could cut it with a knife, an' found the kid an' wropped him up in a blanket an' tossed him down to a couple of fellas on the shed roof, an' they tossed him to some folks on the ground—an' when they onwropped the blanket off'n him, damn if he wasn't laughin'—like it was some game he was playin'! An' before the guy could get back out through the winder the fire musta et up through the floor an' touched off a gas pocket, er somethin', 'cause there was a kinda dull roar, an' a hell of a bust of flame, an' the guy got blowed out through the winder an' hit the shed roof an' rolled off. An' the next minute, the walls caved in an' the roof fell an' sent the sparks flyin' that ketched the roof of the next house."

"Oh, thank God! Thank God!" the woman was sobbing and laughing hysterically. "I don't care about the house—if my baby is safe!"

Most of the men and some of the women had dashed from the room to help fight the fire, but a few remained on the outskirts of the crowd of women who surrounded the sobbing woman and the narrator. "The man who saved the baby?" someone asked. "Who was he? Was he killed?"

"No, mom, he worn't killed. Scorched up pretty bad, an' mebbe bunged up some, what with hittin' the shed roof an' then the ground. They've took him to the horspital. They say his name's Dean—some chechako from up Sixtymile way. He's sure got guts! Stubborn as hell, to boot. Keepin' on goin' up that ladder with everyone hollerin' at him to come back—an' the smoke pourin' out through the winders, an' flames lickin' up the walls! Cripes—there worn't a chanct in a thousan' he could of got in that room through all that smoke—let alone findin' the kid after he got in there! But—he done it! An' he got the kid! An' checha-ko, er no chechako—that's what I call a man!"

Clyde Barto was among those few men who had not gone to help fight the fire. At his side on the edge of the crowd, he heard Marjory Benton gasp. "Tommy Dean!" she cried. "Oh, is—is he badly hurt?"

"Couldn't say, mom," the man who had mentioned his name answered. "They'll know to the horspital. If he ain't, he'd ort to be—gittin' blow'd out through a winder, an' hittin' a shed roof, an' then the ground."

The girl turned to Barto. "Take me to the hospital right this minute!" she cried, starting toward the door.

Barto laid a detaining hand on her arm. "Hold on, Marjory. There's no hurry. You can't do any good there. It's his own fault if he got hurt. That kid was nothing to him. Why didn't he listen to 'em when they tried to call him back? I warned him that he'd learn the hard way that stubbornness don't pay. It's probably cost him his life."

The girl shook off the detaining hand, whirled and faced the man, her eyes flashing. "You—you cur!" she cried as the words left his lips, then turning abruptly, she disappeared through the doorway.

Apparently unperturbed, Barto smiled into the outraged eyes and scornfully curled lips of those women who had overheard his words. "Hero worship," he said lightly. "If that fool dies she'll forget all about him in a month's time. But whether he lives or dies, I intend to marry that girl. I like her spunk."

Some of the women sniffed scornfully, others turned away. "You don't hate yerself none, do you?" one taunted. "Why ain't you out with the rest helpin' fight the fire?" Then she, too, turned away.

In the small waiting room at the hospital Marjory Benton paced the floor restlessly, pausing now and then to throw herself into a chair, pick up a magazine, and turn the pages, staring at the illustrations with unseeing eyes. A nurse had promised to let her know when they brought Tommy Dean from the operating room. Oh—wouldn't the doctors ever finish? He must be terribly hurt! Or—or maybe—maybe they would never bring him from that room—alive! Why did they take so long? It seemed that hours passed before the uniformed nurse appeared in the doorway. "They've finished now," she said. "He's in Number 18."

"Can—can I see him?" Margy asked.

The nurse nodded and smiled. "Yes. But not very much of him. He's pretty well bandaged."

In the hall the girl accosted young Doctor Sutherland. "Oh, doctor," she faltered. "Will he—is he badly hurt?"

"He ought to be hurt a good deal worse than he is—judging from what the men who brought him here said. I'd say he got off mighty lucky. Superficial burns—multiple bruises—not a broken bone in his body. He's a tough one, all right. Be good as ever in a couple of weeks. Go on in, if you want to."

IN THE doorway of Number 18, the girl paused and gasped. Two arms, bandaged to the fingertips lay stiff and inert as a pair of white stovepipes on the counterpane, and on the pillow a head bandaged so as to leave only a narrow slit for the eyes, and another through which the lips and nostrils were visible. Beyond the bed stood a nurse, who smiled. "He looks a lot worse than he is," she said. "He won't come to for an hour—and even then he won't be able to do much talking through the bandage. You can sit here, if you like. I've got some other patients to look after. If you want anything just touch that button. We've got the electric bells installed at last."

Slowly the minutes dragged past as Margy sat there beside the still form on the bed—a form that looked more like some hideous mummy than a man—her man. Yes—her man! She knew now that she loved him—had loved him all along. Her face flushed with shame at the recollection of her persistent pestering him to give up his location and take the lay her father had offered. She had called him a fool, and headstrong, and stubborn. Others had called him stubborn, too—her father, and those men who had yelled at him as he climbed into that burning house and rescued the baby. He was brave—braver than any of the others. She realized now that his stubbornness was a cardinal virtue and not a fault. Because he was stubborn enough to disregard those warning cries he had saved that baby's life—and because he was stubborn enough to stick to his location against her wish, maybe his claim would pay out as big as he thought it would. She felt a growing resentment within her against those who had called him stubborn—her father, and those men at the fire. Clyde Barto had called him stubborn, too—at supper and again in the dance hall. At recollection of his words a flaming anger surged up within her—"his own fault if he got hurt"—"that kid was nothing to him."—"Why didn't he listen when they tried to call him back?"—"I warned him he'd learn the hard way that stubbornness don't pay—"

"He learned the hard way, all right," she muttered to herself. "But if he could have had just one glance into that poor woman's eyes when she learned her baby was safe—he'd have learned that stubbornness *does* pay! That *damn* Barto—how I hate him! There was positively a gloating note in his voice when he said 'it's probably cost him his life.' The dirty lowdown coward—he wouldn't even go and help the others keep the fire from spreading. And—only to think—I turned Tommy down to go to the dance with *him!* But—if I hadn't—that baby would have burned up in the house. I—I'm glad I did turn him down—the way things turned out—and I'll have all my life—all our lives to make it up to him."

The bandaged head on the pillow turned slightly, a bandaged arm moved stiffly and leaping to her feet she bent over the bed, her eyes peering into the slit in the bandage. "Oh, Tommy—it's me—Margy! I'm here—and the doctor says you're going to be all right!"

The eyes staring up through the slit lighted with recognition. The lips moved. "Margy. I—I'm all right. But—where am I?"

"You're in the hospital—and they've got you all bandaged up—but everything's all right. The doctor says so. And—oh Tommy—as soon as you get well we're going to get married and live on your claim—there in the gulch!"

The bandaged arms raised as though to encircle her, and the lips moved. "That's swell, Margy! It's a good location—it'll pay out big—when we get the water. We'll stick to it, Margy—no matter what they say."

The nurse came in and glanced at the patient. She turned to Margy. "You'd better go, now, and get yourself some sleep. He'll be all right. You can come back this afternoon."

VI

THE STUD GAME in the Tivoli broke up suddenly at the cry of fire, and the sourdoughs joined the hastily formed bucket brigade that soon had the fires on several adjoining roofs under control. The story of Tommy Dean's rescue of the Saunders baby was told and retold a hundred times as men and women milled around the smoking embers. As the sourdoughs returned to resume their game, Black John accosted Clyde Barto entering the door of Cuter Malone's notorious Klondike Palace. "What's the matter, Barto?" he asked. "Get tired of the dance?"

The man scowled and passed on into the Palace. Lotta de Atley, one of Dawson's professional dance hall girls, who happened to overhear the question, snickered. "You'd of got tired of it too, John—if your girl had told you off in front of all the folks like his did when she heard about this young Dean savin' that kid. But he didn't answer—jest claimed the girl was a hero worshipper, bragged he'd marry her whether Dean lived or died. Maybe he will—but if he does, she's a damn fool if she don't feed him rat poison for the weddin' supper!"

Black John laughed and joined the other sourdoughs in the Tivoli. The game lasted all night and along toward breakfast time, as the big man was making his way toward the hotel, he saw two men come out of Scougale's store. Both were dressed for the trail. Both carried packs and his brow drew into a frown as he watched them make their way toward the river. Then, casually, he sauntered into the store and accosted Scougale. "Seen Clyde Barto this mornin'?" he asked.

"Clyde Barto? Hell, he was in here not more'n five minutes ago—him an' that damn Slim Aker that hangs out around Cuter Malone's. They can't be very far off."

Black John grinned. "Birds of a feather, eh?"

Scougale glanced about and nodded. "You said it. I wouldn't trust neither one of 'em as far as a one-legged frog could jump.

Barto, he's got plenty of dust, an' claims to be respectable. But Aker is nothin' but a damn bum."

"Might be useful, though, if Barto was figurin' on pullin' off some kind of a shady deal somewheres."

"Could be. Barto, he buys a couple of weeks' grub, an' three, four rock drills, an' fifty sticks of giant, an' some caps an' fuse, an' they hit out with it. Claimed they was hittin' out on a prospectin' trip. Looks to me like Barto aims to fool around with some kind of a hard rock proposition."

"He might, at that."

"He's a slick one," Scougale continued. "I know several deals he's pulled off an' got away with 'em. He's crooked as a dog's hind leg, but he's smart enough to always stay within the law. He took some British minin' company's agent for a hundred thousan' not long ago, an' I happen to know that he's got better than two hundred thousan' in the bank right now."

"H-u-u-m. The amount is worth contemplatin'," Black John said. "The minin' company's loss don't give me no pain in the neck—but it shore irks me to know that a damn tinhorn like Barto got it. Well, so long. I got to go ketch me some sleep."

In the lobby of the hotel he came face to face with Margy Benton. "Hello, Sis!" he greeted. "Just gettin' in from the dance?"

"Just getting in from the hospital," the girl replied. "Oh Uncle John, didn't you hear about the fire? And about Tommy Dean climbing in through an upstairs window and saving a baby with everyone yelling at him to come down?"

The big man grinned. "Oh shore—I heard all about it. Stubborn cuss, ain't he? Just like you claimed. I rec'lect you told me he's stubborn as a mule. Guess you're right, at that."

"I was a fool. But you don't have to rub it in!" the girl said. "I'm glad he is stubborn. He's the only man in Dawson who had nerve enough to save that baby, and I'm going to marry him as soon as he gets out of the hospital."

The grin behind the black beard widened. "What—him an'

Barto both! You better keep about four jumps ahead of Downey, if you do. It's bigamy, er poligomy, er some sech matter."

"I hate Clyde Barto!" the girl cried. "I never did intend to marry him. I just said that to try and make Tommy give up his location on that gulch and take dad's proposition. But now I don't want him to. I'm going to marry him and we'll stick to that location till we make it pay out—just like Tommy believes it will."

Black John nodded. "You ain't makin' no mistake there, Sis."

"Oh, do you really believe he's got a good thing in that gulch?"

"I know damn well he has."

"You were the only one who stuck up for him—everyone else, even dad, said he's a stubborn fool."

"Um-hum. Well, Sis—just let 'em keep on sayin' that. The longer I live, the more convinced I am that stubbornness is more often a virtue than a fault. Run along now. By the looks of yer eyes a few hours sleep ain't goin' to hurt you none. I'm goin' to hit the hay myself."

VII

ON THE DAY after the big Fourth of July celebration, Black John accosted Steve Benton and Margy in front of the N. A. T. & T. store. "Hi, Steve! How you feelin' this fine mornin'? An' Sis, here—she looks happy as the cat that et the canary, as the sayin' goes."

"I am happy, Uncle John!" the girl exclaimed. "I just came from the hospital and Doctor Sutherland says Tommy can go home in two weeks! Daddy and I are pulling out today. Tommy and I are going to be married in a month, and I've got a lot of sewing to do between now and then." She turned and flashed a smile on Steve. "Poor daddy—he isn't feeling so good, this morning."

"I'll say I ain't," Steve growled. "Time was when a four, five days drunk would roll off me like water off'n a duck's back. But not no more. Gittin' old, I guess. I shore feel like hell."

Black John laughed. "Cripes, Steve—a week from now you'll begin countin' the days till the Chris'mas jamboree!"

"Not me—not no more. I've be'n sayin' that fer the last four, five year, but this time I mean it! There ain't no jamboree worth the way I feel this mornin'."

The two entered the store and Black John passed on down the street and stepped into the Tivoli Saloon to see Clyde Barto standing before the bar. The man greeted him, "Hello, John! I'm just about to enjoy my morning's morning. Won't you join me?"

"Don't care if I do," the big man said, ranging himself beside the other, and filling the glass the bartender slid toward him. "Just be'n talkin' to Margy Benton. Her an' old Steve is hittin' out for home today. Margy told me that she an' Tommy Dean are getting married in a month."

"They are, eh? Well, I wish 'em luck—and all the happiness in the world. This Dean seems to be quite a fellow, made quite a hero of himself at that fire, I hear. Sort of a grandstand play—but he got away with it. Talking with Doc Sutherland last evening, and he says Dean will be out of the hospital in a couple of weeks."

"Yeah, that's what Margy claimed. Well—have one on me, an' I'll be on my way. Guess all the excitement's over. I'll be hittin' for Halfaday Crick."

Later in the day, he ran into Bettles, who wanted him to go to Bonanza with him and inspect a proposition he was thinking of taking over. Several days later he headed up the Yukon, but instead of continuing toward Halfaday Creek, he turned up the Sixtymile, cached his canoe near the mouth of Tommy Dean's gulch, and proceeded to the rock dike that held back the waters of the little lake, high on the rim. As he stealthily approached the spot he could hear the sound of a hammer on a drill. Worming his way through a thicket, he lay concealed by the closely knit spruce boughs and watched Aker at work on the narrowest part of the dike. Presently, when the man knocked off for the evening, and went to his tent, some distance back from the rim, the big man waited till the smoke from his supper fire curled above the spruce tops, and slipped to the dike and inspected the work. "The rock's a damn sight softer'n it looks," he muttered, "or he'd never have got all them holes drilled. Cripes—they're all loaded, an' tamped an' connected up! He's just finishin' the last one. Another hour an' she'll be ready to shoot."

TURNING AWAY, he cut across the ridge toward the Benton claim on Sixtymile, a distance of only a couple of miles. On the way he pondered the situation. "When that shot lets go, an' that lake comes roaring down, every damn thing in the gulch is goin' to be swept out into the Sixtymile—trees, cabin, the whole works. An' Tommy Dean along with it—if he'd happen to be in the gulch when she went off. It'll be three, four days before he'll be out of the hospital an' a couple of more before he gets home. Barto's scheme is to wait till Tommy gets here, then touch off the shot—an' there won't be no more Tommy Dean to stand between him an' Margy. An' the hell of it is, he might get away with it because lots of folks know that Tommy intended to let the water out of the lake into his gulch, an' no one—not even the Bentons—know how far he might have got with his drillin'. They'd figure he tried to blow a hole in the dike an' overdone the job.

"Barto, he'll have to trail Tommy up an' then slip the word to Aker when to shoot. I'll lay around an' be on hand about the time they're ready to touch her off. I'll queer their game all right—but hell, long as Tommy don't suffer no loss, they can't do nothin' to Barto. The damn onderhanded cuss would claim he put in them shots on a prospectin' venture—an' I guess a man's got a right to prospect hard rock if he wants to. An I can't let him go ahead an' shoot it, without wipin' Tommy out. Recollectin' that two hundred thousan' Scougale claimed Barto's got in the bank, I'd shore like to figure a way to make some slight profit out of the venture—but I guess I can't."

He stepped into the little clearing before the Benton's door to be greeted by Margy, all excitement—her eyes shining like stars. "Oh, Uncle John! Have you seen Tommy? He just left here about an hour ago! He got along faster even than the doctor figured he would, so he let him go home. And he's looking just fine. His face and hands look sort of red and peeled—but the burns have all healed."

"Where'd he go?" Black John asked, in a voice he strove to make sound casual.

"Why, he went to his cabin. He only stopped there for a few minutes, coming up. Then he came on here—to tell me he was back."

"Guess I'll saunter down an' see him," the big man said, turning abruptly away.

"Hey! What's the big idee of hittin' down there now?" Steve Benton called as he stepped from the cabin. "Stop here overnight an' we'll all go down in the mornin'. You had supper?"

"Oh, shore. I et down the river a ways. Thought you folks would be all through supper."

"Where's yer canoe?" Steve asked, eyeing the other.

"I left it down where I et. Snagged it on a rock, an' come on up a-foot. Got to patch it in the mornin'."

"Cripes—it'll be dark agin you git to Tommy's!" Steve exclaimed. "Stop over with us tonight."

"Nope. Much obliged. Fact is, I want to talk over a proposition with Tommy. Figgered on sort of hangin' around till he got back. Be seein' you in the mornin'. So long."

The moment he was out of sight, Black John broke into a run.

MARGY TURNED perplexed eyes on her father. "Uncle John

acted—somehow—kind of queer. It's funny he wouldn't stop overnight with us. He always has before. And what kind of a proposition would he want to talk over with Tommy that couldn't keep till tomorrow?"

Steve shook his head. "Ain't no one ever figgered John out yet. He's apt to up an' do the damndest things at the damndest times without no apparent reason—but I take notice he's generally got a reason—an' a damn good one. You don't never want to be surprised at nothin' John does. He's allus about two jumps ahead of other folks."

"Especially the police," the girl laughed.

"Yeah—about four jumps ahead of them."

But despite his admonition Steve Benton would have been surprised at Black John's use of the word "saunter" if, at the moment, he could have seen him dashing across the ridge, crashing through brush, leaping over rocks and fallen logs in the fast gathering darkness.

AT THE shore of the lake he paused momentarily, then skirting the edge of the water, plunged through the spruce thicket toward Aker's camp. Suddenly the ground trembled slightly beneath his feet, a thunderous explosion rent the air, followed by the dull roar of rock and water crashing into the gulch, and then the sound of rock fragments that had been blown high into the air splashing into the lake and crashing through the spruce boughs as they fell. Halting in his tracks, with the rock fragments crashing about him, Black John stared at the surface of the lake. The air was filled with the roar of water cascading into the gulch. Before his eyes the shoreline was rapidly receding, while stumps and the limbs of fallen trees seemed to be rising rapidly out of the depths, like eerie denizens of the underworld emerging from an age-old captivity.

He plunged on and came upon Aker's camp just as the man was swinging a stampeding pack to his shoulders. The man whirled as Black John broke from the surrounding thicket and stared wide-eyed into the muzzle of the big man's .45.

"Goin' somewheres, Aker?" Black John asked.

"What—what the hell you doin' here?" the man gasped.

"Who—me? Why I thought I heard a slight noise a few minutes back, an' figured I'd better investigate. Take it, livin' out in the bush like us fellows do, it don't pay to ignore them stray noises. Throw off yer pack an' set a while."

His eyes on the .45, the man swung the pack from his shoulders and sat on it. "What—what do you want?" he asked, in a low wooden voice.

"You know who I am, don't you?"

"Sure. Yer Black John Smith, the king of them outlaws that hangs out on Halfaday Crick."

"Yer information is accurate, if a bit garbled. But seein' you've got the gist of the matter, I s'pose you've heard how we hang damn miscreants like murderers, claim jumpers, thieves, dikeblowers, an' other skulldugs on Halfaday."

"Yer damn right I have—but this here ain't Halfaday."

"A feeble argument, at best—a mere quibble, as a lawyer would say. I'll explain that accordin' to our construction of the eternal verities, our jurisdiction extends beyond the confines of Halfaday Crick to include any an' all contiguous an' subtendin' territory, which, *pro bono publico,* involves this gulch an' its rims."

"By God, you can't hang no one fer shootin' down a rock face!"

"The hell we can't! You wait an' see. When the boys hears how you blow'd out this dike an' let that lake into Tommy Dean's gulch an' sent Tommy an' his cabin roarin' down the Sixtymile, they'll pass sentence before Pot Gutted John can get the proper knot tied."

"Mebbe this here Tommy Dean ain't dead."

"A mitigatin' circumstance, but hardly worth bringin' up as a defense. Dike-blowin' with intent to defraud would be sufficient to win you a hangin' without the murder, not to mention cabin-smashin'.'"

"By God, if you hang me you've got to hang Barto, too!"

"Barto? What's Barto got to do with it?"

"He's got plenty to do with it! It was him paid me to do this job. He give me two thousan' dollars to blow this dike an' let that lake into the gulch on account he hates this here Tommy Dean. He figgers if he'd git rid of Dean, he'd git Steve Benton's gal, an' then locate Tommy's claim hisself. He looked the claim over, an' he knows it's a good proposition when he got water onto it. He even kinda give me the creeps when he says 'if it's water Dean wants he'll git it—an' it won't cost him a damn cent, either.' He know'd damn well that when this dike let go Dean would go whirlin' to hell in the flood."

"So that's your story, eh—tryin' to drag Barto into it. Well it don't quite jibe. Fer instance, Tommy Dean's be'n in the hospital in Dawson on account of some burns he got in a fire Dominion Day evenin', an' the doctor claimed he wouldn't be out fer two weeks. Bein' right there in Dawson, Barto would know that—so if he aimed to kill Dean, why would he tell you to blow this dike before Dean was out of the hospital?"

"That's right," Aker agreed. "Barto know'd that, all right. So he tells me to hold off on firin' the shot till he let me know. I jest finished the job this evenin'—got everythin' all ready, an' figgered on waitin' till Barto give me the word. Well, he give it to me—not more'n a couple of hours ago. He come here an' says how Dean has got well an' is back on his claim, an' I should wait till jest about dark an' then touch her off—an' that's what I done."

"Where's Barto now?"

"Damn if I know—he didn't hang around—jest paid me my two thousan' an' beat it. He's prob'ly camped in the bresh, about two hours along his back-trail to Dawson."

"H-u-u-m—an' interestin' complication—if true."

"It's true—every damn word of it!"

"An' in case we was to involve Barto in this hangin', would you be willin' to tell the boys about his part in it, at the miner's meetin'? I ain't makin' no promises—but it's just possible that sech procedure might induce the boys to hang Barto an' turn you loose with a warnin'. After all, there's only one murder."

"Yer damn right I'll tell 'em—an' I'll prove it, too! I know some of them boys on Halfaday, an' they know me. I'll show 'em the money Barto passed me. They know I never had no two thousan' dollars at one time in my life. Hell, if I had even a hundred dollars, I wouldn't be hangin' around the Klondike Palace cleanin' spitoons, would I?"

"W-e-e-l-l, yer argument seems sound. I never heard of spitoon cleanin' bein' a hobby of the wealthy. Where was you hittin' out for jest now—Dawson?"

"Not by a damn sight! I never want to see Dawson agin. I was hittin' fer the Dalton Trail. I come in that way—helped Jack Dalton fetch in a bunch of steers, an' I aimed to go back out. To hell with this hull country! I was headin' back to the States."

"Okay. You wait here till I go down the gulch to Tommy Dean's cabin—er where his cabin was, an ascertain the extent of the damage. I'll be back in the mornin'."

"I'll wait."

"Yer damn right you'll wait. Lay down while I tie you. You look to me like a man whose word should be augmented by a few turns of good stout rope." A few minutes later he rose to his feet, and looked down at the man, bound hand and foot with babiche line.

"Cripes," the man whined, "it gits cold up here, nights! An' besides, the mosquitoes'll eat me up!"

"I'll throw a couple of blankets over you—what few mosquitoes gits under 'em won't hurt you none."

VIII

PICKING UP AKER'S lantern, Black John lighted it, and made his way down into the gulch. The lake bed was completely drained, and as he proceeded he noted that most of the small spruce trees had been swept away by the flood, and the sand and soil along with them. He walked, for the most part on hard rock and boulders. As he rounded the last bend, the flicker of a fire caught his eye, and the bobbing light of a lantern. The bobbing stopped as the one who carried it evidently saw his light, and Steve Benton's voice cut the silence. "Who's there?" he yelled.

"It's me—Black John!" the big man answered, and hurried on to the fire, where Margy stood sobbing and wringing her hands. He was quickly joined by Steve, who had been searching with the lantern below the site where the cabin had stood. "Oh," cried the girl. "It's terrible! Oh—why did he do it? Why didn't he tell us he was going to try to get that water from the lake? We didn't even know he'd done his drilling. He knew nothing of such things! Why didn't he ask daddy—he would have told him it was dangerous!"

Steve nodded. "Hell yes! By the sound, he must of put in enough giant to blow the hull damn ridge down! All he needed was a few sticks, an' shallow shots, at that."

They tossed more wood on the fire, and the yellow flames shooting skyward disclosed an eerie and unfamiliar scene. They stood on the edge of the little plateau that had been the cabin site. But the plateau was now a deep pit, and a solid rock dike rose a full fifteen feet above the floor of the pit—a dike that ran transversely across the gulch from rimwall to rimwall. Against the upper side of this wall, lay a mass of twisted tree trunks. Steve pointed at the obstruction. "Look, John—that there dike never showed before. By God, the top of it was in under the surface. It was filled in clean to the top with sand an' gravel that's all worshed out now. I've be'n here a hundred times, an' I never know'd that dike was there."

"Maybe you didn't," Black John replied. "But Tommy did. He told me about it the time we went up an' looked at the lake. He'd heard about that cross dike where Moosehide Charlie made his big strike, an' he heard about others, too. He knew he had a good thing, here. He showed me some big nuggets he'd picked up behind that dike. He didn't show you folks—he was keepin' it for a surprise."

The girl was sobbing aloud. "And—oh—I called him a fool—and stubborn—and—and—now he's—"

"He's right here! And doggone glad to get back."

"Tommy," the girl cried. "Tommy Dean!" And the next instant she was in his arms, sobbing against his breast.

"How the hell did you git out of it?" Steve asked, eyeing the younger man.

"I wasn't in it," Tommy grinned. "When I left your place I didn't stop here. When I came up from Dawson today I was in such a hurry to see Margy that I left my stuff at the last portage on the river and went on up light. When I left your place I went on back to the portage, and was packing my supplies to the head of it, when I heard a roar like thunder and the water in the river began to rise so fast I dropped my stuff and hit for high ground. It rose for a while, and then went down as fast as it rose, and when I climbed down to the river again, I didn't have any canoe or supplies, or anything. I've been making my way back a-foot and it's some job—dark as it is."

"Oh Tommy—nothing matters, now I know you're safe. But—we've lost everything—even the cabin is gone."

Staring out into the firelight Tommy Dean's eyes widened as they fixed on the rock wall. "Good God!" he cried suddenly. "My rock dike!"

Leaving the girl, he snatched the lantern from Black John's hand, dashed to the edge of the jamb pile, dropped to his knees and began to work his way beneath the loosely piled tree trunks. Five minutes passed—ten, and the girl called to him. "Where are you, Tommy? What are you doing down there? Come on out—you can't find anything from the cabin! It's all gone down the river."

"Be there in a minute," came the voice from the jamb pile, and a few moments later Tommy Dean wriggled free of the logs. He approached the fire, his hat grasped by the two brims to form a bag. As he approached his singed head gleamed red in the firelight. Stepping up to the girl, he extended his hands. "Hold my hat a minute, Margy," he said.

THE GIRL reached for the hat, her fingers closing about the brims, and as Tommy let go, she exclaimed loudly as the hat dropped to the ground. Then all four stood speechless, staring down at the heap of yellow nuggets that lay at her feet. "Oh— it was so heavy I couldn't hold it!" she cried. Then, staring at the yellow pile. "Tommy! Why—Tommy—it's—it's gold. Nuggets— great big ones."

Steve Benton was on his knees staring at the two handfuls of nuggets he had picked up. "Fifty pound of nuggets in ten minutes—out of a jamb pile," he cried, in an awed voice.

"That's right," Tommy grinned, "and believe me there's plenty more down there. I only picked up what I could find right on top among the gravel and the logs. When I get that jamb pile moved, I'll really show you gold!"

"But," the girl cried, "what happened? If you didn't shoot down that rock dike that held back the lake—who did?"

For a long moment the four glanced into each other's faces. Steve was the first to speak. "It's beyond me. John—do you know?"

"W-e-e-l-l, just cast yer wits around amongst the folks you know, an' see if any one of 'em would like to see Tommy wiped out."

"Clyde Barto!" cried the girl. "Oh, he tried to kill Tommy!

He ought to be hung."

Tommy Dean laughed and, throwing his arm about the girl's shoulders, drew her close. "Why hang a man for doing you a good turn? Look," he pointed to the rock dike, "he's done in half an hour what it would have taken me years to do with a controlled stream of water. Just think, Margy—we can clean up the whole proposition in a month or two—and you won't have to spend your life in a dry gulch, after all. I think we owe Barto a vote of thanks!"

"Well," Steve said, "we can't do no good here tonight. Let's go on up to my place. Came on, John—you've got to go with us—it's a cinch you can't spend the night with Tommy, now."

The girl glanced into the big man's eyes. "Uncle John," she said, "I'll bet you know a lot about this business—showing up just when you did. And I thought you acted kind of funny, when you refused to stop overnight with us. I know, now, what that proposition was, you were in such a hurry to talk over with Tommy. You wanted to warn him!"

The big man grinned. "You guessed it, Sis—part of it, anyway. I had an inklin' Barto was up to some sort of skullduggery, an' when I swung around an' looked that dike over, I knew it. So I figured to warn Tommy about Barto, an' then I was goin' to try to argue him into makin' a loan off'n me to finance his proposition here. I knew it was an A-1 investment, an' I'd have to let him have it at a low rate of interest. First an' last, Sis—I'm a business man. An' I was tryin' to promote a deal that might show some slight profit. I figured I had plenty of time. But when you told me Tommy was back, I knew I had to hurry."

"It's too damn bad that Barto knocked you out of that profit, John," Steve grinned.

IX

THE FOUR PROCEEDED to the Benton cabin and spent the night. In the morning, Black John said good-by.

"Where you headin'?" Steve asked. "Up to Halfaday?"

"No, guess I'll swing down Dawson way. Fact is, seem' how Barto knocked me out of my profit on this venture, I'm goin' to enjoy seein' his face when I tell him how his little scheme of murder worked out. So long. It's a good thing I cached my canoe on the river above the mouth of Tommy's gulch, er I'd had to hit out for Dawson a-foot."

Instead of going directly to his canoe, Black John crossed the ridge to the place he had left Aker. Throwing the blankets off the man, he cut the thongs and seated himself comfortably while Aker built a little fire and prepared his breakfast. With his teapot nested against the flame, and salt pork in the frying pan, the man asked a question. "Was you down there—to Dean's shack?"

"I was down to where Dean's shack was before you fired that shot last evenin'. There is nothin' there now—no shack, no Dean, hardly even a tree left in the gulch."

"Like I told you last night—it's Barto's fault. I never figgered out the deal. I jest worked fer him."

Black John filled his pipe and lighted it. "Aker," he said, "yer nothin' but a lowlived murderer, an' my conscience shore pricks me fer turnin' you loose on society."

"What do you mean—turnin' me loose?" the man asked, a gleam of hope in his eyes.

"I mean I've be'n doin' some thinkin' since I was talkin' to you last night. You'll have to admit that both you an' Barto richly deserves a hangin', an' all the trimmin's that goes with one. But then I says to myself, 'John,' I says, 'who are you to judge these men? You ain't a policeman. They didn't harm you.' So—I decided to go about my business an' forget the whole thing."

"You mean yer goin' to turn me loose!"

"That's right—under certain conditions. The first one bein' that you'll hit for the Dalton Trail, an' keep on pickin' 'em up an' layin' 'em down as fast as God'll let you till you get plumb over into American territory, an' agree never to set foot in the Yukon agin."

"By God; I'll do it!"

"Okay. You claimed, I believe, that Barto paid you two thousan' dollars to pull off this venture. Is that right?"

"That's right."

"An' have you got it on you?"

"Sure I have."

"It strikes me that one thousan' will be entirely sufficient for your needs an' requirements on your journey back to the States, so I've decided to split that two thousan' between us—fifty-fifty."

"You mean, I've got to hand you over half my money?"

"Certainly. Cripes, you couldn't expect me to go to all this trouble without makin' some slight profit on the venture, could you?"

"Okay. I'll pay it," the man said, and handed out ten one hundred dollar bills, which Black John pocketed. Then he rose to his feet. "So long, Aker," he said. "If I was you I wouldn't lose no time gittin' out of the Yukon. Steve Benton's girl is liable to put up a hell of a squawk about Tommy Dean bein' murdered, an' Downey's liable to be on yer trail."

PROCEEDING TO Dawson, Black John headed for the Tivoli Saloon, glancing through the window of the little office where Barto carried on his business, he saw the man was busy at his desk. In the Tivoli he joined Bettles at the bar. After a couple of drinks, he inquired, "You rec'lect that location on Dewar that you picked up, last year, off'n that chechako—what was it you paid for it?"

"You mean that Number Ten Above Discovery? I give fifteen hundred for it. Why?"

"What'll you take for it?"

"Take fer it! Hell, you can have it if you want it. It ain't worth a damn."

"I'll give you what you paid."

"You'd be a damn fool to. What do you want of it?"

"I want to sell it to a man. I figure I might make some slight profit on the venture."

"Cripes, John, you wouldn't stick some pore devil with a worthless claim, no more'n what I would!"

"Not some pore devil. A well-heeled devil."

"Who."

"Clyde Barto."

"Him! Say, if you kin work that claim off on Barto, take it fer nothin', an' welcome! He's the crookedest crook in the Yukon! I'd shore be proud to donate the claim, if I thought you could soak him with it! But—they claim he's smart, John. Damned if I believe you kin do it!"

"Won't hurt to try. It's the smart ones, an' the well-heeled ones, if they're also blessed with larcenous souls, that I like to go after."

"It's a deal! I'll go get the papers an' make 'em over. Meet you at the recorder's in ten minutes."

HALF AN hour later Black John strolled into Barto's office. The man greeted him genially. "Hello, John. Pull up a chair and sit down. What's on your mind? As the sayin' goes—what can I do you for?"

"Well, that's accordin'. I just come down from the Sixtymile. Hell of a thing, happened up there couple nights ago. A rock dike that held back the water of a little lake on the rim above Tommy Dean's cabin let go, an' the whole damn lake went roarin' down his gulch."

"It did! My God, man—is Dean safe?"

"Safe! Hell's fire, he's gone! His cabin's gone! An' damn near every bush an' tree in the gulch is gone along with 'em! How the hell could he be safe—with a wall of water hittin' his cabin—an' him in it?"

"Oh—that's too bad! I'm sure sorry. And that poor girl—Margy Benton—and they were to have been married soon, according to reports."

"Yeah, so I heard. But getting down to business—what I come in for, I've got a proposition up on Dewar I thought you might like. You deal in locations, don't you?"

"Sure I do. But Dewar—where 'bouts on Dewar is it?"

"Number Ten Above Discovery."

Barto laughed. "No go, John. Hell, I wouldn't give a dime a dozen for any claim on Dewar between Five Above and Thirty-two Above. You'll have to shove that one off on someone else."

"Just thought you might be interested," Black John said. "Speakin' of that there disaster on Tommy Dean's gulch, I run acrost a fellow up there name of Slim Aker. Know him?"

Barto's eyes went suddenly hard. "Never heard of him," he snapped. "What are you driving at?"

"Only that Aker done some talkin'—there was jest me an him. I happened along just about three minutes after he touched off that shot—caught him red-handed, you might say. He spilled his guts, Barto. In other words, he sung like a canary. An' what's more, he's promised to tell it to the judge an' the jury when the time comes. He figures he can save his own neck by turnin' Crown's evidence, an' swearin' a rope around yours. Your scheme for gettin' rid of Tommy Dean so you could get his girl an' his location was a clumsy one, Barto. Looks like it kind of backfired on you, don't it?"

BARTO'S FACE had gone paper white, and his lips moved stiffly. "What—what did you mean about that Dewar location, John?" he said, his eyes meeting the big man's gaze.

"W-e-e-l-l—to tell you the truth, Barto, the claim ain't worth a damn to me. I sort of figured maybe you'd be interested in it.

Of course, in case you are interested, Slim Aker, an' what he said could be considered irreverent an' immaterial—an' forgot."

Barto was silent for several minutes. "But—there's the Bentons?" he said. "They'll be sure to put up a squawk about what happened to Dean."

"Nary a squawk. I was talkin' to Steve an' Margy both. They think Tommy blow'd up that dike himself, tryin' to get that water into his gulch. They knew he talked of it—an' they figure he overplayed his hand—put in too big a shot."

"And Aker? What about him?"

"I'm holdin' Aker incommunicado, as the sayin' goes, until I find out how you feel about buyin' this claim. If you feel that you need the proposition, I might let you have it—for a consideration—in which case Aker will disappear up the Dalton Trail, never to show up in the Yukon agin'. He knows his own neck ain't much safer than yours."

"How much do you want for the claim?"

"The price is two hundred thousan'."

"Why—you damned outlaw! That's more cash than I've got."

"No it ain't. I happen to know that you've got more than that in the bank, right this minute."

"How do you know that?"

The big man grinned. "The ways of us outlaws is entirely too devious for your limited intellect to grasp, Barto. Are you goin' to take it, or leave it? If you ain't interested, I'll slip over an' have a chat with Downey."

"You damned crook!" Barto said, in a hard, grating voice. "I'll take it. You've got me. There's no other way. How do you want it?"

"Spot cash," Black John replied. "First though, we'll slip over to the recorder's an' enter the transaction on the books—just in case you might try to make out at some later time that I tried to use coercion, or blackmail, or some such onderhanded scheme. It's better, in a deal of this kind, that everything should be open an' aboveboard."

From the recorder's office they proceeded to the bank, where Barto drew a check which Black John presented for payment. The cashier took the check and consulted a book. "How do you want it?" he asked.

"Thousan' dollar bills will do," Black John replied. "I like to have a little loose change in my pocket, in case them old sourdoughs would want to start a stud game."

"I sure hope I can depend on you to keep what you know under your hat," Barto said, as they left the bank.

"You can. I'm a man of my word. Honest John, they should be callin' me—instead of Black John."

"Some crazy guy might," Barto said bitterly. "You're the damndest crook in the Yukon. You've put me in a hell of a fix, gouging me for that two hundred thousand. I haven't got enough left to operate with!"

"Cheer up, Barto," the big man grinned. "There's a sucker born every minute—you ort to know that, you're one of 'em. Look! Yonder—comin' up the street—damned if it ain't Tommy Dean, himself. He must have come down to replace them supplies he lost in the worshout!"

THE PARTNERSHIP BUSINESS

IN THE TIVOLI SALOON, in Dawson, Swiftwater Bill yawned and stretched as he watched Black John Smith rake in the pot and stack the chips in orderly columns in front of him. "That'll be all fer me," he said, shoving back from the table. "I got to be hittin' fer Squaw Crick. A man's a damn fool to play cards all night when he's got to hit the trail in the mornin'.'"

"I'd ort to went to bed, myself," Burr MacShane admitted. "I'm pullin' out after breakfast, too."

Old Bettles, dean of the sourdoughs, snickered. "You fellas give me a pain in the neck. Hell, there's plenty of nights when there ain't no stud game fer a man to sleep. Ain't that so, John?"

"That's be'n my thesis. Sleepin's all right, when there ain't nothin' else to do." As the others rose from the table, the big man picked up his chips and led the way to the bar where he cashed them in. "I'm buyin' a drink," he grinned, as he gathered the bills into a roll. "I figure you boys can lick yer wounds better if your tongues are wet."

"Yer luck was runnin' tonight," Swiftwater grinned. "But this ain't the last game you'll be settin' in. Luck like that can't hold."

Three men entered and stepped to the bar. Bettles slanted them a glance as a bartender set a bottle and glasses before them. "There's that damn Tom Brower," he said. "Prob'ly found him a couple more suckers to trim."

Swiftwater Bill nodded. "Yeah, he's a slick one, all right. Beat old Mort Dolan out of every damn cent he had—an' his location, to boot."

"Yer damn right he did," Moosehide Charlie concurred. "An' he beat Clem Johnson out of his steamboat. Clem, he had a good thing in that there *Aurora* till Brower bought in pardners with him."

"Clem was a damn fool to have any dealin's with him," MacShane opined.

"Well," defended Moosehide, "come spring, the boat needed overhaulin'. An' you know Clem—he hangs around all winter an' blows in the money he makes in the summer. Brower finds out how Clem's up agin it fer money to pay fer the overhaulin', so he offers to pay the bill on a pardnership proposition which looks like a good thing, so Clem takes him up. I don't know how he worked it, but it worn't no time at all till he owned the boat, an' Clem didn't have nothin'. Then Brower sold the boat fer seventy thousan'."

"Pardnerships is his game," Camillo Bill said. "He's got plenty of ready money, an' he lays around an' finds someone with a goin' proposition which needs cash fer development, an' he offers to put up the money fer a half interest in the proposition. He's a lawyer, an' he draws up the papers, an' clutters 'em up with 'whereas', an' 'be it known', an' 'party of the first part'—now you see it, an' now you don't see it—till the first thing you know he's got the hull proposition—an' the other guy's out."

"H-u-u-m," said Black John, eyeing the three at the far end of the bar, "doin' pretty well for himself, eh?"

"I'll say he is! An' it's a damn shame," Bettles said. "I'd shore like to see someone take him fer every damn dollar he's got. It would damn well serve him right. He's turned half a dozen crooked tricks that I know of, an' God knows how many more. Always works the same game—pardnership. An' he's smart enough to always keep inside the law."

"How come these suckers go to him for their development money instead of the bank?" Black John asked.

Swiftwater Bill shrugged. "Prob'ly some of these propositions ain't far enough along so the bank will take a chanct," he hazarded. "An' then again—mebbe they do put out a feeler at the bank—an' the bank tips Brower off."

"But hell, Swiftwater," Moosehide Charlie cut in, "why would the bank do that? Cripes, if they done that they'd lose the interest on the loan!"

"The bank wouldn't tip him off—as a bank. But, some teller or clerk might. It wouldn't be no money in their pocket if the bank made a loan—but if they was to slip the word to Brower, an' he made it, he might make it worth their while."

BLACK JOHN shook his head slowly. "Tch, tch, tch, the ways of these damn scoundrels is devious in the extreme. Human nature, in some of its aspects is shore sad to contemplate."

Bettles grinned. "Yeah. I'll bet that's the way Clyde Barto looks at it, too. He faded plumb out of the picture after you took him fer two hundred thousan' on that Dewar location. But at that, John, I'm bettin' this here Brower is smarter even than Barto."

"Anyone," Black John opined, "that would lay around preyin' on the needs of his fellow man is nothin' but a damn vulture. Personally, I ain't never be'n averse to turnin' an honest dollar at the expense of sech damn scoundrels."

"You mean," inquired Swiftwater Bill expectantly, "that you figger on takin' this here Brower?"

"W-e-e-l-l, the idea sort of intrigues me—as a sportin' proposition. Of course, if the transaction netted me some slight profit, it wouldn't irk me none. But it's an ondertakin' that would require a certain amount of thought an' meditation—not one to be entered into on the spur of the moment, as the sayin' goes. Everything would have to be open an' aboveboard. I wouldn't want no lint of onderhandedness about it. Drink up, an' I'll buy another. Then I'm goin' to breakfast, an' after that I'll be hittin' out for Halfaday. I'll most likely be back in about a month er so an' give you boys a chanct to even up this stud score. Meanwhile, if you can find a woodshed somewhere, my advice is that you go out behind it an' practice dealin'."

II

OLD CUSH, PROPRIETOR of Cushing's Fort, the combined trading post and saloon that served the little community of outlawed men that had sprung up on Halfaday Creek, hard against the Yukon-Alaska border, set out the inevitable bottle, glasses and leather dice box as Black John stepped into the room and crossed to the bar. "How's things down along the river?" he asked, after the big man had beaten him for the drinks.

"Nothin' startlin'. I took the boys down to the Tivoli fer three thousan' in a stud game.

"There's be'n three, four chechako stampedes to different cricks, but they didn't turn up nothin'. By the way, Cush, speakin' of cricks, reach in the safe an' get me the transfer paper to that location I bought off'n young Ellis. You rec'lect he's the lad that located last fall on the gulch we named Spruce Crick. You know I bought it off'n him after he'd got discouraged workin' it, an' had the transfer recorded the next time I went to Dawson."

Cush fumbled among various papers in the safe and tossed the transfer onto the bar. "That location ain't no good—an' never was," he granted. "No one but a chechako would of recorded it."

"Gold's where you find it."

"Yeah—but it ain't where you don't find it."

"Your postulate is ontenable. There might be plenty of gold—"

"Oh, shore," Cush interrupted, "an' if big words could git it out of the gravel, you'd be the richest man in the world! But jest the same, that there young Ellis never took no gold outa there, an' you was a damn fool to buy the location—like I told you when you done it."

"Oh, I don't know. I felt kind of sorry for the kid. All he wanted was enough to pay you for what he owed for supplies, an' buy his passage back to the States. That's the best place for him. He'd never have made good up here. He wasn't the type. An' then again—a man can't never tell when some odd piece of property might come in handy."

"Like fer what?" Cush grunted. "You goin' to start a moose farm, er somethin'?"

"No. Fact is, I'm goin' to work that location. I swung around by Sebastian's Village an' fetched up half a dozen Siwashes. They can knock out one end of Ellis's cabin an' make it a little bigger, an' then go ahead an' sink a couple of shafts. Better shove out enough supplies to last 'em a month er so, an' they can start packin' 'em up there."

"You gone crazy, er somethin'? You know damn well Ellis never even took wages outa that location. Spruce Crick—hell! There ain't no water in it only in the break-up. You couldn't never sluice out yer dump."

"There's a little spring-fed lake back off the rim. A man could pipe water from it."

"Huh," Cush snorted disgustedly, "so on top of payin' them Siwashes wages, yer figgerin' on blowin' in eight, ten thousan' dollars fer pipe, eh? You'd ort to stayed down to Dawson an' got yer head examined. I'll bet Doc Sutherland would laugh like hell when he found out what you're tryin' to use fer brains."

IGNORING THE comment, Black John continued. "An' not only that, but I'm goin' to get some of the boys to locate on the rest of Spruce Crick. There must be room fer half a dozen locations besides Ellis's Discovery claim."

Cush shrugged. "Who you goin' to git? There ain't that many more damn fools on Halfaday."

"Some of the boys ain't doin' much better'n wages—Pot Gutted John, an' Long Nosed John, an' a few others. I'll guarantee 'em double what they're takin' out on their own locations to file on Spruce Crick an' work their claims there."

"Looks like the older some folks grows the less sense they git," Cush grunted. "But it's your money."

The big man grinned. "You wouldn't, perchanct, care to go into this proposition on a fifty-fifty basis?"

"Not by a damn sight! When I want to throw money away, by God, I'll go down to Dawson where I'll have some fun doin' it! Not sink it in some damn dry gulch."

"Okay. I'll slip down along the crick an' speak to some of the boys. I want 'em to get their stakes in on them locations so I can take the papers down to Dawson an' record 'em."

A MONTH after his departure for Halfaday, Black John stepped into the Tivoli and joined the group of sourdoughs at the far end of the bar. "Figured I'd come down an' give you gravel hounds a sportin' chanct to get yer money back," he grinned. "Fill up. I'm buyin' one."

"Speakin' of sportin' propositions, I rec'lect the last time you was down you claimed you might try to put one over on this here Tom Brower that's be'n gyppin' folks along the river on them pardnership propositions. But I notice he's still flyin' high. Don't look like his wings has be'n clipped none."

"Oh—yeah—Brower. Hell, I'd fergot all about him. Fact is, I've be'n busy ever sence I left here on a location I bought on Spruce Creek."

"Spruce Crick?" Bettles asked. "Where the hell is Spruce Crick?"

"It's a little crick that runs into Halfaday a little ways above Cush's. Young fella name of Ellis located on it last fall, an' this spring I bought the location off'n him so he could go back to the States."

"You mean, yer workin' the location?" Burr MacShane asked.

"Shore. Got half a dozen Siwashes sinkin' a couple of shafts. An' when some of the boys seen that, they filed the rest of the crick. I fetched the papers down with me an' recorded 'em. They're all busy up there sinkin' shafts of their own."

"You takin' out any dust?" Moosehide Charlie asked.

"W-e-e-l-l, we ain't only be'n at it ten days—an' I fetched down the dust we panned out." Swinging his pack to the floor, he reached into it and tossed half a dozen little moosehide sacks onto the bar, and called to the bartender. "Hey, Curley—weigh up these pokes, will you?"

One by one the man placed the sacks on the scale as the sourdoughs looked on, wide-eyed. "Five hundred ounces, she figgers altogether," he announced as he totaled the figures he had jotted on a paper.

"Fifty ounces a day!" Swiftwater Bill exclaimed. "Good God, John, you've shore hit it lucky!"

"Yeah," Black John admitted, "kinda looks like I might of, at that. Trouble is, this here Spruce Crick is dry most of the time, an' I ain't got no water. But I located a little lake back off the rim. I can pipe water from there. But it'll take quite a bit of pipe, an' I ain't in no shape to swing the deal."

Moosehide Charlie gasped. "What! Cripes, John—if you can't swing it—who the hell could?"

"I don't figure I can finance the venture alone. I need some outside capital. I can't very well go to the bank for it, on account of it's bein' a new location of onproven worth. But I was thinkin' that if you boys know'd where I could get holt of a pardner, someone with plenty of loose money to invest, I might—"

A GREAT light broke upon Bettles, who roared with laughter and smote the bar with his fist. "By God, John, yer all right! I figger we might find you jest the man! Fella name of Tom Brower—"

At mention of the name the others saw the light, and several rounds of drinks were had amid much laughter and back thumping.

"Of course," Black John continued, "this Brower, he ort to hear about the Spruce Crick proposition in a roundabout sort of way, an' somehow get wind of the fact that a chechako name of John Smith, an Iowa farmer, is sort of lookin' around for a pardner." Reaching down he raised his pack sack from the floor, stowed the sacks in it, and swung it to his shoulder. "I'll be seein' you boys after supper," he said. "I'm goin' over to the bank now, an' deposit this here dust."

SHORTLY THEREAFTER Bettles left the Tivoli and, sauntering down the street, spotted Brower seated at the window in the lobby of the Northern Hotel, idly awaiting the supper call.

Almost at the same instant, Black John, pack sack dangling from his shoulder hove in sight from the direction of the bank. Bettles accosted the big man. "Yonder's Brower sittin' there in the hotel," he said, and falling in beside him, spoke hurriedly for a few moments.

Entering the hotel, with Bettles following, Black John strode to the desk, registered, and picking up the key the clerk tossed onto the counter, turned and headed for the stairway with Bettles still arguing. At the foot of the stairs he turned. "No!" he growled. "By God, you don't buy in on that Spruce Crick proposition fer no lousy fifty thousan'! You'll have to double it—er I'll find someone that will!"

"I'll have to see the boys first," Bettles replied. "I don't know if we can scare up that much right off hand—but you come over to the Tivoli after you've et, an' we'll see what we kin do."

Black John grunted an assent, and went on upstairs.

As Bettles turned toward the door, Brower accosted him with a grin. "Your friend don't seem in a very amiable mood," he said.

Bettles scowled and dropped into an empty chair besides the other. "Name's John Smith—claims he's a farmer from down in Ioway, er somewheres—er was, till he come to the Yukon. Says he's prospected around on a lot of cricks without doin' much good till he hit this Spruce Crick proposition."

"Seems to me I've seen him in town from time to time," Brower said. "So he struck it lucky, eh?"

"I'll say he did! Last fall some damn chechako name of Ellis located on this here Spruce Crick an' didn't do no good there, an' this spring Smith bought the location off'n him fer jest enough to git Ellis back to the States. Then he puts half a dozen Siwashes to work on the location an' damned if they didn't take out five hundred ounces in ten days! He fetched the dust down with him an' Curley weighed it up right there on the Tivoli scales. He sluiced out them ounces with snow water, but now the crick's went dry on him, an' he's got to git water. He found a little lake back off the rim, an' figgers he kin pipe all the water he needs out of this lake—but he ain't got enough cash to swing the deal fer the pipe. He claims he tried to git the money at the bank but they turned him down on account of Spruce Crick not havin' no claims of proven worth on it. So he come over to the Tivoli an' offered us boys a half interest in the proposition. We seen the dust he fetched down—an' we know he couldn't of be'n workin' the claim much longer than the ten days he says—because he was down here not so damn long ago. First off, we figgered on stampedin' up there an' locatin' on the crick. But Smith says, it ain't only a short crick an' when news of his strike got around prospectors from nearby cricks come in an' staked the whole crick. Smith, he fetched down the papers an' recorded 'em for these boys. So we talked it over, an' I jest offered him fifty thousan' fer a pardnership—but he turned it down. Like you heard him."

Brower nodded with apparent unconcern. "Yeah—said he wants double that. Do you figure the proposition's worth it?"

"Worth it! Hell—figger it out fer yerself—fifty ounces a day—that's eight hundred dollars—twenty-four thousan' a month, an' his pardner gets half of it—an' they ain't hardly into the grass-roots! So long! I got to go tell the boys."

AS BETTLES disappeared down the street, Brower made a beeline for the recorder's office and verified the transfer of the Ellis Discovery location on Spruce Creek to one John Smith. Verified also, the fact that numerous other locations had been recorded that very day. Then he returned to the hotel, and finding the dining room door open, peered in to see the big man seated alone. Pausing beside the table, he smiled down. "Mind if I sit here?" he asked. "Brower's my name. Sort of boring eating alone."

"Help yerself. Smith's the name—John Smith."

Seating himself, Brower glanced at the bill of fare and laid it aside. "Prospector?" he asked.

"Yeah."

"Lots of hard work—prospecting."

"Well, it is, an' it ain't" Black John replied. "Take farmin' now, an' it's all hard work. A man's got to git up 'fore daylight, an' clean out the barn, an' milk the cows, an' feed the horses, an' slop the hogs, an' when he gets that done, his day ain't started yet. Prospectin', a man can get up when he wants to, an' knock off when he wants to, an' when he strikes it lucky he can hire someone else to do the work."

"I guess most of 'em don't strike it that lucky."

"No—most of 'em don't—but some of us does."

"You mean you're one of the lucky ones?"

"Oh, shore. I am now. But I ain't always be'n lucky. I've had my ups an' downs, same as the rest."

"But now you're fixed so you can just sit back and let someone else do the work, eh?"

Black John eyed the other frowningly. "Listen, mister—there's a damn sight more to runnin' a proposition than jest settin' around an' lettin' someone else do the work. It's like farmin'. Take it like when a man gets his farm in shape so he can hire hands to do the work, he's got to stay right on the job himself. He can't jest move to town, an' buy a house, an' a fast-steppin' team of horses, an' a fancy rig an' r'ar back an' take it easy. Not by a damn sight, he can't! A lot of 'em does—an' the first thing they know their farm's gone to hell. Either the hired hands don't rotate the crops, or they don't spread no fertilizer, er they leave the hay sp'ile an' when that happens them fancy town farmers has got to get back into overalls, er by God, the bank gits their farm."

"I guess that's right," Brower agreed.

"Shore it is—take me, now. I've had a bunch of Siwashes up there on Spruce Crick shovelin' gravel fer ten days 'fore I left there. We sluiced out the dump with snow water, an' I fetched down five hundred ounces of dust an' stuck it in the bank. But—can I jest set around an' take it easy whilst them Siwashes shovels out the dust? Not by a damn sight I can't. This here Spruce Crick ain't no reg'lar crick. It goes dry after the snow water runs off. Dust ain't no good layin' in the gravel on a dump, no matter how rich it runs. It's got to be sluiced out. So it's up to me to get water onto the crick. I can do it. There's a spring lake back off the rim, an' I can pipe all the water I need from that lake. But it'll take some workin' capital to do it. It ain't no use goin' to the bank, on account of 'em not knowin' nothin' about Spruce Crick. So I went to a bunch of sourdoughs, like they call the old-timers up here—men that knows dust when they see it. I showed 'em them five hundred ounces, an' their eyes shore bunged out, 'cause they knew I hadn't be'n workin' that proposition only a few days. I offered 'em a half interest in the location on a pardnership basis, an' they offered me fifty thousan'—but hell, I ain't goin' to let go a half-interest in a proposition like that fer no fifty thousan'—not by a damn sight, I ain't! I want a hundred thousan'—an' not a damn cent less."

"Hum. Where is this Spruce Crick?"

"It's up the White River a piece. The White runs into the Yukon about eighty miles above here. Spruce Crick's a gulch that runs into a crick that empties into the White."

"I'd like to look the proposition over."

"You!"

"Yes. That's my business—looking around for investments. I suppose you'd call me a speculator. I've got capital to invest in gilt-edge propositions, preferably on a partnership basis."

"You got a hundred thousan'?"

For answer the man nodded, and drew from his pocket a balance sheet and a packet of canceled checks. "Just picked this up at the bank this afternoon," he said, and selecting the sheet, handed it to Black John, who scrutinized it, and handed it back.

"Accordin' to that," he said, "you've got a hundred an' thirty-seven thousan' four hundred an' sixty-two dollars an' fourteen cents in the bank."

"That's right. But of course you understand that I would have to look this proposition over before I put any money into it."

"Oh shore. But—I don't know. There's them sourdoughs— Bettles, an' Swiftwater Bill, an' the rest of 'em. I offered them the chanct to get in on this proposition. They claimed they could scrape up fifty-thousan' between 'em—but I turned em down. I was talkin' to Bettles in the hotel jest before supper, an' he claimed he'd go back to the boys an' see if they could scrape up another fifty thousan'. Them boys knows a half interest in the proposition's worth a damn sight more'n a hundred thousan'. It's jest that they mightn't be able to raise that much on short notice. It kind of looks like I'd ort to go over to the Tivoli where they hang out an' see if they got the money, bein' as I was dickerin' with 'em."

Brower leaned forward and eyed the big man shrewdly. "Listen, Smith," he said. "Don't be a damn sap. Those men know you're a farmer—a greenhorn in this country—a chechako, they call 'em. And they're tryin' to take advantage of you. Don't think for a minute that those men couldn't raise a hundred thousand—or twice that much on a moment's notice—if they wanted to. They're stalling. They figure that if they can make you believe that fifty thousand is all they can raise, you'll take it. They know you can't get a loan from the bank on a proposition on an unknown crick, so they figure you'll have to deal with them— on their own terms. In other words, they're trying to beat you out of fifty thousand. It's nothing but a damned swindle!"

Black John's eyes widened and his brow drew into a frown as he smote the table with a fist that made the dishes rattle. "Why—the damn scoundrels! I'd ort to go over to the Tivoli an' knock hell out of the whole bunch of 'em!"

Brower smiled. "That wouldn't get you anything. There's too many of 'em. They'd gang up on you—and if they didn't beat hell out of you, the police would probably pick you up for disorderly conduct, or something. I've got a stampeding pack all ready, and I happen to know that the *Sarah* is pulling out for upriver at eight o'clock tonight. Why not take a canoe along and get the captain to set us ashore at the mouth of the White, then go on up to Spruce Creek?"

"By cripes, we'll do it! An' it'll serve them damn sourdoughs right fer tryin' to beat me out of fifty thousan'. I'll learn 'em that they can't play John Smith fer no sucker!"

III

SOME TEN DAYS later they beached the canoe at Cushing's Fort, and Black John led the way up the steep bank. At the summit Brower paused and glanced about him. "Well—quite an establishment here!"

The big man nodded. "Yeah. Tradin' post an' saloon. Some fella name of Lyme runs it. Does pretty well fer himself. There's quite a few prospectors located along the crick, an' they trade here." Stepping into the saloon, with Brower following, Black John crossed to the bar. "Lyme," he said heartily, "I want you should meet Tom Brower. Tom, he's come up to look my Spruce Crick proposition over. Kind of figgers on buyin' a half interest in it, if it looks good to him."

Cush set out a bottle and three glasses. "Fill up," he said. "This un's on the house."

They drank and Brower bought another round. "Quite a place you've got here," he said, glancing about the room.

"'Tain't bad."

As the man's glance lingered on the array of card tables, Cush caught Black John's eye, winked, and shook his head emphatically.

The big man looked puzzled for a moment, but as Brower again faced the bar, he tossed off his drink and ordered another.

Brower shook his head. "No more for me, thanks. Two's plenty."

Black John grinned. "Okay. I ain't much of a hand fer licker, neither. Well—shall we shove on up to Spruce Crick? My cabin's there on the crick bank about a hundred yards from here. But if we hustle we can get up to Spruce Crick an' back before dark."

Brower shook his head. "Not me. Not today. I don't mind telling you that I'm plumb tired out. Tomorrow, maybe—but not today. It was a man-killing pace you set coming up from the Yukon. I don't see how you stand it. But I suppose your work on the farm has hardened your muscles. Gosh, my shoulders feel about ready to drop off. I'd like to crawl into a bunk and sleep for hours."

"Well, there ain't nothin' to hinder you," Black John replied. "I've got an extra bunk in the cabin. I'll take you over an' you can roll in an' sleep as long as you like. I s'pose when it comes right down to hard work, us farmers has got it over you city fellas."

In the cabin, Brower pulled off his shoes and threw himself on the bunk. "This sure feels good," he sighed.

"Go to it. I don't feel sleepy, myself. I'll loaf over to Lyme's, I guess. I'll be back later an' cook supper."

Brower nested his head on the pillow. "Listen," he said, "if I don't wake up when you get supper ready, for God's sake let me sleep. I don't care if I don't eat till breakfast."

Back in the saloon Old Cush eyed Black John somberly as he set out the bottle and glasses. "So that's why you was so damn anxious all to onct to work that there Ellis location, eh?"

The big man grinned. "You guessed it. This here Brower is an ornery skunk that makes his livin' swindlin' honest folks out of their money—"

"How come he'd tackle you, then?"

Ignoring the jibe, Black John continued. "His specialty is buyin' a pardnership in some good proposition, then beatin' his pardner out of his share. The boys was tellin' me about him last time I was down to Dawson, so, as a sportin' proposition, I figured it was my duty to teach him a lesson. He beat old Mort Dolan out of his location an' Clem Johnson out of his steamboat—an' he's swindled plenty of others besides, accordin' to the boys."

"So you figger on sellin' him a half interest in the Ellis location, eh?"

"That's right—for a hundred thousan', spot cash."

"How come he figgers yer a farmer?"

"Oh, I don't know. My looks, mebbe. Mebbe somethin' I might of let drop over the campfire in the evenin'. You know how it is, Cush, them early reminiscences crowd into a man's mind—settin' there in the firelight—an' he jest naturally talks."

"Huh," Cush grunted, "them early remisses you'd be thinkin' about wouldn't inclood no farm—by a damn sight. But speakin' of this Ellis location, how about lettin' me in on it?"

"Not by a damn sight! You called me a damn fool when I bought the location off'n Ellis. An' you called me a damn fool when I put them Siwashes to work on it. I offered to let you in on it fifty-fifty, an' you turned me down cold—said when you wanted to throw money away you'd go down to Dawson where you could have some fun doin' it, an' not sink it in some damn dry gulch. But now when you can see a good profit in sight, you want to horn in on it! No, sir—that hundred thousan' goes into my pocket—an' no other. An' that reminds me—jest shove me out three, four sacks of dust. I'll slip up to Spruce Crick tonight whilst Brower's asleep."

"Figger on saltin' the dump, eh?"

"W-e-e-l-l, a judicious sprinklin' of dust on the right place might sort of influence Brower in drawin' a conclusion. Mind you, Cush—I wouldn't stoop to saltin' a claim under ordinary circumstances. But Brower's a damn swindler. His sole idea in buyin' into this location is to beat me out of it. So I deem it my duty to teach the damn crook that crime don't pay."

"An' you won't sell me a half interest in it, eh?" Cush asked again, filling his glass.

"Nope. That's final. You had your chanct, an' you passed it up. The only half interest I'll sell in that location goes to Brower."

Cush nodded somberly. "And I'd ort to let you go ahead an' sell it, but I can't do it, John—much as it would serve you right."

The big man frowned. "What do you mean—serve me right?"

"Serve you right if I let you go ahead an' git beat out of that location fer a hundred thousan' dollars. Hell, man—it's worth a million! I guess that sayin' 'a fool fer luck' is about right. I told you you was a fool fer buyin' that location—an' you was. An' now it turns out to be a million-dollar proposition."

"What ails you?" Black John asked. "You drunk? Or jest crazy?"

"I ain't neither one. Didn't you see me shake my head nix when you said you was sellin' this here Brower a pardnership in the location?"

"Shore I did. An' I wondered what the hell you meant. But what's this about that million-dollar proposition?"

"Couple of days after you'd hit out fer Dawson, Pot Gutted John an' Long Nosed John come bustin' in here like the devil was after 'em, an' they told how them Siwashes of yourn had busted into the damndest richest pocket they ever seen. You rec'lect you got them two an' some of the other boys to locate on the crick below yer Discovery claim? Well, they happened to pass yer dump an' looked down an' seen yellow dust showin' up, so they grabbed a pan an' started pannin'. I'm tellin' you, John—they panned, twenty, thirty, an' even fifty dollars to the pan right off'n the top of yer dump! It's jest like Bonanza that first year! The boys is up there now workin' their own claims— an' they're all doin' better'n wages. But they ain't struck nothin' like yourn. An' here you was figgerin' on saltin' that dump, with three, four sacks of dust! Say, rich as that gravel is, if you throw'd *forty* sacks onto that dump it would weaken it!"

"H-u-u-m—that shore is important news, if true," Black

John said. "Guess I'll slip up to Spruce Crick an' look her over before Brower wakes up."

On Spruce Creek, before he reached the Discovery claim, Cush's estimate of its worth was verified by Pot Gutted John and the others he had induced to stake locations on the creek. Procuring water from a spring he made a dozen test pannings and stared wide-eyed at the butter-yellow residue in the bottom of the pan. Then, as he squatted there beside his pan, a slow grin widened the lips behind the black beard. "Well—I'll be damned!" he muttered. "Ain't that jest my luck? Right when I've got it all rigged up to take Brower on this proposition—this had to happen!" For several minutes he squatted there staring down at the gold in the pan, then the grin became a low chuckle. "I told Cush I deem it my duty to teach that damn Brower that crime don't pay—an' I ain't the one to shirk my duty when I see it. Besides, onct I engage in a sportin' event I like to see it through—if I don't them damn sourdoughs never would quit ribbin' me."

POT GUTTED JOHN and Red John, who had knocked off work for the day, strolled up and the big man eyed them. "How's your dumps pannin' out?" he asked.

"Not bad," Pot Gutted replied. "We're takin' out anywheres from three to six ounces a day, an' the stuff is gittin' better as she goes down. When we hit bedrock she might be a real strike."

Red John grinned at Black John. "Yeah—an' when you hit bedrock, here on Discovery, I'll bet there won't be but damn little gravel mixed in with yer dust!"

"That's what I'm afraid of," Black John replied gravely. "I done a little pannin' here off'n the dump, an' she's entirely too rich to suit me."

Pot Gutted John regarded the speaker with a puzzled stare. "What!"

The big man nodded. "Yeah," he continued, seriously, "the fact is, I'm figurin' to sell a half interest in this location—

speculator from Dawson—Brower, his name is—I'll fetch him up here tomorrow to look the proposition over. In the meantime we've got to get busy an' thin this here dump out." He turned to Red John. "You slip down and get all the boys that's located on Spruce Crick to come up here pronto. Tell 'em to fetch buckets an' sacks an' whatever they've got that they can pack gravel in."

Red John eyed the speaker with a puzzled frown. "But—"

"No buts about it!" the big man interrupted. "Get goin' an' fetch the boys back with you!" He turned to the Indians. "Get busy now an' shovel lean top gravel into the shaft—a good two foot of it." As they complied, he picked up a shovel, and tossed in rich gravel from the dump, shovel for shovel with the lean.

WHEN RED JOHN returned with half a dozen men at his heels Black John ordered them to get busy and throw lean gravel onto the dump, covering it to a depth of at least a foot, while he and Pot Gutted John, who worked under his orders with a bewildered look on his face, mixed rich gravel into the lean.

At the end of two hours the job was done and Black John issued his final instructions. He ordered the Indians not to disturb the present shaft, but to start a new one in the morning over near the rimwall, and turned to the others. "I'll come back tomorrow with a guy that's figurin' on buyin' in on this Discovery location. I want to make this sale, an' I don't want any of you boys to say nothin' that might queer it—like blurtin' out how rich it is. If Brower asks you any questions, tell him it's a damn good proposition—but don't go no further than that. He'll prob'ly do some test pannin' out of the dump, an the bottom of the shaft, an' find out for himself that it's good enough to invest in."

Pot Gutted John removed his hat and scratched his head, a puzzled frown on his face. "But—hell, John—if you want to sell a location, the richer it is, the more the guy would want it!"

"Yeah," the big man replied. "That's what I'm afraid of."

"Oh—you mean you don't want him to buy in on it! Well, then why in hell didn't you cover the dump with lean gravel without mixin' no rich stuff into it?"

"Why in that case, he wouldn't invest in it. No one's damn fool enough to buy into a proposition that don't even show a color! Well, so long boys, I've got to hit back to Cush's. Mind what I told you—tell Brower the claim's good—but not too good. So long!" And before any of the bewildered men could find voice Black John had disappeared around the first bend of the gulch. They stood there eyeing each other. Pot Gutted John was the first to speak. He eyed the others solemnly. "He worn't drunk," he said. "I edged up an' got a whiff of his breath, an' there worn't no more licker on it than nach'el."

"Mebbe he's went kinda cuckoo," hazarded Short John. "By heck, I've know'd fellas to salt a claim—but this here's the first time I ever seen one onsalted!"

"He's shore as hell got his wires crossed somewheres," Long Nosed John opined. "When Pot Gut p'ints out that the richer a claim is the more a guy would want it, Black John says that's what he's afraid of. An' when Pot Gut asks him if he didn't want the guy to buy it, why he mixed in any rich stuff at all, Black John says in that case this here Brower wouldn't want to buy in on it! Cripes—he's augerin' both ways from the middle!"

"Halfaday Crick'll go to hell in a handbaskit if Black John's gone nuts," Left Handed John said ruefully. "Me—I'm goin' to hit out fer somewheres else."

Red John eyed the others calmly. "Listen, you guys—Black John worn't drunk, an' he ain't gone cuckoo—you kin bet on that. I've heard him talk like a damn fool—an' I've saw him act like one before this. But I never seen him be one. I can't figger out what he's up to, no more'n what you boys kin. But believe me—he knows. An' don't you fergit it!" Only half convinced, the men returned glumly to their shacks.

Back in the saloon Old Cush eyed Black John across the bar as they filled their glasses. "Well—how'd she look?" he asked.

"She's a better proposition than I ever hoped to own."

"She's that, all right," Cush agreed. "When you wouldn't let me in on a half interest, I'd ort to let you go ahead an' sell that pardnership to Brower. But hell, John—I couldn't do it. Sort of a pride I've got in the crick, I guess. I don't like to see none of the local boys git took—not even you. I guess this here Brower might's well head back fer Dawson in the mornin', eh?"

Black John shook his head and regarded the other gravely. "No, Cush, we'll be headin' up to Spruce Crick. Fact is, I've be'n thinkin' the matter over, an' I've come to a decision. Brower's gone to considerable trouble an' expense comin' up here—an' he came on my promise to sell him a half interest in that location. Ethically, I feel bound to carry out my part of the con-tract—cost what it may."

Cush stared aghast. "But—I thought you claimed this here Brower wasn't nothin' but a damn crook—a swindler—an' you was aimin' to learn him a lesson, shovin' off a half interest in that worthless claim on him!"

"That was my intention. There's no gettin' around it. But a promise is a promise, Cush. I give him my word that if he liked the location, I'd sell him a half interest in it. An' I feel duty bound to hold to that agreement. That promise was made in good faith, without no qualifications regardin' Brower's moral status. An' you know as well as I do, Cush—I ain't a man to go back on his word."

"I know this," Cush growled, in disgust. "Yer the damndest fool I ever seen—an' there ain't no moral statuses mixed up in that, neither!"

IV

BROWER SLEPT ON through until breakfast. The meal over, Black John reached for his hat. "Come on," he said, "we'll slip up to Spruce Crick an' you can look that proposition over."

Brower yawned. "What's the hurry? Why not wait till tomorrow. Cripes, I was never so tired in my life. I could sleep all day today, and all night, too."

"It ain't only a little ways," Black John said. "I'd like to get the deal closed as quickly as possible so I can go down to Dawson an' order that pipe. We want to be shore of havin' water on the crick when we need it."

Reluctantly Brower put on his hat and followed the big man up the creek. On Spruce Creek Brower stopped to question several of the men who were working their claims. Their replies seemed to satisfy him—to a man they stated that their locations were good—but not as good as Black John's Discovery claim. All were careful not to mention its extreme richness, merely admitting that it was a mighty good proposition. Brower made several test pannings, both from the dump and from the bottom of the shaft. "She's good," he admitted, "providing we can get water."

"Oh, we can get the water, all right!" Black John assured him. "We'll go up, now an' I'll show you the lake we'll tap. It lays a little piece back from the rim, right opposite here."

Brower eyed the almost perpendicular rimwall. "How do we get there?" he asked.

"Climb up, an' then walk back a piece."

"You mean—climb that damned wall—and then walk back in those hills!"

"Oh, shore. It ain't but a little ways, onct you get to the top of the rim."

"To hell with climbing that wall!" Brower said. "I'm tired out already just walking up here practically on the level. I'd never make it. I'll take your word that the lake's there. After all, you're as much interested in getting the water as I am."

"Okay—if yer satisfied. I'd rather you'd take a look at it, though. Jest to make shore there ain't nothin' onderhanded about this deal."

"I'm satisfied. Let's go back to your cabin and I'll draw up the contract, and we'll close the deal."

"Did you fetch the hundred thousan' with you, in cash?" Black John asked.

"Certainly not," Brower replied. "I'm not damn fool enough to hit out into the wilderness with a perfect stranger, and a hundred thousand in cash in my packsack."

"You can draw up the contract in my cabin," the big man said, "but the deal won't be closed till I get the hundred thousan'."

"You'll get that in Dawson just as soon as I can draw the money out of the bank."

"Okay. Let's go."

Back in me cabin, Brower drew several sheets of legal cap from his pack and arranged them on the table. "This will be a partnership agreement, equally binding on both parties," he said. "Now regarding the firm name—how do you want it—Brower & Smith, or Smith & Brower?"

"Suit yerself," the big man replied.

Brower wrote steadily for half an hour. Then he paused and looked up. "Regarding this hundred thousand I'm turning over to you—as I understand it, part of this money will be available to the firm for such expenses as arise in connection with the business of mining, such as the purchase of the necessary pipe and so forth?"

"You don't onderstand it very good," Black John replied, eyeing the man shrewdly. "That hundred thousan' goes into my pocket, an' the pardnership ain't got no strings on it whatever. It's what you, personally, pay me, personally, fer a half interest in the location. All operatin' expenses will be stood by the firm."

Brower smiled. "Okay. You can't blame a man for trying." Shortly afterward he wrote out a duplicate, and handed both copies to the big man for inspection. Black John glanced at the script, and after a few moments handed them back. "Got so damn many 'whereases' an' 'be it knowns' an' parties of the different parts that I can't make head nor tail to it—but I did take particular notice that you set it down in both copies about that hundred thousan' bein' paid to me, personally, an' the operatin' expenses to be assumed by us jointly, as pardners. That's the main p'int, as I see it. To hell with the rest of it. I ain't no lawyer. I'll take your word that it's draw'd up proper—same as you took mine about the lake. That's fair enough."

"That's right," Brower agreed, and handed over the pen. "So now, when we set our John Hancocks down here we'll be full partners and each will have a copy of the agreement."

Both signed, folded and pocketed their copies, and Black John glanced at the clock. "I'll fry us up a moose steak, an' then we'll be hittin' out fer Dawson," he said. "I want to git back here an' git to work on the claim."

"Good God, man—you mean pull out for Dawson, today!"

"Oh, shore—it's only noon. We can git a hell of a ways by dark with the days as long as they be."

"But I'm tired, I tell you! I feel like I could sleep for a week."

"Goin' back down won't tire you none. You'll be in the bow, an' it's all downstream. You won't even need to pick up yer paddle, if you don't want to. You can lean back on the packs an' snooze all day. I don't want to lose no time. The quicker I git back an' git to work, the quicker we'll begin makin' money."

"Okay," Brower grinned. "One thing I won't have to worry about is a lazy partner. I sure wish I had your stamina."

"Yeah, stamina's a good thing to have," the big man agreed. "We'd ort to do all right—I've got the stamina, an' you've got the brains."

IN DAWSON Black John waited outside while Brower stepped into the bank. When he came out the two proceeded to the hotel where Brower paid over the hundred thousand in big bills. Black John pocketed the money, and stepped to the door.

"Okay, pardner," he said. "Good luck to us. I'll slip over to Al Scougale's store an' order that pipe." After a few minutes closeted with Scougale in the little office, he proceeded to the

Tivoli, where the sourdoughs eyed him expectantly.

"We figgered you'd be showin' up pretty quick," Moosehide Charlie said. "Swiftwater, he seen you an' Brower pull in at the landin' an' hit fer the bank."

"Did you take him?" Bettles asked. "By God, if you did yer the first one to do it, that I ever heard tell of."

Black John grinned broadly, and producing his packet of bills, riffled them as the men stared at the denominations. "If these are good genuine bills I took him—I hope."

"What do you mean—'you hope'?" Burr MacShane asked. "Hell, you've got the bills, an' they shore look good to me."

"Well, it's jest possible there might be some kick-back to the deal. Brower draw'd up them papers, an' he's tied up with me, hard an' fast, as a pardner. But as we stepped into the hotel I seen Cuter Malone eyein' us from the door of the Klondike Palace. Brower, he frequents the Palace, an' it might be that Cuter will tip Brower off that his pardner is an outlaw."

"What the hell do you care? You've got the cash." Camillo Bill asked. "S'pose he does tear up the contract!"

Black John's grin widened. "That's jest what I want him to do. If he don't, I'm in a hell of a fix."

Depositing his pack sack in his room, Brower stepped across the street, entered the Klondike Palace, and stepped to the bar behind which Cuter Malone stood, the inevitable big black cigar cocked at an angle from the corner of his mouth.

"Where the hell you be'n fer the last three, four weeks?" he asked.

Brower grinned and winked. "Been way up the White River. Got hold of a sucker, and bought in on a location that ought to net a good profit—after I ease the sucker out. Shove out the bottle and I'll buy a little drink."

"Who was this here sucker?" Cuter asked, slanting Brower a glance as he set out a bottle and two glasses.

"Oh a boob by the name of John Smith—some farmer from

down in Iowa, or somewhere."

"You mean the fella I seen you go into the hotel with a few minutes ago?"

"Yeah, that's him. Big, black-whiskered cuss."

MALONE MOUTHED his cigar to the opposite corner of his lips and eyed the man before him. "You didn't, I hope, let go of any real mazuma to this here sucker, did you?" he asked softly.

"Sure. I paid him a hundred thousand in cash for a half interest in a proposition on Spruce Creek, that I'll double my money on easy. He's got nothing from me that I won't cash in on. You can bet on that."

"Uh-huh," Cuter replied dryly, "nothin' but a hundred thousan' of your cash. An' when you come to work that claim, you'll find out it ain't worth the powder to blow it to hell."

"Why—what do you mean?" Brower asked sharply.

"Ever hear of a guy named Black John Smith?"

"Why—yes. Some kind of an outlaw, or something, isn't he?"

"He is. An' he's yer sucker, Brower. It was him I seen you go into the hotel with."

THE COLOR drained from Brower's face, and the hand that raised the glass trembled so that much of the liquor slopped down his front. "You mean—you mean—that—"

"I mean that Black John has trimmed another sucker," Cuter said in a low, hard voice. "An' you ain't the only one—he's took me fer plenty. He's prob'ly over to the Tivoli, right now, countin' them bills."

"By God, he must have salted that claim then! I made the test pannings myself—and I know the dust was there in the gravel!"

"So what?"

"So I'm hitting for the Tivoli right now, and demand my money back."

"An' all you'll git back outa Black John will be a good horse-laugh."

"I'll take it to court!"

"How you goin' to prove he salted the claim? That's one thing you never kin prove—leastwise I never heard it proved, an' I've saw lots of 'em try it."

Brower's eyes were fixed on the glass before him in a widening stare. "But—but—but—" His lips formed the word stiffly and got no further.

Malone shoved the bottle toward him. "Snap out of it!" he said. "Take another drink. You've kissed that hundred thousan' good-by—but there's more where that come from. As the feller says, there's a sucker born every minute. Cheer up."

"But—there's a clause in that partnership contract that might let him clean me out! He could incur any amount of expense for operation—and I'd be liable for half of it! By God, I've got to get hold of that contract and tear it up!" Abruptly he turned and dashed from the room.

A few minutes later he stepped into the Tivoli where Black John was drinking at the bar with the sourdoughs. The big man greeted him heartily. "Here's my pardner now! Come on over here Brower, an' meet the boys. Boys, this here is Tom Brower. Him an' I are pardners on a sweet proposition up on Spruce Crick." As he spoke he drew a paper from his pocket and held it so Brower could read. "You see, Brower, I didn't let no grass grow under my feet, as the sayin' goes. Here's the order for that pipe—ninety-six thousan' dollars worth of it, all signed up by Brower & Smith. I jest stopped in an' fixed it up with Scougale. So I'll have to trouble you fer forty-three thousan' dollars."

"Ninety-six thousand dollars—worth of pipe!" the man said in a dull voice, as though trying to grasp the idea.

"Yeah, you see, that little lake I spoke of—"

"You said it lays only a little piece back from the rim. My God, man—ninety-six thousand dollars!"

"It ain't only a little piece back from the rim, in comparison to the distance it might be. This here's a big country, Brower. It could lay ten times as far. But it's only a matter of ten mile—an' this order ain't all fer pipe, neither—you'll notice there's several syphons, an' valves, an' pumps, an' what-not. You see there's a couple of ridges lays between the lake an' the rim that we've got to h'istin' the water over. It'll cost a lot more before we git it workin'—but we'll sure have the water when we need it!"

Brower's face flamed a brick red. "By God, I won't pay it! I won't pay a damn cent!" he cried in a voice that rose to a scream.

"Oh, yes you will," the big man said, and drawing the partnership contract from his pocket, he shook it in the other's face. "That stuff is ordered, an' you're legally liable fer your half."

Quick as a flash the man's hand shot out and snatched the contract from Black John. An instant later he had torn it to shreds and dashed them onto the floor. Drawing his own copy from his pocket he tore that up, too. Scraping the bits of paper into a pile with his toe, he reached down and touched a match to it. Then he eyed the big man with a sneer. "There's your damned contract," he said. "You took me for a hundred thousand—but that's every damned cent you'll ever get out of me! I'm no damned fool!"

White teeth flashed behind the black beard. "That's what you think, Brower. Later, when you hear about that there Discovery claim on Spruce Crick runnin' into a million, you'll know different."

SLIGHT MISUNDERSTANDING
ON HALFADAY

THE SPARE, SHIFTY-EYED man with the sharp rat-like face raised his glass halfway to his lips and returned it to the bar untouched as his glance shifted from the open doorway of the Klondike Palace to the face of Cuter Malone, the burly proprietor of the combined saloon and dance hall, who faced him across the bar, the inevitable black cigar protruding at an angle from a corner of his mouth. "Well, I'll be damned!" he muttered. "Look who's comin' in the door!"

Malone frowned as his muddy eyes rested for a moment upon the figure of the huge black-bearded man who had just stepped into the barroom, a limp packsack dangling from his shoulder. "Black John Smith," he grunted. "What's so funny about that? He stops in here now an' then, when he's in Dawson—damn him!"

"But—he ain't s'posed to be in Dawson."

"What do you mean—s'posed to be? There's sure one hombre that wherever he's at, that's where he's s'posed to be! There ain't no one tellin' *him* where to go—not even Downey."

"What I mean—how the hell did he git here?"

"How the hell would he? In a canoe, or a boat—er mebbe he walked. How does anyone git around the country?"

The big man had stepped to the bar, well toward the front of the long room, allowing the limp packsack to slip to the floor at his feet, as a bartender set out a bottle and glass. As he poured his drink, the rat-faced one eyed him with a puzzled frown.

"Listen here," he said, again glancing into Malone's face, "I an' the Swede kin git around the country as quick as anyone when we want to—an' this time, I'm tellin' you, we wanted to! It's like this—you rec'lect, it's damn near a month ago, a couple of chechakos which claimed their names was Freeman an' Evans was in here throwin' their dust around an' braggin' about makin' a strike on some crick way to hell an' gone up the Stewart. Big Rosy, she froze onto this here Freeman an' hung to him till she got him soused an' frisked him fer 'leven ounces in one of the dance hall booths—"

"Hold on!" Cuter interrupted, and turning, reached for a notebook that lay on top of the huge iron safe behind him. Thumbing the pages, he paused and scowled at an entry. "Here

it is, June the thirteenth—'leven ounces, did you say? I git a fifty-fifty cut on whatever the girls pulls in, an' here Rosy only turns in my cut on eight ounces—that's what she claimed she got. The girl's crooked as a dog's hind leg. Wait till she shows up tonight, an' I'll tell her where to head in at! It's gittin' so an honest man can't make a livin' no more, the way he gits gypped."

"Hold on, now, Cuter—it might of be'n eight ounces Rosy told me she got. I most likely fergot—"

"Fergot—hell! You ain't no better than any of the rest of the damn crooks. You'd try to cover up fer her. Seems like a man can't trust no one in this damn country!"

"Well, anyhow, Rosy, she tips off me an' the Swede, that these two guys claims they've got better'n two hundred ounces in their cache, so when they pulls out we follers 'em.

"Gee—talk about a trip! Way to hell an' gone up the Stewart, an' then up a crick—an' the water higher'n hell, an' havin' to lay around in the bresh fer four days after we got there gittin' damn near eat up with the black flies an' mosquitoes waitin' fer them guys to go to their cache so's we could locate it. We grabbed off a hundred an' eighty ounces—all there was in it—not two hundred like Rosy claimed. We promised her a twenty-five percent cut, so we told her we only got eighty ounces, an' give her twenty. All she done was tip us off—so what the hell!

"Well, anyways, whilst we was waitin' there in the bresh—it was the last day before we found their cache—Black John an' a Siwash come by there. An' they was headed the other way— up the Stewart! That evenin' them fellas went to their cache to put in some more dust, an' when they'd went back to their shack me an' the Swede grabs off the dust an' hit hell-bent fer Dawson. We got here this mornin'. Now, what I mean, how in hell could Black John of got here damn near as quick as we did when he'd went on up the Stewart? 'Cause, believe me, brother, we high-tailed here all the way!"

Cuter rolled the cigar to the opposite corner of his mouth and regarded the man critically. "Did Black John see you an' the Swede hidin' out there in the bresh when he went by?"

"Hell, no! We didn't let no one see us—him most of all. He'd of know'd damn well what we was hangin' around there fer, an' it's claimed he won't stand fer no cache-robbin', not on Halfaday Crick, nor nowheres else. Not even if the guys that gits robbed is chechakos, he won't. Cripes, like as not if he'd of saw us he'd let us clean out that cache, an' then throw'd a gun on us an' took the dust away from us, an' either kep' it, er give it back to them guys, an' hung us. I've heard how him an' that Halfaday Crick bunch has hung guys before now fer somethin' they done."

MALONE NODDED. "Yeah, they've hung guys up there—plenty of 'em. An' I've know'd Black John to give guys back dust an' money, too, that they've be'n robbed of. An' him the damndest crook in the hull Yukon! Trouble is, a man can't never figger out what Black John will do. He don't never rob no pore guy, an' like I said, if someone else robs one, like as not Black John robs him, an' gives the dust back to the guy that lost it. Then the damn cuss'll turn around an' rob, er swindle a guy like me fer all he kin git. He's took me fer plenty, off an' on. An' if someone robs some big outfit, like the Consolidated, like as not Black John will lay fer him, an' rob him. But he don't never give them big outfits back their dust, by a damn sight! No sir—he grabs it off'n the thief an' keeps every damn ounce of it. He hates the big outfits—claims they're ruinin' the country fer the pore man. He's right, at that—but he's smart enough never to rob no one but a thief, an' slick enough to do it so the police can't git onto it. So the law ain't never ketched up with him. I'm tellin' you that if him an' I could make a deal—sort of throw in together—with me down here slippin' him the word, like on gold shipments, or guys that had struck it lucky, an' him an' his gang pullin' off the jobs, there wouldn't be no limit to our take. But somehow him an' me, can't seem to git together on nothin'.

"You claim he didn't see you an' the Swede when he passed by where you was at, up the Stewart. That's what you think. But you might be wrong. He might of saw you an' never let on, an' then follered you on down here. Anyways, that's the way it looks from here. Er else why would he be here so quick—an' him headed the other way? If I was you I'd lay low till he gits outa town. There ain't no one in Rene LaBlanc's shack. You an' the Swede better hole up in there, an' I'll slip you the word when he's gone."

The shifty-eyed one cast a furtive glance in the direction of the bearded man, who was refilling his glass from the bottle, and slipped hurriedly from the room by way of the back door.

WHEN HE had gone, the bartender who had served the bearded man stepped the length of the bar and addressed Malone in an undertone. "The big guy there, he wants a word with you when you've got time. He's been waitin' around till you got through talkin' with Lefty. Claims he's got some connections down in the States that passed him the word that you're okay, an' to hunt you up when he got here."

Malone eyed the man with a frown. "What the hell you talkin' about? You mean Black John, there?"

"Black John! Hell, that ain't Black John!"

"What!" Malone's eyes suddenly widened, and he stared at the bearded one at the other end of the long bar. "By God, if that ain't Black John I'll eat him!"

The bartender grinned. "Better start eatin', then. An' believe me, if he's as hard as he claims he is, yer goin' to chaw some damn tough steak. Shore looks like Black John, though. I thought he was him when he come in the door."

"Tell him to come over here," Malone grunted, a note of skepticism in his voice. "I'll know damn quick whether he's Black John er not."

The man moved along the bar and faced the burly proprietor. "You Cuter Malone?" he asked abruptly.

His eyes on the man's face, the other nodded. "That's me," he replied. "Who the hell are you?"

The stranger grinned, showing a double row of uneven yellow teeth behind the black beard. "It would depend on what part of the country you seen me in. I've got several different monikers. Spokane Blackie'll do as well as any of 'em. So, bein' as we're acquainted, I'm tellin' you you got recommended to me."

"Yeah?" Cuter replied, a wary note in his voice, "an' I'm askin' you who done the recommendin'?"

The other grinned. "Ever hear of a guy named Slim Aker? An' another one name of Jim Quantum? An' Stanton? An' a dame name of Frisco Nell?"

Malone nodded. "Yeah, I know all them folks. Every one of 'em's left the country—gone outside."

"That's right. On account of who?"

"On account of Black John Smith."

"Right agin. An' that's where I come in."

"You?"

"Yeah—me. Accordin' to them folks I'm a dead ringer fer this here Black John. Fact is, Jim Quantum damn near swallered his cud when I stepped into a saloon in Frisco where him an' Aker was havin' 'em a drink, an' Aker, he turned sort of green like around the gills. When they found out I wasn't Black John, they rung in Stanton, an' all of 'em agreed I'd pass fer Black John anywheres. Jest to make shore they figgered out a joke on Frisco Nell, her bein' a dame they claimed hated Black John's guts on account of him shovin' off a batch of queer bills on her an' gittin' her picked up when she tried to pass 'em down in Frisco. She done time on account of 'em an' had jest got turned loose. They claimed that if I'd fool Frisco Nell, I'd fool anyone—even you an' some guy in the Mounted, name of Corporal Downey.

"So they rigged up a date with this here Frisco Nell in the back room of a dump an' was in there chawin' the fat with her over a couple of bottles, when I walks in on 'em. It was a hell of a joke, if you ask me. The minute I steps in the door, this here dame grabs up a bottle by the neck an' heaves it at me, an' then she reaches fer a long wicked blade she's got strapped to her leg, an' she's halfways acrost the table with it, 'fore Quantum an' Aker grabs her an' holds her whilst Stanton pries the knife out of her hand. Cripes, another minute an' I'd be'n sliced like a side of bacon!

"Well, she quiets down when she finds out I ain't him, an' then the four of 'em figgers out that if I was to come up here an' git in touch with you the minute I got here, an' before I'd showed up to anyone else, betwixt the two of us we might rig up some damn good plays—an' Black John would git blamed fer 'em. They all hate this here Black John's guts, an' would be glad to see him knocked off, er put away by the Mounted. Then they could come back here. They figger you could dope out some jobs, an' I could pull 'em off—mebbe in cahoots with some kind of a gang you could git together—like I was the leader of the mob—an' if anyone got sight of me, they'd swear it was Black John an' some of his Halfway Crick gang done it."

"It's Halfaday Crick—not Halfway," Cuter corrected, an avaricious gleam flashing in his muddy eyes. Turning abruptly he picked up a bottle and two glasses from the back bar. "Foller me," he said, in a low terse tone, "before anyone sees you. We kin talk things over in the back room."

II

JUST ON THE edge of darkness, about a little fire above which a kettle of moose stew was bubbling, four men sat before a tent pitched well within a grove of spruce that grew on a tiny plateau at the bend of a creek that flowed into the Yukon, some fifteen miles below Dawson. They were an evil crew, hand-picked by Cuter Malone from among the thugs and sinister characters who frequented his notorious Klondike Palace in Dawson. The man known as Lefty took a long pull at a bottle, and passed it to the Ape, a person of unbelievably long arms and eyebrows so shaggy as to almost conceal the wicked gleam of a pair of beady green eyes. "The hell this here ain't the place!" he replied to a doubt expressed by the other. "This here's the first crick that comes in on the right hand side below them red rocks, ain't it? An' we're a couple of miles up it, ain't we—jest like Cuter said?"

The Ape grunted, pulled at the bottle, and passed it on to Slim Carew, a hard-eyed, tight-lipped individual, who glanced across the fire at the speaker. "If it's the right place, why ain't nothin' happened?" he demanded, drank from the bottle and passed it to Big Mike, a huge hulk of a man who was said to have packed his eleven hundred pound outfit over the Chilkoot in three trips. It was also hinted among the Klondike underworld that he had obtained this outfit by the simple process of strangling its owner and "tromping" his body into the quagmire on the outskirts of Sheep Camp. Mike held the gurgling bottle to his lips until it was empty, tossed it into the bush, and wiped his lips with the back of a hairy hand.

"Yeah, why ain't they?" he seconded Slim's question. "What the hell we here fer, anyhow?"

"You know damn well why we're here—'cause Cuter told us to be—that's why!"

"I don't notice Cuter hittin' out on no crick an' hangin' around fer two days gittin' et up by the dam' skeeters an' black flies," the Ape said. "No sir—he stands there back of his bar smokin' them big seegars, an' h'istin' a drink whenever he wants, with that big yellar diamon' flashin' in his necktie, watchin' the money roll in."

"Cuter's smart," Slim ventured. "He wasn't made in a minute. He knows his way around, all right. I'm willin' to go along with him. He never sent us here fer nothin'."

"Yer damn right he didn't," Lefty agreed, heartily.

"I'll say he didn't!" Big Mike sneered. "Whatever he sent us down here fer, he gits a fifty-fifty cut! Whatever there is to do, we do it—an' he sets back doin' nothin' an' grabs off the half of what we git."

"He doped out the play—whatever it is," Lefty defended. "Hell, a man's got to git paid fer his brains, ain't he?"

"It don't take no hell of a lot of brains to send four guys out in the bresh to git eat up by skeeters, does it?" the Ape queried.

"Not if that's what he sent us out here fer, it don't," Slim agreed. "But if you know'd Cuter like I do, you'd know he don't never do nothin', that don't show a profit. You fellers kin do as you damn please. Me, I'm stickin' here till somethin' happens. What it's goin' to be, I don't know. But when it comes, there'll be somethin' doin'—an' whatever it is, we'll be in on the play, an' there'll be plenty of dough in it. Cuter, he don't fool around with no small-time stuff."

"An' I'm stickin' along with you," Lefty said, lifting the lid of the pot, and prodding the meat with a pointed stick.

The Ape shrugged. "We all got to stick, I guess," he said. "If we don't, Cuter, he'd be sore at us, an' we wouldn't have no place to hang out."

"That's right," assented Big Mike, and glanced at Lefty. "Ain't that stew about done? I'm hungrier'n hell."

"Git yer plates an' fly at her," Lefty replied, as he swung the pot from the fire.

FIVE MINUTES later, as the four were engrossed in gorging themselves on the savory stew, a man stepped into the circle of the firelight. So noiseless had been his approach that no hint of his presence reached the four, until he appeared at their side.

"Good evening, gentlemen," he said. "Go right ahead. Don't let me interrupt yer meal."

The four sat as though petrified staring up into the face of the huge man, whose snaggy yellowed teeth showed behind a black beard that concealed his features.

"My God," Lefty gulped. "Black John Smith!"

The big man nodded. "That's right, Lefty. The last time I seen you was in the Klondike Palace a few days ago standin' there at the bar chawin' the fat with Cuter Malone. That was only a few days after I seen you an' the Swede up a crick that runs into the Stewart. You was layin' in the bresh waitin' to spot a cache belongin' to a couple of chechakos. I was headin' into the back country with a Siwash, an' I seen how you seen us go by, so I kep' on goin' fer a ways. Then I left the Siwash to make camp an' I slipped back that evenin' an' watched you two lift a couple hundred ounces outa the cache, an' hit out downriver."

"It—it wasn't only a hundred an' eighty ounces," Lefty managed to say, his eyes on the big man's face.

The other grinned. "Oh, well, what's twenty ounces amongst friends?"

"Friends? Did you say friends?" Lefty exclaimed, a hopeful note in his voice.

"That's what I said—an' meant it, too."

"You et?" Lefty asked.

"Not sence noon. Me an' Cuter had dinner together in Dawson."

As the big man seated himself Lefty produced a plate, heaped it with stew and passed it to him. The meal proceeded in silence. When it was finished the bearded one began. "You see, it's like this: I've be'n playin' a kind of a big-time game up there on Halfaday—not botherin' to pull no jobs except there was big money in 'em. That's all right except it's gittin' harder an' harder to find out where the big money's at—an' me located way up there on Halfaday. I never bothered with no small-time stuff, like robbin' chechakos, an' the like—never figgered it was worthwhile. Hell, I've even robbed fellas that's robbed chechakos, an' then give the chechakos back their dust—jest fer the hell of it—kind of a joke, like.

"But like I said, them big jobs is gittin' further an' further between, so couple weeks ago when a Siwash come along an' told me about a crick he'd found way up the Stewart, where the gold laid thick in the gravel, I hit out with him, figgerin' that if it was as good as he claimed, mebbe I'd turn to prospectin' fer a change. We was headin up there when I seen you an' the Swede, so, like I said, I sent the Siwash on to make camp an' I snuck back an' laid in the bresh watchin' you boys, an' then, when I seen you lift them pokes from that cache, it set me to thinkin'. 'Cripes,' I says to myself, 'there's a couple hundred ounces them boys lifted in a couple of minutes! No matter how rich a strike is, it ain't that rich! An' I got to thinkin' about all the hard work there is in shovelin', an' pannin', an' sluicin', an' choppin' wood, an' burnin' in, an' crankin' a windlass, an' how a man's way to hell an' gone up there with no one but a damn Siwash to talk to, an' nowheres to buy a drink, an' no one to play a game of cards with. An' layin' there in the bresh slappin' the mosquitoes I got to thinkin' how many chechakos there is in the country, an' how many of them small caches there is, an' how easy it was fer you boys to pull that job, an' how a man was overlookin' a hell of a lot of bets by passin''em up. 'John,' I says to myself, 'yer a damn fool.'

"So I hits back to where the Siwash had made camp, an' I tells him to go on up to his crick an' start pannin', an' I takes the canoe an' hits out fer Dawson. I done some more thinkin' on the way down, an' I figgers that along with them little jobs, a man hadn't ort to pass up the big ones, neither. 'If I could hook up with someone,' I says to myself, 'that could git wise to stuff like gold shipments, an' which chechakos had made big strikes, an' tip me off to 'em, then I an' a few other guys could pull 'em off.'

"It was then I happened to think of Cuter Malone. 'He's the guy kin do it, if anyone kin,' I says, an' then I got to thinkin' that mebbe Cuter wouldn't throw in with me on account of a couple of deals I'd pulled off where Cuter hadn't come out so good. 'Mebbe he's so damn sore he won't have nothin' to do with me,' I says. But then I got to thinkin' that Cuter he's first an' last, a business man which don't never overlook a chanct to turn a dollar—honest er dishonest. 'He'd be a damn fool to turn down a hook up like that,' I says, 'an' Cuter ain't no damn fool. Anyhow,' I says, 'it won't do no harm to try.'

"So when I git to Dawson, I hits fer the Klondike Palace, an' it was then I seen you an' Cuter standin' there at the back end of the bar talkin'. So I waited till you'd went, an' then I goes back where Cuter's standin' an' him an' I goes in the back room an' has a powwow. First off, he's kinda sore about them deals I'd pulled on him, but when I p'ints out that bygones is bygones an' how a man can't never git nowheres lookin' backwards, an' how a hook up betwixt us would be onbeatable, an' might be good fer a million, he seen the light, an' we dickered. 'I'll hit fer Halfaday,' I says, 'an' pick out about four of my boys, an' come back down, an' we'll git to work.'

"But Cuter, he balks at that. 'Not by a damn sight!' he says. 'Not you an' yer Halfaday Crick bunch! By God,' he says, 'if I go into this here thing you'll be boss of the gang, all right—but it'll be my gang. I trust you like a brother, John,' he says, 'but I know damn well if you worked with yer own boys, I'd never git a damn ounce of the take. If we go into this, I handpick the four guys that you work with. I want to be shore I'm gittin' my cut.'

"I done some objectin', but Cuter he stood pat, so finally I agrees, an' we works out the deal. It's simple. Cuter he tips me off to where the dust is at—an' we git it. Then we split fifty-fifty with Cuter. Seems fair an' reasonable, on the face of it. What do you boys say?"

THE APE tamped tobacco into his pipe bowl, lighted it with a brand from the fire, and scowled. "I ain't kickin' on you bossin' the mob," he said. "'Cause I've heer'd how yer good. But damn if I see how it's fair an' reasonable if we pull off the jobs an Cuter sets back an' grabs off a fifty-fifty cut, fer just fingerin' 'em."

Big Mike agreed. "Yeah, I figger we'd ort to git the big end of the cut—us doin' all the work."

"'Special," Slim Carew added, "when there's five of us to divide our half of the cut. That there leaves us only ten percent apiece, an' we take all the resk."

"A fifty-fifty cut looks like a hell of a lot fer Cuter to take, even if he does figger out the jobs," Lefty opined.

The bearded one grinned. "Glad to know jest how you boys feel about it," he said. "Bein' how you was Cuter's own hand-picked men, I didn't know but what you'd be hell-bent to see that he got all that was comin' to him. He will, at that—but you boys is overlookin' one angle—it's us that does the jobs, an' takes the resk, as you boys p'inted out—an' likewise, it's us that does the dividin', after we git the dust. How the hell will Cuter know how much we take? He won't—till we tell him. Somehow, I figger the deal will be even more fair an' reasonable than appears on the face of it—fer us."

Slim Carew offered his hand. "Put her there, John," he said.

"By heck, you're all right! How about it, boys?"

The others agreed wholeheartedly, and the bearded one eyed them. "I seen a little of Lefty's work when him an' the Swede lifted that there cache up on the Stewart. Him an' the Swede had the patience to wait around till they located that cache, which is recommendable. I asks Cuter if you two would be in the gang, an' he says how Lefty would, but not the Swede, him bein' ontrustworthy."

Lefty nodded. "Yeah, he's all right, some ways, the Swede is—but he's a crook, at that."

The big man turned to the others. "You boys is total strangers to me," he said, "an' bein' as how we've got to sort of depend on one another in a pinch, I'd kind of like to sort of git a line on you."

"My grift is strong-arm work—stick-ups. Frisco, Chi, an' points between. I'm figgered handy with a gat."

The Ape grinned. "Sort of all-around yegg, I guess you could call me. I've worked up an' down an' acrost—pretty much all over—peterman, gum-shoe worker, hister, eight-wheeler—all down the line."

Big Mike growled surlily. "I could swing fer plenty of mine," he said. "I ain't talkin'. But I'll be there when the fun starts."

THE BEARDED one nodded. "Guess you boys will do, all right. Now about me—any of you got any doubts about me bein' able to run this gang? Any questions you'd like to ask? Might's well know where we stand before we start."

Lefty grinned. "I ain't never, what you might say, know'd you, John. But I've saw you quite a few times in Dawson. An' I seen you an' that Siwash when you passed me an' the Swede, up there on the Stewart—an' believe me, you shore was slick enough not to let on you seen us. But I've heard tell enough about you an' that there Halfaday Crick gang, an' the jobs you've pulled off, so even if the half of it was true, you'd be good enough fer me to throw in with, any day in the week."

The Ape shrugged. "I'm like Lefty," he said. "I've heer'd enough about you so's I'm satisfied."

Slim Carew nodded. "That goes fer me, too."

Big Mike knocked the dottle from his pipe. "I'm takin' Cuter's word fer it. If you've got the guts an' the savvy he claims you've got, yer all jake by me."

The bearded one smiled. "Okay. An' seein' we're all satisfied, I'll fetch up my bed from the canoe. It's down around the bend. In the mornin' we'll have some target practice. I'd like to see how good you boys be—in case we'd have to shoot it out with some of our clients, er mebbe the cops."

III

IN THE TIVOLI saloon in Dawson a little group of sourdoughs had foregathered toward the rear end of the bar early one evening when they were joined by Burr MacShane, himself one of the elect. Old Bettles, dean of the sourdoughs, greeted him vociferously:

"Fill up, Burr. We've been waitin' for some old gravel hound to show up so we can get a game of stud goin'. Where the hell you be'n for the last month, er so?"

MacShane filled the glass the bartender slid across the bar. "I've be'n down Forty Mile way," he said, "lookin' over a proposition on a crick I heard about."

Swiftwater Bill laughed. "The proposition didn't turn out so good, eh? Yer face is longer'n the moral law."

"What the hell's the moral law?" asked Moosehide Charlie.

Bettles grinned. "I ain't got time to go into details, right now. But the gist of it is, if you mind yer morals the law won't bother you. Ain't that about right, Burr?"

MacShane failed to join in the laugh that followed. His brow puckered in a frown. "Fact is," he said, "it's the law that's botherin' me—an' not that there proposition on that crick."

"What the hell you be'n up to git the law on yer tail?" Camillo Bill asked.

"It ain't me. It's Black John."

"Black John!" Bettles roared with laughter. "Shorely you don't mean to hint that Black John would break the law!"

The others joined in the guffaw. "Why, that old sin-blister has broke it in so many pieces they never will git it put together agin," Swiftwater Bill exclaimed.

"Guess you don't need to worry about the law ketchin' up with Black John," Moosehide chuckled.

"That's the hell of it," MacShane replied. "It's already caught up with him."

The laughter was stilled and the faces of the sourdoughs became suddenly grave. "What do you mean—caught up?" Bettles asked. "Hell, Downey was in here not over an hour ago, an' he didn't say nothin' about it. Claimed he was hittin' to hell an' gone up the Klondike to investigate a corpse some guy found up there. Stopped in here for a drink before he started. Cripes, if Black John had got mixed up with the law, Downey'd have said somethin' about it, shore as hell."

"Downey don't know about it yet," MacShane replied. "An' I'm damn sorry to hear he's pulled out. If ever he was needed right here it looks like it's now."

"Who does know, if Downey don't?" Swiftwater Bill asked.

"A rookie constable name of Rollo Buck."

"Oh—him!" Camillo Bill sniffed. "Keeps his shoes shined nice, an' his pants is always pressed. Don't tell me he's arrested Black John!"

"If he tried it," Bettles opined, "Black John would turn him over his knee an' paddle his hind end."

"He ain't arrested him yet, but he claims he's goin' to," MacShane replied. "Fact is, there's a couple of guys with Buck that claim they was robbed of better'n three hundred ounces. I an' Sam Crombly was paddlin' upriver an' we run acrost Buck an' these two guys. They'd stopped to cook dinner on a point. We landed there fer a few minutes an' they told us about it. Both them guys claimed there was five men in the gang that robbed 'em an' both of 'em claim Black John was bossin' the job. They both claim they know him by sight, an' they swear they ain't mistaken. We'll be hearin' more about it before the evenin's over. They'd ort to be pullin' in before long."

Camillo Bill frowned. "Anyone saw Black John lately?" he asked.

Bettles shot him a glance. "Why?" he demanded.

Camillo shrugged. "Oh—nothin' much. Couple days ago I was over to police headquarters chawin' the fat with Downey, an' a chechako comes in an' claimed he'd be'n held up an' robbed of eighty-two ounces downriver, an' that there was five men in the mob, an' the leader of 'em was a big guy with a black beard."

"Black John was in here, couple weeks back," Swiftwater Bill said. "Him an' a Siwash. He bought quite a bill of grub from Al Scougale. Claimed he hittin' way to hell an' gone out in the hills to look over a crick the Siwash claimed he'd found. According' to John the Siwash showed him a poke of coarse gold."

Bettles refilled his glass and for several moments he stood staring at the little beads that rimmed the liquor. "Five, six days ago," he said thoughtfully, "me an' Downey was in here havin' us a little snort, an' a couple of chechakos come in an' claimed, they'd be'n robbed downriver a piece. They claimed they were fetchin' in a hundred ounces to deposit in the bank, when five men took out in two canoes an' forced 'em ashore an' robbed 'em. One of the guys claimed that the leader of the gang was Black John. He claimed he know'd Black John by sight, havin' seen him here in Dawson a time er two. Downey told the guy he was crazy if he thought Black John would pull a stunt like that. An' I told him the same thing. But the guy insisted he wasn't mistaken, an' Downey detailed Constable Peters to investigate the complaint. 'Whatever faults John's got,' Downey says, 'they ain't little ones like robbin' chechakos,' an' we had a good laugh over it."

MacShane nodded. "That's the way I'd look at it, too. But when you come to think about it, Bettles, there ain't so damn many men in the country John's size that's wearin' a heavy black beard."

A STUD game was started and along toward midnight Constable Buck stepped into the saloon accompanied by two chechakos. The officer glanced about the room and, leaving the men at the bar, stepped over and paused beside the stud table. The sourdoughs glanced up as Swiftwater Bill riffled the cards.

"Any of you men seen Black John Smith?" Buck demanded, frowning into the upturned faces.

Bettles nodded gravely. "Yeah, I've seen him," he replied.

"Where is he?"

"Damn' if I know."

"Where did you see him?"

"W-e-e-l-l, a year ago come Dominion Day, he was here in the Tivoli, an' last Chris'mas—"

Constable Buck flushed angrily. "Cut out the nonsense!" he snapped. "You're talking to the law. Any of you men seen Black John lately—within the last ten days? There's been a robbery committed, and Black John's at the bottom of it."

"Did you git to the bottom of it an' see him there?" asked Camillo Bill, guilelessly.

The officer pointed toward the bar. "Those two men were robbed downriver a couple of days ago, and they both swear that Black John was the leader of the five-man gang that robbed them. Both of them know him by sight. And that's not all—I just reported at headquarters, and Constable Nevers said there had been two other robberies, and that one of the victims said the man who robbed him was a big man with a black beard, and the other one said that the five-man gang that robbed him was led by Black John. Corporal Downey detailed Constable Peters to investigate one of these complaints, and put Constable Cox on the other one."

"Looks like robbery's gittin' to be quite a pastime along the river, don't it?" observed Moosehide.

Burr MacShane grinned. "If it's Black John that's pullin' off all them robberies it looks like he's workin' up quite a business."

"What does Downey think about it?" Swiftwater Bill asked.

Constable Buck scowled. "Corporal Downey is not at head-quarters. He is very conveniently investigating a corpse someone reported finding somewheres up the Klondike. There's no one at headquarters except Constable Jones. I'm hitting out for Halfaday Crick."

Swiftwater Bill gave the cards an audible riffle. "That's about as safe a place as you could be—if Black John's workin' along the Yukon," he opined.

Constable Buck flushed. "Halfaday Crick is Black John's reputed headquarters," he replied hotly, "and I'm going up there and get him. I'll bring him back here and let these men iden-tify him."

Bettles grinned. "Looks like you've ondertook quite a chore, sonny," he said. "Did Downey leave orders for you to go up there an' fetch Black John down?"

"No. I'm not taking orders from Corporal Downey. I'm working out of Forty Mile, under Inspector Steele. I ran onto this robbery complaint while making a routine patrol along the river inspecting fish nets."

Bettles' grin widened as he allowed his eyes to travel from the constable's well-shined shoes to his face. "Oh, yes. I knew I'd seen you before. You're the lad that Black John found camped upriver chawin' loon meat that you thought was duck, after missin' a few shots at some moose. Downey was tellin' me about you ballin' up a trap-stealin case, an' Black John clearin' it up, an' about how you'd be'n passed on from one detachment to another clean from Saskatchewan. He inherited you from Whitehorse, an' then wished you off on Sam Steele down to

Forty Mile. Sam, he can't pass you on without shovin' you clean over into Alaska. At that, you'd ort to make a swell U. S. Marshal, after you'd got a little more age an' fat onto you, an' got acquainted with a few politicians. Better stick to yer net inspectin', Rollo, an' let someone else go up after Black John."

Under the studied needling of the sourdoughs Constable Buck blew up. "Damn you oldtimers! You're all alike—every damn one of you! You think just because you've been in the country since God knows when, you know it all—and no one else knows anything! And Corporal Downey's just like you! I told him long ago that when I got the chance I'd clean up on that Halfaday Crick gang—and I told Black John that, too—right to his face! I'm not afraid of 'em—even if Downey is. Believe me, I'm heading for Halfaday after a live man—and a damn bad one, at that—not up the Klondike to investigate a corpse."

"Looks from here," Moosehide Charlie observed, "that Downey's goin' to have two corpses to investigate."

Burr MacShane nodded. "Better let Downey handle Black John," he advised. "Believe me, it ain't no job fer a rookie to tackle."

Constable Buck scowled. "It's Downey this, and Downey that! To hear you men talk you'd think there was no other policeman in the country besides Downey. Downey's had plenty of time to arrest Black John if he wanted to. If you men think it's good policing to allow a notorious criminal to go about his work without any interference by the police—I don't. It's high time Black John's career was brought to a close—and if Downey won't do it, I will!"

Camillo Bill grinned. "Yer guts is more commendable than yer brains, Rollo," he said. "But go ahead. It's your funeral—not ourn."

THE WORDS had scarcely left his lips when a wild-eyed chechako dashed into the saloon, paused in mid-floor for a moment, and spotting Buck's uniform, hurried up to him. "I went to the police station to report a robbery and murder, and the cop on duty there says you're the one to talk to, on account of all the other cops is out on detail, an' he's got to stick there at the desk."

"A robbery, you say? And a murder?"

"You're damn right its robbery an' murder! Me an' my pardner was camped on a point about ten miles up the river, when all of a sudden five men busts out of the woods and pulled guns on us, an' told us to throw up our hands. I put mine up, but Bill, he's my pardner, he made a dive for his rifle and the leader of the gang—a big man with a heavy black beard—the one that ordered us to throw up our hands—shot poor Bill dead. Then they dumped our packsacks upside down, and took our dust— two hundred and ninety-five ounces, and they took what grub we had, and smashed our canoe, and threw our rifles in the river, and then, while one of 'em waited there keeping me covered with his revolver, the others shoved two canoes into the water, and the other one joined them, and they headed upriver, leaving me to find my way here afoot."

"When did this happen?" Buck asked.

"Last evening. It took me all day today to get here clawing my way over rocks and through the brush."

"How about your partner—the man you say was shot?"

"How about him! Hell—he's dead! The big man fired two bullets into his head. Poor Bill never had a chance."

Constable Buck glanced into the faces of the sourdoughs. "There you are!" he exclaimed. "I knew it would be only a question of time till Black John added murder to his long list of robberies. But that spells his finish! This robbery and murder were pulled off upriver from here. The others were below— between here and Forty Mile. That shows that Black John and his gang are headed back to Halfaday Crick, leaving a trail of crime behind them that a blind man could follow. And believe me, they'll find me right on their tail when they get there! This is my chance—the big chance I've been waiting for. The chance to show Inspector Steele who's the best man—Downey, or me. I'll bet he'll never detail me to inspect another fish net!"

"That's right, Rollo," Bettles agreed somberly. "He won't. An' BUCK ain't no long name to carve on a slab, neither."

IV

OLD CUSH, PROPRIETOR of Cushing's Fort, the combined trading post and saloon that served the little community of wanted men that had sprung up on Halfaday Creek, close against the Yukon-Alaska border, laid aside the month-old newspaper he had been reading and peered over the top of his steel-rimmed spectacles as Red John Smith burst into the room.

"What the hell's your hurry?" he asked, as he set a bottle and two glasses onto the bar. "When did you git back from Dawson?"

"I jest got here, right now!" the other replied, grasping the bottle, filling his glass, and downing the fiery liquor at a gulp. "Where's Black John?"

"He ain't got back yet from that prospectin' trip him an' that Siwash hit out on 'bout a week 'fore you hit out fer Dawson. Why? What do you want of him?"

"I wanted to tell him to git to hell over acrost the line as quick as his legs will let him! Downey's comin' up here!"

Cush eyed the man sharply as he refilled his glass. "What the hell's ailin' you? You drunk? S'pose Downey is comin' up here? What's that got to do with John?"

"It's got plenty to do with him! Fact is, Cush, John ain't off on no prospectin' trip with no Siwash. He's be'n down along the river pullin' off a bunch of robberies—him an' four other guys. I hung around couple of days an' heard 'em talkin' about it—Peters, he's investigatin' one of them robberies, an' Cox another one—an' God knows how many more there'll be by now. Downey, he let on he was hittin' up the Klondike to look over some corpse he claimed some chechako had found, but I mistrusted he'd hit fer here, so I follered him, an' las' night I slipped around him when he was camped on the White a little ways below the mouth of Halfaday. He'll be gittin' here sometime today."

"What kind of robberies was these here John's s'posed to be pulling off?" Cush asked.

"Reg'lar common robberies," the other replied. "Them five is stickin' up chechakos an' robbin' 'em of their dust."

Cush scowled. "Yer crazy as hell if you think Black John's got anything to do with piddlin' little jobs like them. How come you figger it's John? An' how come Downey does?"

"We figger it was Black John 'cause every guy that got robbed claims it was him—that's why. These guys have all saw Black John in Dawson, now an' then—an' they all claim it's him that's bossin' them jobs."

"They're a bunch of damn fools, then," Cush replied. "Jest like all chechakos is."

"Shore they're damn fools," Red John agreed. "But even a damn fool might know what he seen." The man paused and glanced uneasily toward the door. "I'm gittin' to hell outa here till after Downey goes back," he said. "He seen me there in Dawson, an' if he was to see me up here ahead of him, he'd figger I come up to tip off Black John."

"Don't go shootin' off yer head about what you heard," Cush cautioned. "You never kin tell how the boys might take it. Someone might figger it would be doin' John a good turn to knock Downey off, an' some of 'em might figger that if John had let go all holts an' was startin' on a round of cheap robberies, they could do likewise—an' hell would be poppin' all around. What we got to do is keep our mouth shet till Downey gits here, an' I'll find out what he's got to say."

RED JOHN disappeared, and a few hours later, Corporal Downey stepped into the saloon, to be greeted by Cush with well-feigned surprise. "Well, damn if it ain't Downey, hisself!" He set out a bottle, and slid a glass across the bar. "Up here fer somethin' special?" he asked, "er jest takin' a walk?"

"Where's Black John?" the officer asked, filling his glass from the bottle, and shoving it toward the other.

"Him an' a Siwash is off on a prospectin' trip way to hell an' gone up the Stewart. This here Siwash, John done him a good turn one time, an' so when he runs onto some crick which he claims is lousy with coarse gold, he lets John in on it. He had the gold, too. I seen it. Nuggets an' dust, too. He had nineteen an' a half ounces which he claimed he scooped outa a rapids behind some rocks in one day—an' that's good money on any man's crick."

"I'll say it is," Downey agreed. "How long has he be'n gone?"

"It's better'n three weeks—yeah, it'll be four weeks tomorrow. Did you want to see him special?"

The officer nodded. "Yeah. The fact is, Cush, there's be'n a series of robberies down along the river, an' every one of the victims claim they was robbed by a five-man gang, an' that Black John was bossin' it."

"They're a bunch of damn fools then," Cush replied. "You know damn well, Downey, that John wouldn't fool around robbin' no chechakos outa their dust! Hell's fire! You know as well as I do, that time an' agin John has robbed guys that's robbed chechakos, an' then give the chechakos back their dust!"

Downey nodded. "That's right," he agreed. "I don't believe John is mixed up in these robberies any more than you do. But these men believe it was John, and they've reported to us it was John. What I'd like to do is to get John to go back down with me an' confront these guys. I'm bettin' they'll find out they're mistaken."

"Shore they will!" Cush agreed heartily. "You know there ain't an honester man in the Yukon than John is, when it comes to robbin' a chechako, er any other pore man. Cripes, Downey, I'd trust John with every damn cent I've got in the world."

"So would I," Downey agreed, "an' never give it a second thought. But," he asked with a twinkle in his eye, "how far would you trust him with say a hundred thousand dollars' worth of the Consolidated dust? Or how far would you trust him if you were a crook?"

"That ain't neither here, nor there." Cush affirmed. "Nor neither I wouldn't trust him if I was shakin' dice with him fer the drinks. But these chechakos ain't the Consolidated nor no other big outfit—nor neither they wasn't the shakin' him fer the drinks. An' the chances is they ain't crooks—jest damn fools."

"You got any idea how long John figured to be gone on this prospectin' trip?" the officer asked.

"No. He didn't say. A prospectin' trip is one of them things a man can't never tell how long he's goin' to be gone on it. I'd say, though, that he's liable to show up any day, now. It looks like a man should orta git clean up to the head of the Stewart an' back in a month."

"Guess I'll jest throw my stuff in John's cabin an' hang around a few days. I'd shore like to get this mess cleaned up. I've got a couple of men workin' on it, down on the river."

V

AS THE SURVIVOR of the two victims of the latest robbery had reported to Constable Buck, the five bandits had headed upriver after committing the crime. But after rounding the first point, they pulled ashore and later, under cover of darkness, slid the canoes into the water and slipped silently downriver, camping before daylight in a thicket of spruce well back from the water's edge almost directly across the river from Dawson.

The bearded leader explained the move as they cooked breakfast over a smokeless fire of dry twigs. "That guy'll hit Dawson sometime this evenin' an squawk his head off, tellin' the police we hit on upriver, an' tomorrow mornin' the police will hit out after us, figurin' we're headin' fer Halfaday Crick. 'Long towards evenin' Lefty, here, he'll slip acrost the river an' git in touch with Cuter. He might have somethin' good doped out by this time.

"I don't know how much them chechakos is goin' to claim they got robbed of—but it'll be plenty—an' Cuter's goin' to put up a squawk when you turn him over his cut. You kin p'int out to him that guys allus lies about how much they lost, an' swear that them four pokes holds his half of the take—an' that we're givin' him a square deal. At that, he's gittin' a little better'n twenty-five percent—which is a-plenty, seem' how we done all the work."

"I'll say it's a-plenty!" the Ape growled. "Not only we pulled the jobs, but we run onto them chechakos without no help from Cuter. What I claim, if he don't tip us off to somethin' good today he don't git a damn ounce outa the next jobs we pull off."

The others agreed, and later in the day, Lefty crossed the river.

The chechako victims of the various robberies had squawked loudly of their losses at the Dawson bars, damning off the police, and cussing the country, in general. On the night after the reported robbery and murder, standing in his accustomed place behind the bar of his notorious Klondike Palace, Cuter Malone bought the survivor of the last outrage a drink and listened sympathetically to his story. As the man turned from the bar, Cuter took a notebook from the top of the big iron safe behind him and added the figure two-ninety-five to the three other entries. "Eight hundred an' three ounces fer the four jobs," he muttered, totaling the figures. "An' my take is four hundred an' one an' a half ounces. That figgers six thousan' an' twenty-four dollars. Not bad fer the time they've be'n at it. It's too damn bad we can't keep the grift a-goin'. But it won't be long now till Black John'll be gittin' back from that prospectin' trip up the Stewart. Lefty an' the Swede seein' him go past 'em, up there, checks with what Red John said when he was in here the other day—about John hittin' out up the Stewart to find some crick a Siwash told him about. If things would break right, an' the police should knock Black John off on sight, everything would be jake. But the hell of it is, when Black John's mixed up in it, things don't never break right—fer me. If the police would arrest him an' charge him with these jobs, the chances is he'd wiggle out of it, somehow er other. They might not take the Siwash's word on where he was at, but God knows how many white men he might of run acrost that could alibi him out of it. I can't afford to take a chanct. I'll slip the boys the word on this Excelsior Development shipment, an' when they pull that one off, we'll close the book. Cripes, if them boys would git picked up, an' find out the guy they think is Black John is a phony, they'd every damn one of 'em spill their guts—an' then where would I be? The best way to work it would be to have 'em knock this here Spokane Blackie off an' then git to hell outa the country."

THE MUMBLED soliloquy was cut short at sight of Lefty, who had entered inconspicuously by way of the back door, and was beckoning with a crooked finger.

Pocketing the notebook, and picking a bottle and two glasses from the back bar, Cuter slipped from behind the bar, led the way to the little back room, and locked the door behind them. Cuter set the bottle on the table, and both filled their glasses.

"Here's lookin' at you," Lefty said, downed the liquor, and refilled his glass.

"How!" Cuter grunted, his pig-like eyes on the other's face. "An' now come acrost with my cut." His glance shifted to the notebook that he had tossed onto the table. "Accordin' to my figgers, it'll be four hundred an' one an' a half ounces."

Lefty laughed. "What the hell you doin'—kiddin' me?"

"What do you mean—kiddin'! I've got it right here, black on white, what you boys lifted off'n these guys—eight hundred an' three ounces."

"That's what they claim," Lefty said. "But you know damn well, Cuter, when a guy gits robbed he allus claims he lost two, three times what he did."

Malone scowled, and pointed to the notebook. "Take that first job—three hundred an' twenty-six ounces is what they claimed you boys took 'em fer."

For answer, Lefty drew a little moosehide poke from his pocket and tossed it onto the table. "There's your half of that take—weigh her up."

Taking a set of scales from a shelf, Malone weighed the dust. "Ninety-two ounces," he roared, "an' it ort to be a hundred an' sixty-three!"

"I wisht it was, Cuter, 'cause we'd of got that much, too. We made a balance scale outa two tin cans an' some string, an' we weighed up the dust even every time we pulled a job, an' put your half in the poke. Here's the four pokes fer the four jobs we pulled."

Malone weighed the dust in the other pokes and totaled the figures. "Two hundred an' twenty-two an' a half ounces," he bellowed, "an you guys got the rest!"

"That's right," Lefty agreed. "An' the rest is jest exactly like you got."

"Yer a damn liar! An' the hull five of you is a bunch of crooks! If a man could only git honest men to work with! But there ain't a guy a man kin trust in the hull damn country." Malone pocketed the dust and eyed the other with a baleful glare. "Well, here's one job you'll come clean on—'cause I know to the last ounce what the take will be! The Excelsior Development Company is shippin' nine thousan' ounces outside day after tomorrow on the *Hannah*. It'll be packed in three wooden boxes—three thousan' ounces to the box. An' when the split comes, I git forty-five hundred ounces—an' not a damn ounce less! An' what's more, we've got to slip the guy that tipped me off to this shipment ten percent of the take—that's nine hundred ounces—an' the half of it comes outa you boys' cut. We don't dast to shave his cut none 'cause he knows how much is in them boxes. He's a clerk in the Excelsior office."

Lefty nodded. "Okay, Cuter. You'll git every damn ounce that's comin' to you—you kin depend on that. You got us boys wrong. Why the hell would we gyp you when we're dependin' on you to finger all our big plays? It don't make sense. You got the half of every damn ounce we took—honest, you have."

Somewhat mollified by the earnestness of the other's tone, Malone shrugged. "Keep on turnin' me in my half then," he growled. "An' remember, on this here job, I know what it'll be. How's Black John workin' out?"

"He's okay. He knows his stuff, all right. Gee, he's hard. He let that guy have it, last evenin' an' never batted an eye."

"He's hard, all right," Cuter agreed. "Mebbe too damn hard."

"What do you mean?"

"It's like this. I got the word, the other day, that Black John's fixin' to doublecross you boys—an' me, too. A guy from up on Halfaday, name of Red John, got drunk in here an' shot off his mouth. Accordin' to him, our Black John figgers on pullin' jest one big job with you boys, an' then hittin' fer Halfaday Crick. If you kick on goin' up there he'll prob'ly tell you he's hittin' fer the outside by way of the Dalton Trail. But Halfaday Crick is where you'll wind up at—an' it's where you'll stay, too."

"Why would he go to Halfaday Crick? Hell, we're doin' all right down here!"

A MALEVOLENT grin twisted the corners of Malone's thick lips. "You'll do all right, up there, too. That is, the four of you'll lay low fer a long time—in under slabs in the little graveyard out behind Cushing's Fort. Black John's game is simple, an' it's safe—onct he gits you boys on Halfaday. All he'll do is call a miners' meetin' an' hang the four of you."

"Hang us! What would he hang us fer?"

Cuter shrugged. "Figger it out fer yerself. Who'd have all the dust you boys has took, if you an' the Ape, an' Big Mike, an' Slim Carew was out of the way?"

Lefty's eyes widened, and he turned a shade paler. "Why—

Black John would."

"Yer damn right he would. That is, onlest you boys beat him to it."

"How do you mean—beat him to it?"

"I mean, knock him off before he gits the chanct to knock you off. It's like this here. You boys lay fer the *Hannah* at the mouth of the White River. Halfaday Crick is up the White. When you've got the boxes of dust, you step behind Black John an' let him have it. An' be shore you git him the first shot. Then you boys come back down here with all the dust. You kin divide his cut up betwixt you—I'll be satisfied with my fifty percent. None of you boys has be'n identified by these chechakos you've took. Every one of 'em spotted Black John, him bein' sort of conspicuous, like you might say—an' none of 'em paid no attention to the rest of you. You four kin lay low here in Dawson till the stink dies down, an' then slip outside with yer dust."

Lefty's eyes lighted with avarice. "By God, Cuter—I believe yer right. I'm tired of the damn country anyhow!"

"You've got to git Black John first."

"We'll git him—you don't need to worry about that. Why the dirty doublecrosser! Gittin' us guys up there on Halfaday an' hangin' us! Yer damn right we'll git him!"

Cuter nodded. "Okay. Better git goin', now—an' don't knock him off till you git that Excelsior dust. We need him on that job."

VI

LEFTY RETURNED TO the bandit camp just on the edge of the darkness.

"Did Cuter put the finger on a job fer us?" the Ape asked.

"I'll say he did! An' believe me, it's a honey! First off, he squawked like hell about us short-changin' him on his cut. He'd set down what them chechakos claimed they lost, an' it figgered up to eight hundred an' three ounces, so when he weighed up them four pokes, he let out a yell. But I told him, like Black John said, how guys allus lies about what they lost, an' Cuter he sort of quieted down. Then he slipped me the word about this here gold shipment. He got the tip from a clerk in the Excelsior Development office—nine thousan' ounces, in three wooden boxes is bein' shipped outside day after tomorrow on the *Hannah*."

"How much does nine thousan' ounces figger in money?" Big Mike asked.

The bearded leader produced a pencil and figured on a scrap of paper. "Gold figgers sixteen dollars to the ounce, up here," he said, "an' nine thousan' ounces would be a hundred and forty-four thousan' dollars."

"The hell of it is," Lefty said, "we ain't got no chanct to short-change Cuter on this deal. He knows what the take is. An' besides that we've got to kick in ten percent of our share fer the clerk that tipped Cuter off to the shipment."

"How much does that figger apiece, fer us guys?" the Ape asked.

Again the leader did some figuring. "It figgers jest thirteen thousan' apiece, after we kick in our ten percent fer the clerk."

"An' how much does Cuter git?"

"He'd git seventy-two thousan' minus the seventy-two hundred he slips the clerk."

"Cuter figgers the best place to pull this here steamboat job would be at the mouth of the White River. Halfaday Crick is up the White, accordin' to Cuter, an' the police would figger we hit fer there, instead of which, we drop back down the Yukon."

The bearded one nodded. "His reasonin' seems sound," he agreed.

"Every damn one of them chechakos claimed Black John was leadin' the gang that robbed 'em. An' a police constable hit out fer Halfaday Crick, today, accordin' to what I heard in

Dawson," Lefty said. "Figgerin' that's where we hit fer, after pullin' that last job. An' other constables is downriver workin' on them other jobs, too."

The leader nodded. "This constable will be already headed up the White, then, by the time the *Hannah* gits to the mouth of it.

"Here's the way we'll work it. Lefty, an' the Ape, an' Slim will slip acrost the river an' buy tickets fer Whitehorse, an' board the *Hannah*. I don't dast to show there, 'cause like Lefty said, all them chechakos seen me an' I'd be knocked off in a minute if I showed up in Dawson. Me an' Mike, we'll hit out tonight fer the mouth of the White, an' be waitin' there when the *Hannah* comes along. Jest before she gits there, one of you boys slip into the pilothouse, an' shoves a gun in the captain's ribs an' tells him to nose the boat up agin the bank. Another one of you pulls a gun on the passengers an' herds 'em into the cabin, an' the other one goes onto the lower deck an' covers the crew. Then when she hits the bank, me an' Mike steps outa the bresh an' carries the boxes ashore. Then we'll slip into the bresh till the *Hannah* pulls away."

"Won't them boxes be heavy as hell?" Big Mike asked.

"They'll go damn near two hundred pounds apiece," the leader said. "They make 'em heavy a-purpose, so guys can't slip off with 'em handy. That's why me an' you's got to handle 'em. These other boys couldn't lift two hundred pound."

"'Tain't right," the Ape growled, "Cuter gittin' better'n sixty thousan', an' us only a lousy thirteen thousan'."

The leader grinned. "If you don't like the arrangement, mebbe, you better jump in the river an' swim acrost an' try to talk Cuter outa part of his share."

"Fat chanct!" the Ape grunted. "An' besides, I can't swim a lick."

The grin widened behind the bearded lips. "You won't have to do no swimmin'. Fact, is, boys, Cuter's cut on this here job is goin' to be jest exactly nothin'. Them there nine thousan' ounces splits five ways—an' we're the five. It's like this—after we pull off this here job, instead of slippin' back downriver an' dividin' with Cuter, we shove on up the White, an' hit fer the outside on the Dalton Trail."

"What's the Dalton Trail?" Slim asked.

"It's a trail that runs along up the White then cuts acrost through the Chilkat an' comes out at Haines. There's only one police post on it an' we kin duck around that. We're settin' pretty. Nine thousan' ounces cut five ways makes eighteen hundred ounces apiece, an' that figgers twenty-eight thousan', eight hundred dollars. That, on top of what we've got will make better'n thirty thousan' apiece—an' that ain't chicken feed in no man's language, fer the time we've put in. I ain't be'n outside in quite a while, an' with better'n thirty thousan' on me, I could have a damn good time!" He paused and glanced into the faces of the others. "How does that strike you?" he asked.

THE SCHEME met with universal approval, and the bearded one turned to Lefty. "Okay, then, you boys know what you got to do. You're bossin' the job on the steamboat—an' see that you work it jest like I said. Me an' Mike's hittin' out fer upriver, right now. So 'long. We'll be seein' you boys at the mouth of the White."

When the two had departed the Ape grinned at the others. "Cuter shore played hell when he picked Black John to run this mob," he said. "He gits short-changed on the jobs we already pulled, an' he don't git a damn cent outa this big job."

"That's right," Slim Carew agreed. "Black John's smart."

Lefty regarded the other two with a cynical leer. "He's smart, all right. But he ain't as smart as he thinks he is—by a damn sight."

"Meanin' like what?" the Ape asked.

"Meanin' his 'rithmatic's a little bit off when it comes to splittin' the take. He claimed she'd split five ways, when the fact is, she only splits four."

"How do you figger that out?" Slim regarded the speaker narrowly.

"Git an earful of this," Lefty said. "Black John never figgered on the dust splittin' five ways. He figgered on keepin' every damn ounce of it hisself."

"Baloney!" scoffed Slim. "How the hell could he do that? There'd be the four of us agin' him."

"Yeah," Lefty sneered, "an' where would us four be when we got on Halfaday Crick amongst that gang of his, up there?"

"We ain't goin' to Halfaday Crick," the Ape reminded him. "We're hittin' fer the outside on the Dalton Trail."

"That's what you think. But I know different. Listen, you guys—Cuter ain't so damn dumb when it comes to figgerin', hisself. A guy from up there on Halfaday Crick gits a load on the other day, there in the Klondike Palace, an' shot off his mouth, fer fair. He brags how Black John's runnin' a gang of punks down here on the river, robbin' chechakos an' the like of that, an' waitin' fer the chanct to pull a big job. An' when he pulls it, he aims to steer his punks up to Halfaday, prob'ly tellin' us he's headin' up the Dalton Trail, an' then call a miners' meetin' an' hang the four of us, an' keep every damn ounce fer hisself, barrin' mebbe ten ounces apiece er so he'd pass out amongst his gang, up there, fer votin' to hang us."

The Ape's eyes widened in horror. "By God," he cried, "I've heered how they hang guys, up there!"

"Shore they do," Lefty said. "Cuter, he's got it doped out like this here—we pull the *Hannah* job at the mouth of the White, jest like Black John said. Then, when him an' Big Mike gits them heavy boxes packed ashore, an' the *Hannah* goes on, we knock Black John off, load the dust in the canoes, an' hit back downriver. Then we slip Cuter his cut, an' we divide the rest of the dust up betwixt the four of us. Then we lay low fer a while, watch fer the chance to hit outside with our dust. That's the way he figgers it. But tellin' you about me—I don't see no sense in us hittin' back downriver an' slippin' Cuter his cut on this here *Hannah* job. We kin find the Dalton Trail, all right. I've heard tell how Jack Dalton drives cattle in over it, so it's bound to be easy to foller. We'll hit fer the outside with them nine thousan' ounces, an' only have to cut it four ways, instead of five."

The Ape smote his palm with a hairy fist. "Black John figgerin' to hang us an' keepin' all the dust fer hisself! The dirty, doublecrosser—yer damn right we'll knock him off! An' me, I be'n figgerin' him fer a square guy. It's gittin' so's a man can't trust no one."

Slim Carew's eyes narrowed. "That's what us guys git fer throwin' in with him. Hell, we know'd he was an outlaw—everyone knows it. It would serve us right if he had of hung us—fer bein' a bunch of saps. But I figgered he was one outlaw we could trust. Damn a man that will go back on a pal! We'll knock him off, all right, an' while we're about it, why not knock off Big Mike, too? That'll only leave the three of us to split that nine thousan' ounces—three thousan' apiece, besides them two's cut on the other jobs."

Lefty agreed enthusiastically, but the Ape frowned. "How long is this here Dalton Trail?" he asked. "There's three of them there wooden gold boxes, an' Black John figgered they'd go damn near two hundred pound apiece. I can't pack no two hundred pound over no trail, an' neither kin you. An' there's our grub besides. Why not save Mike to help with the packin' till we git to the end of the trail?"

"We'll git the dust over the trail, all right, onct we git it," Lefty said. "We'll kill us a moose, an' make pokes outa his hide, an' knock them boxes apart an' stick the dust in the pokes, an' then we kin double back on the trail."

"I agree with Lefty," Slim said. "I don't trust Mike. He's crooked as hell. He might lay fer a chanct to knock us off an' keep all the dust fer hisself. We better git him when we git

Black John, jest as quick as the *Hannah* gits out of sight."

"Okay," Lefty said, "she's all settled then. An' jest so there won't be no mistake—like all of us jumpin' the same guy—I an' the Ape will both take Black John, an' Slim will 'tend to Mike. We'll slip around behind 'em an' let 'em have it."

VII

CONSTABLE BUCK REACHED the Ogilvie trading post as darkness settled over the Yukon. The trader recognizing him as the rookie that had manhandled the old Indian Blackbird, greeted him with a none-too-cordial nod as he announced his intention of spending the night:

"I'm on my way up to Halfaday Crick to arrest Black John Smith," Buck announced importantly.

"Goin' to git even with him fer showin' you up, that time you balled up that trap-stealin' job, eh? I thought Downey sent you on down to Forty Mile to answer charges of misusin' a prisoner. Sam Steele must be out of his head—sendin' you up after Black John. I'll bet Downey'd never done it."

Buck flushed hotly. "Corporal Downey is not sending me anywhere," he snapped. "I'm not taking orders from Downey. I'm working out of Forty Mile under Inspector Steele. But I'm making this trip on my own. I found out that Black John and four of his gang have been robbing chechakos along the river, and have hit for Halfaday Crick. So I'm going up there and get him. I'll show Corporal Downey that if he won't bust up the Halfaday Crick gang, I will! Can I get something to eat?"

The trader regarded him gravely. "Supper's over, sonny," he said, "but I'll see what I can do. What would you like—a sugar tit?"

"There ought to be a law against insulting policemen," Buck replied, "and never mind about the grub. I'll cook my own supper down by the river."

The trader grinned. "Downey, he's shore goin' to be glad of

your help, up there on Halfaday Crick," he said.

"Downey's not on Halfaday. He's gone off up the Klondike to investigate a corpse some fellow found. It's a damn sight easier to investigate a corpse than it is to handle Black John Smith."

"Guess yer right, at that. But if Downey's gone up the Klondike he shore took a hell of a roundabout way to git there."

"What do you mean?"

"Meanin' that he went through here a few days back. Stopped in fer some terbacker, an' shoved on upriver. He said he was headin' fer Halfaday."

"Why would he go up to Halfaday when he knew Black John was operating along the river?" Buck demanded.

The trader shrugged. "He didn't tell me, an' I shore as hell didn't ask him. Mebbe he didn't know Black John was operatin' along the river. If he did, mebbe he figgered the best way to git him would be to slip up to Halfaday an' wait for him to go back there. Or mebbe he jest went up there to pick some flowers. You can't never tell about Downey."

BUCK SCOWLED, a gleam of suspicion in his eyes. "I don't believe Corporal Downey hit for Halfaday Crick. And I'm not so sure you're not just telling me that to head me off. I noticed that time I arrested Blackbird and brought him in here, you seemed mighty friendly with Black John—and so did Corporal Downey. It may well be that I've stepped right into the middle of a damn dirty mess—a mess that will involve you and Downey and God knows how many more—a mess that may explain why such a notorious outlaw as Black John has never been arrested and brought to book."

The trader nodded gravely. "That's right, bub—mebbe you have. If I ever stepped in a mess like that I'd shore track it around some."

"If Downey's gone to Halfaday he'll find me right on his heels, and if I can get to the bottom of this conspiracy there's no telling where I'll go. It's the big chance I've been waiting for."

The trader chuckled. "Well, you've got it. An' there shore ain't no tellin' where you'll go. 'Cause when you explain this here conspiracy to Sam Steele, he's goin' to blow a gaskit."

Owing to certain misadventures anent the handling of his canoe on the upriver journey, two days passed before Buck camped late in the afternoon on the west bank of the Yukon, a mile below the mouth of the White River. Dog-tired from bucking the current, he sat with his back against a rock and filled his pipe. A steamboat hove in sight downriver, and he eyed her with a frown. "Gosh, if I'd known the *Hannah* was due upriver, I could have had her put me off at the White River and saved myself a hell of a lot of work," he muttered. Then his brow cleared. "But I'm glad I didn't. If I had I'd never tumbled onto that conspiracy. That trader's going to find he talked too much for his own good. If Downey really is on Halfaday, and I can slip up and get the evidence that he's playing in with Black John, I'll get my corporal's stripes right away. Inspector Steele might even put me in command of the Dawson detachment!"

The frown again returned to his brow as the *Hannah* suddenly altered her course and headed for the bank a mile or so above. "Going to land some prospector," he muttered. "Maybe that's the mouth of the White River. It sure can't be much farther along. I've been expecting to hit it all day."

The steamboat backed away and continued on upstream. Then suddenly the sound of a shot, and another, and another reached his ears from the spot where the steamboat had landed. "What the devil!" he exclaimed. Then, suddenly his muscles tensed. "Maybe that's Black John and his gang! Maybe they found some prospector was going to land there, and laid for him! If I can slip up and get the drop on Black John, he'll have to order his men to throw away their guns to keep from getting plugged. Cripes, if I can round up that gang single-handed it will sure show Downey up! Even if they do start shooting I'll have the advantage. I'll be under cover, and they'll most likely be in the open. I'll show 'em I didn't get my target medal, and my rapid fire medal down at Regina for nothing!"

Be it said to Constable Buck's credit, that his courage was far and away ahead of his judgment. Drawing the service revolver from its holster, he checked the loaded cylinder, then returning it, he proceeded cautiously on foot though the bush. It was slow going, clambering over rocks, and inching his way through the thick scrub, being careful to make no slightest noise.

An hour later, he crept behind an upstanding sliver of rock and peered around it to see three men seated beside a small fire, above which hung a tea pail. Beyond them two bodies lay face downward upon the sand. With tight-pressed lips, he drew the revolver from its holster and leveled it at the three beside the fire.

VIII

ONE BY ONE, Lefty, the Ape, and Slim Carew slipped aboard the *Hannah* at the Dawson wharf and mingled with the passengers. As the boat approached the mouth of the White River, Lefty edged toward the pilothouse. On the upper deck the Ape took his place in the bow, while Slim Carew slipped below where the deckhands lolled about on the boxes of freight. As they approached the mouth of the White, the Ape suddenly drew a revolver from beneath his shirt, leveled it, and bawled an order for the passengers who were seated in chairs or strung along the rail, to bunch in front of the cabin—or else. At the same moment, Lefty slipped into the pilothouse, and shoved the muzzle of his gun into the captain's ribs. "Head fer shore!" he commanded, in a low, hard voice. "Run her in there at the mouth of the White. An' do it quick." On the lower deck Slim covered the crew.

As the boat nosed against the bank, two big men leaped

aboard, and without a word, each picked up a small heavy wooden box, from a spot indicated by Slim, and carried them ashore. Then the heavily bearded one returned, and picked up the last of the three boxes and stepped ashore with it. From the deck the passengers watched the procedure, wide-eyed. "Black John!" someone gasped, and the Ape grinned.

"You guessed it. That's him, all right. So 'long, folks. Glad I didn't have to knock none of you off. We don't hurt no one that don't hurt us."

A moment later, he was joined by Lefty, and as the two big men on the shore covered the passengers with drawn revolvers, the three bandits leaped ashore, and the *Hannah* backed out into the stream and headed upriver.

As the boat reached midstream, the bearded one regarded the others with a grin. "Everything come off jest like clockwork," he said. "An' here's nine thousan' ounces that Cuter don't git no part of. We'll pack the stuff couple hundred yards up the White, where that sand patch is. The diggin's easy there, an' we'll cache it till mornin'—jest in case. Then we'll split her up, an' start packin' it up the trail." Reaching down, he picked up one of the boxes. Big Mike picked up another and followed him toward the sand strip. The Ape glanced at Lefty and reached under his shirt. Lefty shook his head and stepped closer. "Not yet," he whispered out of the corner of his mouth. "Wait till they git the stuff over on the sand. No use in us liftin' our guts out when we got them to do it. One of 'em'll come back fer the other box, then we'll foller 'em over to the sand, an' when he stoops to let it down, we'll blast the two of 'em to hell. Remember—me an' you takes Black John, an' Slim 'tends to Mike."

Big Mike returned for the third box, and as he lifted it and headed for the sand strip where the bearded one waited, the three fell in behind him. As he stooped to lower the box to the sand three shots rang out almost simultaneously. Big Mike pitched forward atop the box, and the bearded one jerked spasmodically as two heavy-calibre bullets tore through his chest, spun half around, and crashed face downward upon the sand.

For a moment the three conspirators stood with drawn guns eyeing the prostrate forms. "They're finished, all right," Lefty said, slipping his gun beneath his shirt. "An' now, like Black John said, we better bury these boxes in the sand till we git organized to begin packin' it out. Gee, think of it—three thousan' ounces apiece, besides what we git when we frisk Black John an' Mike."

The three set to work and soon had scooped out a shallow hole into which they rolled the three heavy boxes. Covering them with sand, they dragged a blanket over it a few times to smooth the surface, then tracked around over the spot till it presented the same surface as the rest of the strip.

"Hadn't we ort to bury them guys?" the Ape asked as they removed the pokes from the dead men's pockets.

"It's too much work," Lefty replied. "Besides, I'm hungrier'n hell. Let's cook supper, an' after we've et, we kin drag 'em over an throw 'em in the river—it's easier."

THE OTHERS agreed, and collecting firewood, they soon had a fire going, and the tea pail set aboil. Squatting about the fire at the edge of the bush, the three were suddenly startled by a sharp barked command. "Hands up!"

Three pairs of eyes focused upon the figure that had stepped from behind a rock, not thirty feet distant—a figure in the uniform of the Northwest Mounted Police.

Lefty's hand shot beneath his shirt, and came out with his revolver. There was a loud report, and he slumped forward across the fire. The Ape reached the bush in a single leap and disappeared from sight. Slim Carew elevated his hands above his head and eyed the officer, who had him covered.

"Unbutton your shirt," Buck commanded, "and let your gun fall out, then back away from it."

The man complied, and as the constable picked up the gun

he could hear the brush crashing with rapidly diminishing sounds as the Ape placed distance between himself and the arm of the law. Keeping Slim covered, Buck stepped over and glanced down at the dead man. "Good God," he cried, "that's Black John Smith!"

Slim favored him with a twisted grin. "That's right," he admitted. "The king of the outlaws of Halfaday Crick. He don't look much like no king, now—the dirty doublecrosser!"

"What do you mean—doublecrosser?" Buck asked, and listened as Slim unfolded a sordid tale of plot and counter plot, being careful, however to make no mention of the three heavy boxes of dust that lay buried directly beneath Buck's feet.

"Nice bunch of guys," he grinned, when the other had finished. "We'll camp here. It's too dark to go back to my camp. We'll eat first, and then you can get busy and bury those three."

"Why not throw 'em in the river? That's what we was goin' to do."

"No. The manual says to bury all bodies where other disposition is impractical. It don't say how deep to bury 'em, so we won't waste much time."

Supper over, Buck watched while the other scooped three shallow graves in the sand, rolled the bodies in, and covered them. Then he handcuffed his prisoner. "Why," he asked, "were you all on the *Hannah?*"

"We wasn't. Only me an' the Ape, an' Lefty. Black John an' Big Mike was waitin' fer us here. We got the tip that a guy was goin' outside on the *Hannah* with a lot of dust, an' we was goin' to pinch him off here, an' then hit outside on the Dalton Trail. But the guy worn't on the boat, so we made the captain land anyhow. Then we know'd Black John an' Mike would be mad, an' mebbe knock us off fer bunglin' the job—so we beat 'em to it."

Buck nodded. "The main thing is that Black John is out of the way for good. I was headed for Halfaday to get him. According to the trader at Ogilvie, Corporal Downey's up there now, so in the morning, we'll go back to my camp a little way down the river and pick up my canoe, and shove on up to Halfaday. I'll bet Downey'll be sore when he finds out he slipped up on the job, and I stuck on you fellow's trail till the gang was wiped out."

Slim nodded. "Yeah, most likely he will. But it was me knocked off Black John—not you. I'd ort to git some credick fer that, when my trial comes up."

"That will be up to the Crown prosecutor and the jury," Buck said.

"Why not hit back down to Dawson?" Slim asked. "By God, if them guys up on Halfaday figger I knocked Black John off, they're liable to knock the both of us off to git even."

"They won't dare to bother me," Buck replied. "They won't bother anyone any more, now Black John's gone. He was the brains of that gang."

"Okay, if yer bound to go up there," Slim said. "But we don't have to go back to yer camp in the mornin'. We got more'n enough grub fer the trip right here, an' the canoe Black John an' Mike come up in, is hid here in the bresh."

IX

WITH THE SHOT that killed Lefty ringing in his ears, the Ape ran crashing through the brush until, completely winded, he paused for breath in a spruce thicket. Hearing no sound of pursuit, his courage returned. "The cop got Lefty," he muttered, "an' that leaves only me an' Slim to split them nine thousan' ounces. If I kin sneak back an' knock the cop off, we kin git away with it."

Slowly and noiselessly he worked his way back until he lay behind the very rock from which Buck had shot Lefty, reaching it after the bodies had been buried and Buck and his manacled prisoner sat talking beside the fire. Slipping the revolver from beneath his shirt, he leveled it at the constable's back. As he was about to press the trigger a thought occurred to him, and he lowered the weapon as a slow grin twisted his lips. "Gee," he muttered to himself, "I come damn near pullin' a boner! If Slim ain't spilt his guts about them boxes, the cop'll take him away, an' I git the whole nine thousan' ounces, myself. If he has told him, an' he starts diggin'"em up, I'll plug him, an' Slim, too. Slim's got it comin', at that, 'cause chances is, if there was jest him an' me alone, he'd lay fer a chanct to knock me off. He's that crooked."

HE LAY there listening to the two talk until finally they rolled in their blankets. Then he slipped noiselessly away, and spent an uncomfortably chilly night in the spruce thicket. In the early morning, he watched from a point of vantage on the hillside as the two breakfasted, made up a pack of supplies, slipped the cached canoe into the water, and headed up the White. As they disappeared around a bend he rose to his feet and headed for the sand spit where the three boxes of gold lay in the shallow cache.

To his vast relief he found that there was food left in the packs of the two big men, and lighting a fire, he fried thick slices of salt pork, boiled a pot of tea and ate ravenously. Then he proceeded downriver afoot. "The cop said his camp is only a little ways down. I'll git his canoe, an' load the dust in it an' git to hell outa here. No tellin' what Slim will do—the crook might tell the cop where the dust is cached, if he could make some kind of a deal."

Returning with the canoe an hour later, he beached it on the sandspit, dropped to his knees, and scooping the sand away with his hands, uncovered the three wooden boxes. Rising to his feet, he stood eyeing the treasure gloatingly. "Nine thousan' ounces—all mine! How much did Black John say that figgers? A hundred an' forty-four thousan' dollars. Gee—I'm rich!"

X

FAR UP A little feeder of a tributary of the Stewart River, Black John Smith eyed the Indian who faced him across the little fire. "It shore looks like we've got somethin' here, Amos," he said. "We'll set our stakes, an' I'll slip down to Dawson an' record the claim. We've be'n away for quite a while, so I'll slip up to Halfaday first an' see how things is goin'. There's no hurry about the recordin'. Way up here there ain't no one goin' to crowd in on us. If this here proposition holds up clean down to bedrock, you're goin' to be richer even than Carmack. I'm shore obliged to you fer lettin' me in on it."

The Indian shrugged. "Huh. You good mans. Me—I'm ain' fergit dat tam you giv' me poke of dus' w'en me an' my woman los' de boat an' all de nets in de ice. Seexty-t'ree ounce, she was een dat poke. I'm say I'm pay you back som'tam—an' I do it."

The big man grinned. "I'll say you done it—with interest. That poke I tossed you that day turned out to be the best sixty-three ounces I ever invested." He rose, tossed his pack into the waiting canoe, and shoved off. "So long, Amos! Be seein' you before long."

He ran the Stewart without incident, and several days later slanted the canoe across the Yukon opposite the mouth of the White. As he approached the west bank he caught sight of a canoe beached on a sandspit a short distance up the smaller river, caught, also, a fleeting glimpse of a man down on his knees, apparently burrowing into the sand with his hands. Then the brush along the bank hid the man from view, and he beached his canoe a short distance below, and proceeding noiselessly through the bush, brought up behind the upstanding rock only a few feet distant, just as the man rose to his feet and stood staring down at the flat tops of three wooden boxes. "Nine thousan' ounces—all mine!" the man exclaimed aloud. "How much did Black John say that figgers? A hundred an' forty-four thousan' dollars! Gee—I'm rich!"

Stepping into the open within a few feet of the man, Black John spoke: "Comparatively so—for a chechako—if the ounces are there. But—why take my name in vain?"

The man whirled at the words, and stood for a moment as though paralyzed, his huge hands dangling limply almost to his knees. His eyes widened in horror, his mouth gaped open, and his whole frame shuddered. The barrel chest heaved convulsively, and with a choking, gurgling scream, he turned and plunged headlong into the canoe which shot out into the river, whirled around in an eddy, and promptly overturned. For a moment or two the long, ape-like arms thrashed the water, then shot straight upward as the misshapen body disappeared beneath the surface, and the empty canoe drifted out into the Yukon.

So sudden and unexpected was the man's behavior that Black John stood speechless for several moments after his disappearance. Then, a slow grin widened the lips beneath the heavy black beard. "Well, I'll be damned," he muttered. "Some miscreant, no doubt." Then, as his eyes came to rest on the three wooden boxes, the grin widened. "The amount he mentioned is worth

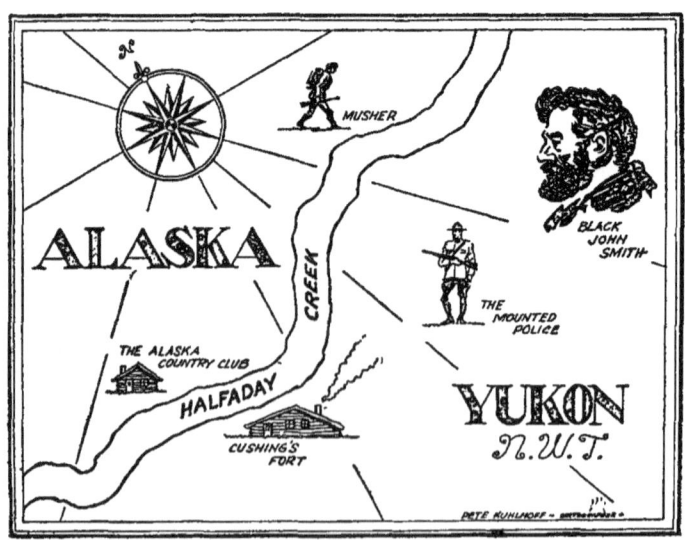

contemplatin'," he muttered. "But the way he acted I shore must be a terrorizin' lookin' object. He mentioned my name. How the hell did he figger I'm mixed up in it?"

Droppin' to his knees, he lifted the boxes from the sand and regarded them with a puzzled frown. "Accordin' to their heft they're full of dust, all right. An' both the Excelsior Development Company an' the Consolidated ships their dust outside in boxes like these. Either one of them big outfits losin' the dust don't give me no pain in the neck. They're ruinin' the country for a poor man with their damn dredges. But how the hell could one man have got 'em here? This ain't a one-man job, by a damn sight. Either this guy knocked off his pals, or he's doublecrossin' 'em by removin' the dust while they're away for some reason 'er other. Any way you look at it, the thing savors of onderhandedness. The ways of these damn crooks is shore sad to contemplate. An' it's my plain duty to see that they don't profit by no sech carryin's on." So saying, he carried the boxes, one by one, to a point some three hundred yards upstream, and deposited them in a recess beneath an undercut bank below the surface of the water.

"It ain't be'n sech a bad month," he mused, as he brushed out his tracks, stepped into his canoe and headed up the White, "what with that strike up the Stewart, an' this here little windfall I stumbled onto. An' when I hit out with that Siwash, Cush claimed I was wastin' my time!"

XI

AFTER WAITING ON Halfaday three days for Black John's return Corporal Downey stepped into the saloon one morning and faced Cush across the bar. "I can't hang around here any longer," he said. "What with these robberies goin' on down along the river, there's no tellin' what'll happen, an' I've got to be there. When John shows up you tell him I want to see him down to headquarters."

Cush poured himself a drink, and shoved the bottle and a glass across the bar. "Drink up," he said. Then, after a moment's pause, "Fact is, Downey, I'm sorta worried about John, myself. Red John was down to Dawson—got back jest ahead of you— an' he told me about John headin' a gang of four robbers down there. I told him he was a damn fool—that John wouldn't mess around in no sech doin's. But where the hell is he? He's had time to go up the Stewart an' git back before this. Tell you what I'm a-goin' to do—I'm a-goin' down to Dawson with you. One Armed John's out back helpin' the klooch smoke some meat. I'll let him tend bar whilst I'm gone. Bein' only one-handed he can't steal only half of what one of the other boys could. Wait till I tell him, an' throw my pack together, an' we'll hit out."

And so it was that at the foot of the Fish Rapids the two met Constable Buck and his manacled prisoner. The constable eyed Downey with just a suspicion of truculence. "Did you arrest Black John?" he asked.

Downey shook his head. "No, he wasn't on Halfaday."

The constable smiled. "You remember that quite a while ago I said that if I ever got the chance I'd clean up on Black John and his gang of outlaws—and I've done it!"

Downey seemed unimpressed. "Have, eh? Was it quite a chore?" he asked quietly.

"I'll say it was!"

"Sam Steele detail you to do it?"

"Inspector Steele had nothing to do with it. In fact, he gave me a very insignificant detail—inspecting fish nets. While on this detail, I heard these reports of the robberies along the river, and realizing that my chance had come at last to show that I can handle a really big situation, I disregarded my orders and hit out after the robbers."

Downey grinned. "That'll prob'ly tickle Sam. Nothin' he likes better'n to have some rookie disregard an order."

Constable Buck flushed. "He'll be glad I disregarded this

one," he replied. "I sure cleaned up on the Black John gang. Black John, and two of the others are dead, and I took this prisoner. Only one of 'em got away."

"Black John dead!" cried both Cush and Corporal Downey in the same breath. "Who killed him?"

"I did," the prisoner cut in. "The damned skunk was figurin' on doublecrossin' us—an' I knocked him off. Him an' Big Mike, too."

"And I got there just after it happened," Buck said, "and shot one of the others, and arrested this one."

For an hour or more Corporal Downey and Cush listened as Slim Carew gave a detailed account of the devious machinations of the gang. At its conclusion Cush shook his head, sadly:

"I shore can't believe it. An' what's more I ain't believin' it till I see Black John's body. He wouldn't of mixed up in no sech doin's if he was sober—nor yet if he was drunk. If it is true, he musta gone crazy. Anyways, if he's dead, us boys'll fetch his body up to the Fort an' bury it decent. Then I'll be pullin' out. Halfaday ain't never goin' to be the same no more, if John's gone."

"If John's gone my work's goin' to be a damn sight harder," Downey added. "He shore kept the men on Halfaday in line."

Slim Carew eyed the officer craftily. "How about me an' you makin' a deal, Sergeant?" he asked.

"Corporal's the word. What kind of a deal?"

"Well, s'pose I'd tell you where nine thousan' ounces of dust is cached in three wooden boxes—dust that was shipped out on the *Hannah* couple of days ago. There's bound to be a big stink about it—an' you'd git the credick for findin' it."

"Nine thousand ounces of dust?" Constable Buck cried. "You never mentioned any nine thousand ounces of dust!"

"A guy don't have to sing his hull song to onct. An' you bein' jest' a common cop, couldn't do no dickerin', if you wanted to."

"The credit belongs to me!" Buck cried. "I was the one who rounded up the gang!"

Downey ignored him. "You mean you men got nine thousan' ounces off the *Hannah?*" he asked, turning to Slim.

"We sure did. An' we've got it cached where you'll never find it if you don't dicker."

Corporal Downey eyed Buck. "How long was it after the landin' of the *Hannah* before you jumped these men?" he asked.

"I'd say about an hour."

"Okay. We'll be pullin' out, now."

SLIM CAREW scowled at the officer. "How about that deal?" he asked.

"I never make no deals with a crook," Downey replied. "Even if I did, I wouldn't have to bother with you. If there was nine thousan' ounces in three boxes, they would weigh right around two hundred pounds apiece, an' there ain't no three men like that could cache them boxes in an hour's time where I can't find 'em in half a day's search. If you'd have left Black John alive to cache 'em, it might be different."

As they were about to step into the canoes, another canoe rounded the bend and beached at the foot of the portage. All four stared at the huge black-bearded man who stepped ashore and regarded them with a grin. Then the grin faded from his lips and he stared in return. "What the hell's the matter with you guys?" he demanded. "You look like yer starin' at a ghost!"

Slim Carew broke the momentary silence with a shrill scream: "It's—it's Black John!"

Whirling about, he headed for the bush, but Downey promptly tripped him, and turned to the big man with a grunt. "This man did think you was a ghost," he replied, "an' the rest of us weren't so sure. 'Specially after Constable Buck, here, reported that he saw you dead and buried." He turned to Buck, who was still staring speechless into the big man's face. "After this, Constable," he said, sarcastically, "when you bury a man John's size, you'd better lay a rock on his grave to keep him from gettin' up."

"But—but—I did see him buried! I—I'd swear to it!"

Black John grinned. "You might swear to it, Rollo," he said. "But damned if *I'll* believe you."

Slim Carew, white and shaking, eyed the speaker narrowly. "You ain't Black John!" he cried suddenly. "I seen it when you grinned. Black John's teeth is yaller, an' kinda snaggy like—an' yourn's white, an' even!" He turned to the others. "This guy ain't Black John. He's a phony."

Cush grasped the big man's hand and wrung it warmly. "By God, John," he said, "when them guys told me you was dead, it seemed like the end of the world."

"There seems to be some slight misonderstandin' here some-wheres," Black John said. "S'pose we onearth this here corpse that's s'posed to be me—that is, if he's buried anywheres clost."

"He's buried shallow in the sand at the mouth of the river," Buck said.

"Let's go," Black John replied. "I'll shore be interested in inspectin' him."

Arriving at the sandpit some time later, Buck led the way to the spot where the three bodies lay in their shallow graves. Uncovering them was the work of a few minutes, and all stared down at the body of the huge black-bearded chechako. "Pretty good replica, at that," Black John opined, "barrin', mebbe, a few moral defects the deceased ondoubtless acquired previous to his demise."

Slim Carew was staring at a hole that had recently been scooped in the sand at a point not far distant. "The dust!" he cried, his voice trembling with rage. "The dust's gone—all three boxes. The Ape musta snuck back an' got it. He's got away with the hull damn works! Nine thousan' ounces of dust! I allus know'd he was crooked!"

Black John regarded the speaker as he shook his head gravely. "Tch, tch, tch—ain't that hell? But—let that be a lesson to you, my good man—shun evil companions, because crime don't pay."

CONSPIRACY ON HALFADAY

CUTER MALONE, PROPRIETOR of the notorious Klondike Palace, a combination saloon, dance hall, gambling joint in Dawson that was shunned by the sourdoughs, but liberally patronized by the horde of chechakos that had surged into the Yukon on the heels of the great gold strike, stood behind his bar near the huge iron safe, the inevitable black cigar cocked at an angle from a corner of his mouth, and eyed the scene complacently. It was early evening and the bar was lined with customers in various stages of intoxication. Several games of stud were in progress at the tables ranged along the opposite side of the room. In the rear the play was lively at the faro layout and the two roulette wheels, and through the wide archway that led to the dance floor the sound of dancing feet was blended with the jangle of the tinny piano vociferously pounded by Joe, the hop-headed "professor". In silver and dust and bills the money was rolling in. It was a good night.

Malone's roving glance centered upon two men who had stepped into the room and advanced slowly across the floor. They were hard-eyed men with weather-beaten faces and slight peculiarities in their gaits, men evidently not used to much walking. "Sailors er cowboys, once," he muttered, "an' believe me, they ain't no punks." The eyes of the larger of the two swept the faces of the four bartenders on duty and met his own squarely. A moment later the two were facing him across the bar.

"You Cuter Malone?" the shorter man asked.

"That's me. Somethin' I kin do fer you?"

"Know a guy name of Slim Aker?"

"Yeah. Used to hang around here. Ain't saw him sence right around Dominion Day. Musta pulled out."

"Yeah," the larger man said, "he pulled out, all right. We run acrost him in Seattle—him an' a bunch of other guys that had pulled out of the Yukon—an' all on account of one man."

"On account of who?"

"Ever hear of a land shark name of Black John Smith?"

"Who the hell ain't? He's the damndest top outlaw that ever hit the country!"

"Accordin' to whose tell?"

"Accordin' to my tell, fer one. He's shore took me fer plenty one way an' another."

"Don't like him, eh?" the short man asked, with a peculiar twisted grin.

"I like him like I'd like a rattlesnake if he bit me."

"What's the matter with the Mounted? Why don't they pick him up, if he's sech a hell of an outlaw?"

"He's too damn smart fer 'em—that's why."

The larger of the men winked. "Er mebbe he's got 'em greased, eh?"

"No. You kin fergit that angle. Corporal Downey runs the detachment here, an' he wouldn't take a crooked dollar from Black John, nor no one else. Hell, I've tried to git to him in a roundabout way several times—but it ain't no go. I hate his guts. Black John's, too."

"Yeah, that's what Aker an' them other guys claimed. That's why we come to you."

A glance of suspicion flashed from Cuter's pig-like eyes, and he rolled the cigar to the opposite corner of his mouth. "About what?" he asked abruptly.

"Why—about Black John. An' this here Corporal Downey, too. But he'll come later. We've got to git red of Black John first."

"Git red of him!" Cuter exclaimed. "You, an' what man's army?"

The man jerked his thumb toward his pal. "Me an' him. The Blue here. He's all the army I need. We ain't afraid of this here Black John, nor Downey, nor no other guy. We come here to make a deal. We aim to cut you in on somethin' good."

"Yeah? Well, listen, you guys—if Black John an' Downey are to be mixed up in it, the only deal you kin make with me is to deal me out."

"It would be worth money to you, wouldn't it, if them two was rubbed out?"

"I'll say it would!"

"How much?"

"Plenty. But if you've got any foolish notions in yer heads about me layin' out any cash on the chanct of you guys knockin' off Black John, er Downey either, yer crazy as hell. A man would have to git up damn early in the mornin' to ketch Black John nappin'."

"Me an Shanghai, here, is early risers," the shorter man grinned. "And we ain't askin' you to lay out no cash till Black John is croaked. Mebbe not no cash then. We got plenty of cash. We got it all doped out. What we want is a hook up."

TURNING TO the back bar, Cuter placed a bottle and three glasses on a tray and, motioning the two to accompany him, led the way to the rear, past the faro and roulette players, unlocked a door and stepped into a small windowless room furnished with four chairs and a deal table. When the two followed, he set the tray on the table, locked the door, and lighted a tin bracket lamp. "Set down," he invited, "an' pour a drink. I'll hear what you got to say, but I'm warnin' you that if you expect me to play along with you, this here scheme, er whatever it is you've got all doped out, better be good. A hell of a lot of guys has tried to outsmart Black John—an' every damn one of 'em that ain't dead is clean outa the country."

The three drank, and Cuter refilled the glasses as the larger of the two spoke. "Me an' the Blue, here, knows about you on account of them bimbos down to Seattle tellin' us. An' we know about Black John, an' this here Corporal Downey, too. But you don't know us. Shanghai's the name I go by. I signs on to see the world through a porthole—see? Down China way I goes over the side. I'm on the beach a year findin' my way around. I hooks up with some Chinks an' a couple of limeys an' two, three more guys, an' we toss a few Chinks over the rail one night an' sail off with their gad yang. It's a couple of years high livin' then—up an' down the coast an' over amongst the islands. Yellow goods, an' ghow mostly—we got it where we could an' sold it where they wanted it. Handled everything from li-yuen to sanlo an' coolie mud.

"Then one night the damn navy blowed us outa the water. It was three of us on a raft in the mornin'—with grub an' water fer one. I'm the one.

"In six days I hit the beach. I ships fer Frisco on a tramp rag wagon with a hold full of copra an' me with half a cargo of five tael tins of ghow in my sea bag. I don't make it an' do a five-year stretch an' then drifts up to Seattle an' runs into the Blue, here. He's got a connection with some express guy on a train, an' we hang around till he gits the office an' then we move up the road a piece an' take the express box for a hundred thousan' after the guy lets us in the car. Then the Blue, he lets the guy have it, an' his helper, too. Claimed it's quicker to pay off in lead than bills—an' a damn sight cheaper. Besides, he cracks that a couple of dead heroes is a damn sight healthier fer us than a couple of live canaries when the song they could sing would keep us in stir from now on. He's quite a card, the Blue is—an' plenty tough. Claim he usta tend cows somewheres—"

"Tend cows! You damn fool! I told you I was a cowhand back in Montana. Rode fer the TU outfit, an' the IX, an' the Bear Paw Pool. I come from down Teton way, an' owin' to me likin' my poker strong, like my licker, I'd keep shovin' blue chips in the pot, so the boys got to callin' me the Teton Blue.

"Then one night in Kid Price's saloon a rookus starts, an' when the shootin's over there's a couple of dead guys layin' there on the floor, and I'm high-tailin' it fer the bad lands.

"I throws in with the wild bunch down there, an' we run horses an' cattle acrost the line for a couple of years, an' then one night five of us done a little railroadin' jest outside of Malta. One of the guys claimed he know'd all about blowin' a box, but the damn fool put in too big a shot, an' blow'd half the car, an' the box, an' all the dough there was in it over half of Montana. A posse cuts us off an' we separate. I cools a sheepherder, strips him, an' rolls him in the river. I takes his clothes, an' rides back to the railroad, caches my outfit, turns my horse loose, puts on the goat loafer's duds, an' hits the rods like I'm a bindle stiff.

"I makes Seattle an' couple days later I see by the paper where the posse wiped out three of the boys an' rounded up another one, a young punk name of Cock-eye which we'd fetched along to tend the horses, an' the paper says how he told 'em the fifth man in the gang was me. But bein' as he didn't know me by no other name than the Teton Blue I didn't worry no hell of a lot. Then I run into Shanghai, here—an' we took that express box, like he told you.

"So now we've give you an earful you know we're guys you kin trust to throw in with. But, bein' as there's a lot of damn liars loose that likes to throw the bull we'll prove we're on the up-an'-up by showin' you the cash—forty-eight thousan' apiece, not countin' some loose change, which is what we've got left out of that express job."

AS THE man spoke he drew several huge rolls from his pockets and tossed them onto the table, and his companion did likewise. Cuter's eyes widened at sight of the money which the men returned to their pockets, and the Teton Blue eyed him. "Money talks. How about it? Are we good—er ain't we?"

"It looks like you boys is all right. I had you pegged the minute I seen you come in the door. 'There's a couple of guys that ain't no punks,' I says to myself. 'They're sailors er cowboys,' I says when I seen you walk, 'cause I know'd you wasn't no regular trail mushers. An' it turns out you was both of 'em! I wasn't made in a minute. I kin generally size a man up. But— about this here Black John business? What kind of a hook up was you figgerin' on?"

"It's like this," Shanghai said. "We go up to this here Halfaday Crick, an' throw in with them outlaws up there, an' hang around long enough to size the place up. Then when we're all set, we knock this here Black John off an' take over. There's plenty of cricks in the country with guys workin' 'em—an' they ain't workin' fer nothin'. There's plenty of gold to be had fer the takin', to say nothin' of the gold these big outfits is takin' out. Then there's the steamboats—this here gold ain't kep' here in the Yukon. It's shipped out on the steamboats. A steamboat could be took as easy as a train—prob'ly a damn sight easier. Then there's the ghow racket. I've got connections, an' when we git goin' I kin show you how to make more dough out of ghow than you make out of yer licker, an' gamblin' an' girls put together. You're here in Dawson where you kin git hep to what's goin' on—who's got plenty of dust on what crick. When a shipment is goin' outside, an' all like that there. You slip us the office—we do the job an' you git your cut. How does that strike you?"

Cuter's brow furrowed into a frown. "Sounds all right," he

admitted. "But there's one item you passed over kinda light, it looks like—where you says 'we knock Black John off an' take over.' Sayin' that is a damn sight easier than doin' it."

The Teton Blue's hard eyes narrowed. "Listen, you," he said, "jest because some other guys has tried it an' didn't git away with it, ain't no sign we can't. Either they made some mistake, er they didn't have no guts. Take me an' Shanghai, here, we've be'n around. We don't make mistakes—an' we've got guts. We don't make no move till we've got every angle figgered out. Take this here Black John—we found out all about him back there in Seattle. We put in a week with them boys that he run outa the country, an' between 'em they told us all about him. But not a damn one of 'em could tell about any big job he done. They all claimed he brags about holdin' up an army an' gittin' away with a payroll somewheres over in Alasky—but no one of 'em knows whether he done it, er if he's jest shootin' off his mouth. His whole reputation as an outlaw hangs on that one job—an' no one even knows if it happened! What I claim—that's a hell of an outlaw! Them boys all says how he won't allow no crime to be committed on Halfaday on account it might fetch the police in on 'em. If he had any guts he wouldn't give a damn if the police come up there, er not. Hell, he's got more men up there that claims to be outlaws, than there is police in the hull damn Yukon! If they had any guts they'd pull off as many jobs as they wanted wherever they wanted an' whenever they wanted, an' to hell with the police. If the police show'd up on the crick, they'd blast 'em down an' be done with 'em. Accordin' to them boys down to Seattle, all he ever done that they know about, is to outsmart some crook that come up there with some money er dust. I'll bet you can't name no job he ever done—like a hold-up er robbery."

"No, he plays it safe. He ain't never run foul of the police this side of the line, anyway. Downey, he goes up to Halfaday any time he wants, an' sometimes he fetches back his man. Black John claims that on Halfaday they don't neither help nor hinder the police."

"That's because he ain't got the guts to hinder 'em. Listen—to show you we ain't afraid of him, an' ain't afraid he kin outsmart us, we're takin' every damn cent of this ninety-six thousan' up there on Halfaday with us. We wouldn't be doin' that if we thought he could outsmart us, would we?"

"Guess that's right," Cuter grinned. "But jest the same, I'm glad it's your money yer takin' up there instead of mine."

"An' you can bet when we git goin', up there, there won't be no rule about not pullin' no crime on the crick! Anyone'll be welcome to pull off any kind of a job he wants to whenever he feels able. Me an' Shanghai ain't afraid of 'em, nor the police neither. We'll blast hell out of this here Downey the first time he shows up there, an' any other police, too. An' like I told you, we'll pull off jobs anywhere's we feel like it.

"You know damn well there's plenty guys on the cricks with dust in their caches—an' they'll tell where it's at, onct we git to work on 'em with a candle. Then, when he does tell, we'll lift the dust an' then knock him off so he can't squawk. There won't no one ever live to identify us. That's why I cooled that sheepherder, an' them two saps in the express car, that Shanghai was tellin' about."

"How about Cush, an' them other boys on Halfaday? Mebbe they won't throw in with you."

"They'll throw in with us—or else. It's a cinch some of 'em will, an' them that don't won't last long. We've got plenty of boys that will throw in with us. Jest as quick as we slip the word back to Seattle that Black John is out of the way, them boys'll hit fer Halfaday. There's Slim Aker, an' a guy name of Shorty, an' another one name of the Phantom, an' Lefty, an' the Parson, an' Simco Sam, an' another guy name of the Chicago Kid. What I mean—when them boys pulls in there'll be a real gang of outlaws on Halfaday Crick. An' we'll do things, not jest stand around an' shake dice fer the drinks like the boys claim Black John does. Believe me—when word gits around the Yukon that we've got

Black John outa the way, an' the Mounted buffaloed, an' after the men out on the cricks sees what's happened to a few of 'em, they'll be fallin' all over theirselves to pay us to leave 'em alone. I'm tellin' you we'll be collectin' from every damn man in the Yukon before we git through—an' that's another place you come in on it."

"Who—me?"

"Yes, you. Located like you be right here in Dawson, you'll be collector fer the gang. When we git strung out we'll figger about how much to ream a guy fer—accordin' to how much he's got—an' you'll keep the list here an' every month when the guys come in an' pay up, you check 'em off. You slip us the word if some guy don't kick in, an' we'll tend to him. Me an' Shanghai's figgered it out that on the jobs we pull that you tip us off to, you drag down a twenty-five percent cut. An' you git a fifty-fifty cut on the protection money you collect. That's a damn good set-up. How about it?"

"It listens all right," Cuter admitted, "the way you tell it. But—it looks from here like you boys are bitin' off a damn sight more'n you kin chaw."

"We don't figger to git everything goin' smooth all to onct," Shanghai explained. "A set-up like that there takes time to rig."

"I'll say it ain't goin' to be smooth goin'," Cuter agreed. "Fact is, yer goin' to hit a couple of big bumps right on the start."

"Meanin' which?" the Blue asked, truculently.

"Meanin' Black John, an' Downey."

"Listen here, brother—a bullet will cool Black John jest as quick as it will cool anyone else—or Downey either."

"Yeah—but it's got to hit 'em first."

"You leave the hittin' to me!"

"Yer damn right I will!"

"Is it a deal, then?"

"There ain't no deal till Black John is plumb outa the picture—an' what I mean—dead."

"He'll be dead, all right—an' Downey, too. An' it won't be long, neither. It's September now. We'd ort to be all lined up in a couple of months. Me an' Shanghai will hit out fer Halfaday in the mornin'. We don't dast to hang around Dawson on account the police is apt to have a hot pick-up on us fer that express car job. We'll locate on Halfaday an' hang around fer a month er so to sort of git acquainted, an' git the lay of the land. We'll separate an' hit the crick a day or so apart. We won't let on we know one another, an' we'll locate in two different places. That way we kin pick up information quicker—what one don't pick up, the other one will. An' they won't suspicion us so quick—like if we was both together they might figger we was plottin' somethin'. We'll play up to Black John, git onto his habits an' take plenty time to figger everything out. We don't want to make no mistakes—go off half cocked, as the sayin' is. We can't afford to have nothin' go wrong."

"I'll say you can't!" Cuter agreed. "There's quite a few men got hung on Halfaday because somethin' went wrong. But if it works out like you've doped it, I'll come in. We'd have the sweetest proposition this side of hell. But if it don't work out, I ain't in on nothin'. I ain't never even saw you guys—let alone talked to you."

II

OLD CUSH, THE proprietor of Cushing's Fort, the combined trading post and saloon that served the little community of outlawed men that had grown up on Halfaday Creek, close against the Yukon-Alaska border, set out a bottle, two glasses, and the leather dice box, as Black John Smith stepped into the room and crossed to the bar. The big man picked up the box, peered into it, gave it a perfunctory waggle, and slid the dice out onto the bar. "Beat them three sixes in one," he said.

Cush picked up the dice, returned them to the box and handed them back. "Slidin' ain't shakin'," he said. "I want to hear them dice rattle."

"Why, you damn crook," Black John retorted. "I shook them dice fair an' square!"

"Yeah? So a guy's a crook if he ketches another guy cheatin', huh? I seen you peek at them dice to see how they laid. Rattlin' an' rollin' 'em might git you a drink—but peekin' an' slidin' won't, if yer tongue was hangin' out a foot."

"It's sad to contemplate the suspicion some folks holds agin friends," Black John said as he rattled the dice and rolled them out on the bar. "There's them three sixes right back at you, an' that proves I shook 'em fair."

"It don't prove nothin' except yer lucky," Cush retorted, rolling out three treys, and returned the dice to the box. He shook again and shoved the box toward the other. "I'm leavin' them three fours. Beat 'em, an' I'll buy a drink."

Black John cast three fives, and Cush shoved the bottle across the bar. As the glasses were filled, an Indian boy stepped into the room carrying two pails of water. Passing around behind the bar he poured the water into the rinse tub, "Me read, now?" he asked.

Cush frowned. "You got the wood carried in? An' the dogs fed?"

"Yes. Tamook got de sore foot. I feex heem oop."

"All right. Carry them buckits out in the storeroom an' come back." As the lad departed with the pails Cush scowled at Black John. "You had a hell of a lot to do—learnin' that kid to read," he scowled. "What good is it goin' to do a Siwash if he kin read?"

Black John smiled. "He's a good kid, an' smart, too. He was so damn eager to learn to read an' figure, that I took pity on him. He carried my wood an water, an' swep' out the cabin, an' kind of looked after things all last winter jest to learn to read an' write. Never saw a kid so hell-bent to learn. Never saw a smarter kid, neither. I took a likin' to him. Used to slip him a little dust on the side. Looked like he was doin' a hell of a lot of work for the little I was teachin' him. I fetched up a spellin' book an' an arithmetic, an' a reader, an' a writin' book from Dawson, an' it shore was surprisin' how he dug into 'em."

"Oh, he's smart, all right, Shocko is. An' like you say he's a good kid. He shore thinks a lot of you—figgers you jest short of God. He'd go to hell fer you any day. But what good is it if he kin read? Hell, I don't know another Siwash in the country that kin. Looks like it'll learn him to waste time."

"How long you had him doin' chores for you?"

"All summer."

"How much time has he wasted?"

"Can't say as he's wasted any, so fer. What I mean, he works like hell till he gits his work done, jest so's he kin read."

"You ain't got no kick comin' if he does his work," Black John replied. "The way I figure it, Siwashes don't get many breaks, an' if the little cuss can get any enjoyment out of readin', I say let him go to it. Besides that, it might stand him in good stead, some day. I got about as much fun teachin' as he did learnin'."

The boy returned to the room and paused before the bar. "What'll it be, the Police Gazette, er the Bible?" Cush asked.

"Bible," the boy replied. "P'lice G'zette all finish."

Reaching onto the back bar, Cush picked up the Bible and peered over the bar. "You worshed yer hands?" he asked. "I seen a smooch mark where you'd thumbed over into Mathoo t'other day. An' when you read in the Bible you got to quit suckin' them lickerish drops Black John fetched you—er the Police Gazette, either. First thing you know you'll be smoochin' up some of them pitchers."

"I wash," the lad replied, holding up his hands for inspection, and picking up the Bible, he crossed the room, drew a chair to the window and seated himself.

One Armed John stepped into the room and exhibited a string of fish. Cush motioned him back. "Git to hell outa here!

The kid's jest got through sweepin' out, an' I don't want them damn fish dreenin' all over the floor, someone's liable to slip an' break their neck. Take 'em around back an' tell the klooch I says to fry 'em up fer dinner. How many you got?"

"Eight. You kin have 'em fer two dollars."

"Okay. Come on back an' I'll buy a drink."

One Armed John filled the glass that Cush slid across the bar. "They's a guy holed up in Olson's old shack," he said. "Claims he come along las' night an' seen how the shack was empty, so he camped there. He wants to know if it's all right, an' I says it is fer all of me, but I wouldn't live there on account it's onlucky. He claims he ain't superspicious an' he'll take a chanct."

"Some damn miscreant, no doubt," Black John opined.

"No, he claims his name is Shanghai. Hell, I never heer'd of no one named Shanghai except a damn big long-legged rooster pa fetched home one time, which he'd boughten him off'n a barber in town 'cause the barber claimed he was a fightin' rooster, an' we had a rooster which he'd got mean an' was fightin' all our other roosters an' runnin' 'em all over the farm. Pa he figgers he'll learn our rooster a lesson, so he turns this here Shanghai loose, an' this here rooster of ourn, which we called him John L, on account of him bein' a fighter, he give this big new rooster one look, an' his hackles begun to stand out an' he come at the big Shanghai, which give him one look an' let out a hell of a squawk an' took out fer the barn an' he seen the hole where the cats got under the floor, an' he crawled in an' died in under there an' the barn stunk somethin' fierce fer a week. An' pa was so damn mad he knocked hell outa the barber the next time he went to town, an' the jedge soaked him five dollars an' costs."

"An interestin' account of a bucolic interlude," Black John observed.

"No, the Shanghai never died of colic—he was jest scairt to death."

The big man grinned. "You're prob'ly right, at that. But layin' aside the woes of that rooster, what for lookin' bozo is this newcomer?"

"Oh, he's kinda biggish like. But not so damn big, neither. He don't look like no chechako—kinda of tanned up, like he's took a hell of a lot of weather. But he don't talk like no sourdough, neither. He's kinda, what you might say, half ways between. He claims he's a prospector. But hell—that's what they all claim. He wants to know where Cushing's Fort is, an' is Black John around. I tells him yes, so he'll prob'ly be up before long."

"Jest another damn crook of some kind," Cush grunted glancing at the big man, "er he wouldn't be askin' about you."

"What do you mean by that?" Black John scowled.

"You know what I mean. If he was a prospector, like he claimed, he'd be askin' about likely locations—not where you was. He's heard about you bein' king of a bunch of outlaws up here, an' he figgers on throwin' in with us."

"Ondoubtless a shrewd deduction, Cush. It's an oncontrovertable fact that a vast amount of heterogenious misinformation has—"

He was interrupted by Cush who beckoned with his hand to the Indian boy across the room. "Hey, kid," he called, "come over here an' git you an' earful! If its eggication yer after John kin learn you more big words in ten seconds than you kin find in the Bible in ten pages! Only the hell of it is, they won't mean nothin' when you git 'em learnt."

The boy smiled. "Damn smart man—Black John—know everyt'ing."

A SHORT time later a man entered the room and crossed to the bar to be greeted by One Armed John. "Hello, Shanghai! These is the two fellas you was askin' about. That's Cush back of the bar, an' this here's Black John." He turned to the others. "This here's Shanghai, him that I was tellin' you about movin' into Olson's old shack."

Cush slid a glass across the bar, and shoved the bottle. "Fill up," he invited. "The house is buyin' one."

The man filled and raised his glass. "Here's lookin' at you," he said, his eyes meeting Black John's squarely. "So you're Black John Smith, eh—the king of the outlaws?"

The big man noted the cold, slatey look in the gray eyes, and he wondered whether there was just the hint of a sneer in the words. He downed his liquor and returned the glass to the bar. "I'm Black John Smith all right," he replied, in a mild tone of voice, "but I shore as hell ain't king of nothin', an' I wouldn't know about any outlaws."

"Heard about you boys in Whitehorse, an' agin in Dawson— what a hell of a gang you've got up here. Figgered most of it was bull. It most generally always is. I come up to look things over. If it suits me I might throw in with you."

"You an outlaw?"

"Well—I don't look like no Holy Joe, do I? What's your guess?"

"My guess," Black John replied evenly, "is that, if you're a prospector, like One Arm claims you told him you are, an' you 'tend strictly to business, you might live quite a while."

"Yeah? An' if I don't?"

"Well, puttin' it mathematically, I'll state that the duration of a man's sojourn on Halfaday is in inverse ratio to his criminal proclivities."

The man scowled and glanced across the bar at Cush. "What the hell's he talkin' about?" he rasped.

Cush shook his head in resignation, as he mopped at a little circle of liquor on the bar. "Only God would know."

"Shrinkin' the statement to fit your mental scope, it's like this—you've ondoubtless come amongst us under a misapprehension. The fact is, there ain't no gang of outlaws on Halfaday—an' never was. If in their past some of the boys has overstepped the bounds of strict probity—oh, hell—I fergot! What I mean is, that what a man done before he come to

Halfaday ain't none of our business. After he gets here though, he's got to watch his step. Robbery, larceny in any form, claim jumpin', an' any other form of skullduggery will earn him a swift an' thoroughgoin' hangin'."

"Huh," the man grunted, "that's about what I thought. The talk is that you birds up here does quite a bit of card playin'. Do you play fer money? Er you got a law agin gamblin'?"

"Oh, no. Draw poker, stud an' cribbage is played here most every night. Various sums of money are involved—an' we play fer keeps. I might add though, that cheatin' in any form, or attempted cheatin', is hangable. We claim to be the moralest crick in the Yukon, but our blue law is flexible enough to wink at minor infringements, like profanity, lyin', gettin' drunk, an' workin' on Sunday."

The man shrugged. "Suits me," he said shortly, and turned to Cush. "Fill 'em up agin. I'll buy a drink." When the drinks were had, he tossed a piece of paper onto the bar. "Here's a little bill of stores I need—salt pork, an' sugar, an' tea mostly. I'm hittin' back to the shack. Be up some night to set in yer game."

The man paid for the supplies with bills he peeled from a sizeable roll, stowed them in his packsack. Black John bought a drink, and the man departed.

III

SEVERAL DAYS LATER another man showed up on Halfaday. He stepped into the saloon and crossed to the bar where Cush and Black John stood, the inevitable dice box between them. "You'd be Black John Smith, wouldn't you?" he asked, ranging himself beside the big man, and elevating a foot to the battered brass rail. Glancing across the bar, he added, "An' you'd be Cush?"

"We would," Black John replied.

Cush spun a glass toward the newcomer, and shoved the bottle, "Fill up," he said. "This un's on the house."

When the drinks were downed, the man tossed a bill onto

the bar. "Which I'm know'd as the Teton Blue," he vouchsafed by way of introduction. "Heard about you boys down along the river. Figgered, if what I heard is true, this here Halfaday Crick is jest the place fer me. I'm an outlaw myself—an' a good one, too. Hell, if the law'd ketch up with me, I'd be doin' time fer now on—if they didn't stretch my neck first. Montana, Wyomin', Idaho, Worshington—all them states wants me—an' what I mean, they want me bad. Murder, train robberies, bank stick-ups, horse runnin', cattle rustlin'. You see, I know I'm amongst friends up here, er I wouldn't be shootin' off my mouth like that."

"Sort of an all around bad man, eh?" Black John asked.

"I'll say I'm bad!"

"An' fairly industrious—fer the time you've lived, if all these pranks you've bragged about ain't jest moonshine."

The other frowned slightly. "I ain't so damn young as I might look. I'll be twenty-nine, come March. Be'n ridin' the range ever sence I was big enough to fork a cayuse. An' what I be'n tellin' you ain't no brag. It's the truth—every damn word of it. I got pieces I tore outa newspapers to prove it. Hell, 'tain't over a couple months ago me an'—me an' my pardner pulled an express job that fetched us a hundred thousan' in bills. How about it? Got a place fer me in yer gang?"

Black John eyed the other appraisingly, noting the slight bulge in. the front of his shirt that was undoubtedly the butt of a six-gun. "W-e-e-l-l, of course, we're always on the lookout for new talent. Better stick around a while till we get acquaint-ed. A man of your experience would realize that we couldn't afford to make no mistakes."

"Oh shore. Suits me all right. But where does a man stay? I didn't fetch no tent—be'n sleepin' out. But the nights is gittin' kinda chilly fer the bed roll I've got, an' they tell me it gits colder'n hell up here in the winter."

"You can throw yer stuff in One Eyed John's cabin. It's only a few rods down the crick."

"You mean bunk in with this here One Eyed John?"

"No. The cabin's empty. One Eyed John ain't used it sence the day we hung him."

"What did you hang him fer?"

"Oh, ondoubtless somethin' he done—er didn't do—damn if I remember. It don't make no difference. I'll step down with you an' show you where it's at. I might add, fer yer own protection, that if you've got any considerable sum of money on you, it might be well to deposit it in Cush's safe. We don't allow no crime of any kind here on the crick—but even so, a man can't never tell when someone might pull somethin'."

"I ain't got enough to bother with," the man replied shortly, "an' if I had, I'd take a chanct on cachin' it where I kin keep an eye on it. Not that I don't trust you boys—but—well, I guess you savvy."

"Oh shore. No offense. When you come right down to it, you don't know no more about us than we do about you."

The man grinned. "That's it. I guess we'll git along."

BLACK JOHN accompanied him to One Eyed John's cabin and helped him in with his pack and bed roll, noting that the end of a stout cord showed inconspicuously beneath a peg in the wall which was the obvious place for a man to hang his hat. "I'll be goin' back to Cush's, now," he said, and grinned. "If you're as lucky in hidin' yer cache as One Eyed John was I guess there ain't no danger of anyone findin' it. We know damn well he had a couple of sacks of dust cached somewheres, an' after we hung him we hunted all over hell fer it—dug up half his location here—but we never found it. Well, so long. Come over this evenin' an' meet some of the boys. We generally have a little game goin' on nights."

When he returned to the saloon Cush eyed him across the bar. "Don't it beat hell, the damn riff-raff that drifts in on us? First it's that damn Shanghai, tight mouthed, an' hard cold eyed—an' then this here Teton Blue, like he calls hisself, with his shifty green eyes, an' braggin' about all them jobs he done."

"Don't like 'em, eh?"

"Who the hell would? An' how come you didn't tell this here Teton party that we didn't have no gang of outlaws up here? You told Shanghai."

"Yeah—an' you know damn well he didn't believe me. Neither would this specimen. I figure jest to let nature take her course. If they're bound to learn the facts of life on Halfaday the hard way—that's their look-out. Me—I don't predict no brilliant future for either one of 'em."

Two weeks passed, during which both Shanghai and the Teton Blue were nightly visitors at Cush's, sitting in the stud and poker games. Apparently they were casual acquaintances who had met at the stud table. From the very first neither seemed to like the other. Then one morning as Black John stepped to the bar, Cush set out the bottle and glasses, without producing the dice box. "Fill up," he said. "I'm buyin' one."

Black John regarded him with mock concern. "What's the matter, Cush? Ain't you feelin' well? Mebbe I better go fetch a doctor."

Cush scowled. "There ain't nothin' the matter with me," he growled. "It's them two damn cusses I'm bothered about—that there Shanghai an' the Teton Blue."

"What's wrong with 'em?"

"That's the hell of it. I don't know what's wrong with 'em. You know how they're allus kinda nickin' at one another, an' a couple of times it looked like they was goin' to scrap. But a time er two, when they didn't know anyone was lookin' at 'em, I ketched 'em shootin' a sort of sideways glance at one another over somethin' that was said. Then agin, some of the boys has mentioned that both of 'em has be'n kinda askin' questions—about you, an' me, an' how much was in the safe, an' if we didn't never pull no jobs, an' stuff like that there. An' this mornin' One Armed John claimed he come by Olson's old shack 'long about daylight where he was fishin' along there, an' he seen the Teton Blue come outa the shack, an' him an' Shanghai stood talkin' fer quite a while, like they was old pals—an' then the Blue hit out fer One Eyed John's. What I claim—things don't look right."

THE BIG man nodded, downed his drink and refilled his glass. Cush refilled his own, an' made an entry in his day book. "These last drinks is on you," he reminded. "How do you figger them two out?"

"W-e-e-l-l, I ain't give 'em no hell of a lot of thought, one way er another. They kinda look to me like a couple of coyotes tryin' to do a wolf's job. Fact is, in saunterin' up an' down the crick at odd moments I run acrost an interestin' bit of lore. Passin' by Olson's one mornin' after Shanghai had set in on a long session of stud, I ascertained, by lookin' in his window, that he was dead to the world, an' out of idle curiosity, I slipped over to that hole covered by the flat rock where near everyone that has sojourned in Olson's shack has used fer a cache, I removed the rock an' found several rolls of bills totallin' exactly forty-eight thousan' dollars. I replaced the bills, an' the rock, an' went on my way.

"Then one afternoon, when the Teton Blue was off on a moose hunt with Red John, I slipped into One Eyed John's shack an' pulled on that string that removes the section of log in the wall, an' in the aperture I found them two sacks of iron filin's that I gilded to resemble dust to a chechako, together with several rolls of bills that totaled exactly forty-eight thousan' dollars. These, also, I returned to the cache.

"Now, it may be pure coincidence that them two boys would have exactly the same amount of money in their caches. But it's an odd amount—an amount that's worth contemplatin'. Jest for the sake of argument, I discarded the coincidence theory, an' assumed that these amounts was the split on some job them two pulled in cahoots. You rec'lect that the Teton Blue mentioned a hundred thousan' dollar express robbery that him an' a pal pulled? An' did you happen to notice, like I did, that he damn near named his pal, but caught himself jest in time? Well, deductin' expenses, they'd have about forty-eight thousan' left. They ain't had to dig into it because both plays pretty good stud, an' have be'n fairly lucky, to boot. So now we're confronted with the problem of why these two damn miscreants are pretendin' to be strangers—an' onfriendly strangers, at that.

"I can't see no reason for it. But when men acts out of the ordinary, there always is a reason—an' on Halfaday, nine times out of ten, it would be an ornery one. I agree with you that them two will bear watchin'."

"Watchin'—hell! Who's goin' to watch 'em? What I claim we ort to call a miners' meetin' an' hang 'em 'fore they git a chanct to pull somethin'. Cripes—they're prob'ly plottin' to rob the safe! If they was on the up-and-up an is pals, why ain't they shackin' together? An' why are they allus quarrelin'? An' like you say, how come they each got the same amount of money? Hell, John—plottin's skullduggery! Why the hell don't we hang 'em?"

The big man grinned. "In the first place we ain't got no evidence that they're plottin' anything. That's jest a surmise. An' it ain't a crime for two men to live apart, nor yet to possess identical amounts of money. We don't want to run hog-wild with our hangin's."

"Yeah—but what if they rob the safe?"

"That would be an overt act. In sech case we'd hang 'em."

"But hell—what if they'd knock me off doin' it?"

"That, also," grinned the big man, "would be an overt act. Don't you worry, Cush—if they knock you off, we'll hang 'em, shore as hell. Fact is, I don't think they've got designs on the safe—primarily. I've got a hunch they've got bigger ideas than that. I've had Short John an' Red John sort of playin' up to 'em, an' settin' down the questions they've asked, an' the answers give 'em—an' the whole thing seems to add up to quite an ondertakin'. But somehow I don't figure they'll get away with it."

Cush eyed the other shrewdly. "Yeah? Well, listen to me. When you grab off them ninety-six thousan', remember I git a split on it! By God, I suspicioned 'em as quick as you did!"

"Hell, Cush, if those boys is honorable an' upright men, their money is as safe where they've got it as it would be in the Bank of England."

"Yeah," Cush retorted dryly. "That's why I'm claimin' my share of them bills. You know damn well that neither one of them two ain't no honorabler'n a couple of skunks."

"When I get yer statement ontangled I'll ondoubtless agree with it," Black John grinned. "But—shet up! Here comes Shang-hai, now."

The man crossed the floor, elevated a foot to the brass rail and tossed a bill onto the bar. "Fill up," he said. "I'm buyin' a drink. Come up to see if I couldn't hire someone to help me cut wood."

"Figger on winterin' on the Olson location, eh?" Black John asked, as he filled his glass from the bottle the other shoved toward him.

"Yer damn right I am. I might have a good proposition there. The boys tells me there ain't no one ever worked it long enough to find out what it's worth."

"That's right," Cush agreed, filling his own glass. "There ain't no one lived there very long."

The man grinned thinly. "To hell with that. This crick suits me. I'll prob'ly be livin' there the rest of my life."

Black John nodded slowly. "Most of the other tenants done that. How's she pannin' out?"

"I ain't done no work there yet. There's a couple of shafts on the place. They ain't very deep, but there's water standin' in 'em. The boys claims it's seepage. They claim the way to work it is to wait for the freeze-up an' then build fires in the shaft an' thaw out the gravel, an' then throw it out on a dump an keep on doin' that way till spring an' then build a sluice an' git out the gold.

They claim in the winter time the water freezes before it kin seep into the shaft."

"That's right," Black John agreed. "You got the right idea."

"Yeah, but it's goin' to take a hell of a lot of wood, an' I ain't no hand with an ax. I figger on hirin' me a helper."

"Labor's scarce along the crick," Black John said. "Most of the boys works their own claims—an' practically all of 'em takes out better than wages."

The Indian boy, Shocko, entered from the rear with a small bundle of laundry which he placed on the back bar. "Neetna say dat better you got some clean bar rag," he announced.

Shanghai eyed the lad. "Hey—you! Want a job? I'll pay you goin' wages to cut wood fer me. There's an extry bunk in the shack, you kin throw yer blankets in there."

"He's doin' chores fer me," Cush objected.

"What you payin' him?"

"Board an' lodgin'."

"To hell with that! I'll give him board an' lodgin' an' an ounce a day on top of it. Hell, there ain't so many chores around here that you an' that squaw wife of yourn can't handle."

"Neetna ain't no wife," Cush retorted. "She's the hired girl. I had four wives a'ready, an' come to think of it if the first three of 'em had be'n klooches I'd be'n better off. But I don't want to stand in the way of the kid betterin' hisself. If he'd ruther work fer wages he's welcome. I won't be holdin' it agin him."

"How about it, kid?" Shanghai. asked.

The lad glanced from Cush to Black John, hesitated a moment, and shook his head. "I like it I stay here," he replied.

Black John turned from the bar. "I got to be goin'," he said. "I run out of meat. Goin' to slip out an' knock down a moose."

"I'm out of meat, too," Cush grumbled. "Looks like mooses is skurse along the crick. I was out all yesterday afternoon an' never seen none—not even no fresh sign."

"I was talkin' to Job Benson couple days ago, an' he says there's some moose hangin' around down by Sam Evans's place. Sam an' Ella May's spendin' a couple of months outside, an' their cabin's handy, on the White only about a mile above the mouth of Halfaday. I could stop there overnight."

Shanghai scowled at the Indian boy. "What's ailin' you? What do you want to hang around here fer, workin' fer nothin', when I'll pay you an ounce a day?"

Black John paused on his way to the door and grinned. "Presumably it's the cultural advantages derived from his present environment that intrigues him," he said, and passed on.

Cush had turned to arrange the glasses on the back bar, and only Shocko caught the glance of murderous venom that Shanghai shot at the big man's back as he stepped through the doorway. The lad stepped from behind the bar, and paused beside him. "I work for you," he said. "I go get my blankets."

IV

WHEN THE TWO arrived at Olson's shack, Shanghai indicated the spare bunk. "Throw yer blankets on there, an' then git to work choppin' down trees. The ax stands there beside the door. I'm outa meat, too. I'll see if I can't shoot us a moose." Picking up his rifle, he struck off down the creek.

With narrowed eyes the boy watched the man disappear among the scrub willows. Stepping outside, he picked up the ax, walked to a stand of spruce at the foot of the ridge and began to chop furiously. A couple of hours later, he paused, glanced at the sun, and returned to the shack. Slipping the short carbine that Black John had given him from his bed roll, he loaded it, and struck off down the creek. "Dat damn Shanghai he no like Black John," he muttered. "Mebbe-so try to keel heem. He know Black John go to Sam Evans cabin tonight. Mebbe-so lay in de brush an' try for shoot heem. By damn I'm shoot Shanghai firs', you bet!"

Knowing every inch of the country, the lad struck straight

across the ridge that flanked the White River in the vicinity of the Evans cabin. "Mebbe-so Shanghai no try to keel Black John. Mebbe-so he jus' hont de moose. Mebbe-so he git back to shack firs', fin' me gone. I tell um I see moose, foller heem to git de shot, but no kin fin'."

Reaching the ridge the lad slipped through the spruce forest silent as a shadow. Presently he halted and dropping to hands and knees, inched his way toward a fallen spruce, behind which crouched Shanghai, rifle in hand. Ten yards away, he flattened himself beneath some low spreading branches. Below, some seventy yards distant lay the Evans clearing, the door of the cabin in clear view of Shanghai's position. The sun sank lower and the shadows deepened. Several times the man behind the spruce raised his rifle and sighted at the closed door, muttering curses, and shifting about impatiently. Twilight deepened into dusk, and the Indian lad smiled as he sighted his own gun at Shanghai's back. "No kin hit Black John, now," he grinned. "No kin see sights."

Suddenly Black John stepped into the clearing below them and walked to the door of the cabin. Shanghai raised his rifle, and immediately lowered it with a curse. "Well, damn the luck! I don't dart to take a chance! If I'd miss, er jest nick him, he'd git me sure as hell. He'd know who took a shot at him 'cause he knows I heard him say he was goin' to hole up here tonight. He's no damn fool, even if he does run a Sunday School bunch of outlaws. Outlaws—hell! They're nothin' but a bunch of damn prospectors. By God, things'll be different when me an' the Blue takes over—an' that'll be tomorrow. 'Cause come daylight, I'll be right here—an' when he steps out that door, I'll git him. I'll slip down there an' lay behind that rock right on the edge of the clearin' so there won't be no chanct to miss, even if it's dark as it is now when he comes out."

Rising, the man struck out for Olson's, some three miles away. When he arrived, long after dark, the Indian boy was preparing supper. "You git moose?" the lad asked.

"No, but I seen two, three of 'em slip into a thicket down the crick a way. I figger they'll bed down in there, an' I'll git one in the mornin'. I'm goin' to hit down there 'fore daylight, so's to be sure of gittin' a shot at 'em when they come out. How'd you git along with the wood?"

"I git 'long all right. Got lot trees cut. Cut lot more tomorrow."

"That's the stuff," the man approved. "But at that, I don't expect a man to kill himself workin' fer me. Fact is, I don't give a damn if you don't git out there so early in the mornin'. I got a little job fer you tonight. The moon's comin' up, an' it'll be pretty light an hour from now. You'll be able to feller the trail to Cush's all right."

The lad nodded. "Sure, me kin follow trail in de dark."

"Okay. You know that guy they call the Teton Blue. He lives in One Eyed John's shack—hangs around Cush's nights."

"Yes. I know."

"I want you should carry a letter to him. I'll write it after we've et, an' you kin take it up there. It might be he'll be to Cush's settin' in a game. If he is, jest you hang around there till the game busts up, an' slip him the letter without no one seein' you. Mind you—be shore no one sees you give him the letter. If he ain't to Cush's he'll be in his cabin. Wake him up an' give him the letter. You git that?"

The lad nodded. "Sure. I geeve heem de letter—no one see."

"Okay. Yer a smart kid, all right. Jest you stick along with me an' you won't lose nothin' by it."

The man spent a half hour composing the letter, which he folded several times and handed it to the boy, who pocketed it, put on his hat, and stepped from the room. A short distance away, he retrieved his carbine which he had cached under a fallen log, and struck off up the trail. Half a mile farther on, he left the trail, circled back, and took a stand behind a tree, watching the trail to see if he was followed. Ten minutes later, he squatted down behind a rock, shredded some birch bark, lighted it and read the letter by the light of the flames. Returning the letter to his pocket he stood up, lips pressed tight, black eyes flashing. "By Gos' I go back an' keel heem where he sleep!" he exclaimed. And headed back for the trail. Abruptly he paused. "Mebbe-so Black John no like I keel Shanghai. Mebbe-so make de miner meetin'—hang me."

TURNING HIS back on the trail he struck off through the bush, and an hour later pounded on the door of the Evans cabin.

"Who's there?" came a sleepy voice from within.

"Me, Shocko. Got letter."

Black John rose, drew on his trousers, lighted the tin bracket lamp, and opened the door. "A letter?" he asked, in astonishment. "Who from?"

"Shanghai."

"Shanghai! What the hell's he writin' to me about?"

"No write to you. Write to Teton Blue." The lad fished the missive from his pocket and tossed it onto the table. "Dat damn Shanghai! W'en I read dat, I'm t'ink I'm go back to Olson— shoot heem dead een hee's bunk! Den I'm t'ink mebbe-so you no like—so I'm breeng de letter to you."

"You done right," the big man commended. "But how come you was down to Olson's. I thought you turned that job down."

"W'en you go out de door in de s'loon, Shanghai look on you back like he like to keel you. You good man—you de bes' man on de worl'—teach me to read an' write an' figger. No odder mans teach me dat. By Gos', I'm no like Shanghai keel you. I'm like I'm keep eye on heem. So I'm take de job."

The big man read the note and regarded the earnest young-ster with twinkling eyes. "You read the Good Book quite a bit, Shocko. Do you rec'lect that piece about castin' yer bread upon the waters?"

The boy knit his brows and shook his head. "No—I'm not t'row no bread in de water."

"It's quite a big book—ondoubtless you ain't come to that part yet. I might add that Cush was way off when he told me I was a damn fool to teach you to read. At that, though," he added with mock severity, "ain't you never learnt that it's wrong to read other folks' mail?"

"No wrong read Shanghai mail. Shanghai skunk."

THE BIG man grinned broadly. "I'm inclined to agree with you, son," he said and seating himself at the table, proceeded to make a copy of the letter in his notebook. Then he handed it to the boy. "Go ahead an' deliver it to the Teton Blue, jest as Shanghai told you. An' I'm shore glad you used yer head. You prob'ly saved my life—but we'll talk about that later. Accordin' to this letter, he waited here to knock me off last evenin', but it got too dark on him. I'm sure glad I didn't git here a few minutes sooner."

"He no shoot you. Me, I'm shoot heem firs'. I'm foller heem here. Got my gon on heem all de time—ten step—no kin miss. He no shoot you—you bet! An' w'en he fin' out it too dark to shoot, he cuss like hell, an' say he git you in de mornin', come daylight. He no hide on de ridge in de mornin'—he hide behin' dat beeg rock rat on edge of clearing, so w'en you come out de door he git you sure—no kin miss."

Black John's eyes met the liquid black eyes raised to his in a long look. Reaching out he took the small brown hand and pressed it in a mighty grip. "Okay—pal," he said, in a voice that sounded unusually gruff. "I think me an' you have now got matters well in hand. Skip along an' deliver that letter—an' you might sort of stick around Cush's tomorrow till I get there."

V

SHANGHAI SLEPT LITTLE that night. After the departure of the Indian boy with the note, he took a bottle from the shelf, poured a small drink, and seated himself at the table with the bottle at his elbow. "Gotta go kinda light on the licker tonight," he muttered, eyeing the little beads that rimmed the glass. "Tomorrow night, though there'll be hell a-poppin' up to Cush's. Me an' the Blue'll be bosses of Halfaday, an' we'll throw a hell of a party. Everything's worked out jest like we figgered. We took our time, an' we ain't made no mistakes. Black John's jest like me an' the Blue figgered—nothin' but a damn dice-shakin' blowhard that's be'n gittin' by on a reputation he ain't never earnt. Hell, there can't be a man we ever talked to name a damn job he's ever pulled, except that army payroll heist that was s'posed to of come off a long time ago—an' they're takin' his word fer that. Most of the guys on the crick'll throw in with us when they know Black John's outa the way fer keeps. He's sure got them damn saps buffaloed. We kin count on Red John, an' Short John, an' prob'ly Pot Gutted John, an' half a dozen more besides them boys down to Seattle that'll come pilin' in the minute they git the word. If there's some that won't throw in with us, that's their hard luck. They'll git to hell off Halfaday— one way er another. Me an' the Blue, we've be'n ready fer a week er more. Jest waitin' fer our chanct—an' this here moose hunt Black John's on give it to us. It's jest made to order, as the feller says—I knock Black John off the minute he sticks his head out that door in the mornin', an' a little while after Cush opens up, the Blue steps into the saloon, throws down on him with that forty-five of his, an' takes over the saloon.

"That's mutiny fer you, by God. We take over the hull damn ship—an' not a shot fired. A damn sight easier than tossin' them Chinks over the side, the time we took over their gad yang. At that, we had a sweet racket out there till the navy butted in. That's one thing—there ain't no navy kin git in here to gum our game—you bet!"

THE MAN dozed fitfully, waking up frequently to consult his watch and cast a longing eye at the bottle. Several times he reached for it, but refrained from pouring a drink. "Gotta have a clear head fer this job," he growled. "Gotta have a sharp eye an' a stidy hand. One good stiff one before I start out, an' that's all."

The moon was low in the west when he left the cabin and threaded his way through the scrub willows. Upon reaching the White, he headed upstream, avoiding the ridge, and a half hour later slipped behind an upstanding rock on the edge of the Evans clearing. The moon set, leaving the valley in total blackness.

It seemed hours the man knelt there behind the rock before the first gray streaks of dawn lightened the eastern sky. The timbered skyline of the opposite ridge showed first, then gradually the outline of the cabin was distinguishable, then the doorway through which Black John soon was to step to his doom. The man's lips felt dry and he moistened them frequently with his tongue. It wouldn't be long now. Any minute he'd see smoke begin to curl from the chimney, then the door would open—one well-placed shot as the man stepped into the open—and he and the Blue would take over. Time and again, in the slowly gathering daylight, the man raised his rifle, rested it on a shoulder of the rock, and sighted the doorway. "It's light enough now," he muttered as he lowered the rifle for the dozenth time. "Let him come."

"Was you expectin' someone?" A deep voice broke the silence and the man started, then whirled to look squarely into the muzzle of a rifle held carelessly in the hands of the huge man who had stepped from behind a rock scarce twenty feet to the left and a little behind his position. White teeth flashed beneath the black beard as the big man continued. "Jest drop the rifle, Shanghai, an' step back a ways."

Only for an instant did the man hesitate—an instant in which he noted the finger on the trigger of the rifle whose muzzle loomed so menacingly close. Then his rifle rang on the loose rock fragments at his feet, and he backed slowly away. "What—what the hell?" he gasped, staring into the big man's eyes.

"Exactly the question I was about to ask," Black John replied. "What the hell?"

"You mean—about me bein' here?"

"W-e-e-l-l—yes. About that—an' about yer sightin' yer rifle on Sam Evans's door yonder, about every three er four minutes fer the last half hour."

The man regained composure. He forced a grin. "Oh—about me sightin' the rifle! Hell, you got me wrong. I wasn't sightin' on the door except to see if it had got light enough to line my sights in case a moose come along. I'm like you—I'm outa meat, an' I heard you tellin' Cush yesterday about how you heard tell they was moose down here, so I come down to try to git me one. I figgered if I got here 'fore daylight one might come walkin' out into the clearin'. Red John, he told me how moose moves around right on the edge of daylight. But—what you doin' here? An' how'd you git so clost without me hearin' you?"

"Fact is," grinned the big man, "I got the same hunch you did. I've be'n waitin' to see if a moose wouldn't be stirrin' around early—same kind of a moose you was waitin' fer, Shanghai. Beats hell how men's minds sometimes runs sim'lar, don't it?"

"Yeah—sure—that is—yeah—I mean—sure it does. But what I mean—I never heard you come."

"I heard you come, though. You see, Shanghai, I was sort of expectin' you, so I got here first. I've be'n watchin' you ever sense it got light. It was right amusin'."

"What d'you mean—you was expectin' me?" asked the man, a look of swift terror in his eyes.

"Meanin' that, after readin' the letter of instructions you wrote the Teton Blue about takin' over Cush's fort, an' explainin' how you was goin' to knock me off, I mistrusted you'd be along here before daylight. Livin' as we do out here, a man can't afford to make many mistakes. Even one's liable to prove fatal—as you'll damn well find out."

"Readin' that letter! You—you mean that Injun kid give that

letter to you!"

"Oh, shore. You see he read it, an' figurin' there was certain things in it that might prove deleterious to my interests, he fetched it here an' give me the chanct to look it over. Because, Shanghai, the kid's a friend of mine—an' a Siwash never goes back on a friend."

"But who the hell ever heard of an Injun—an' a damn kid, at that—bein' able to read!"

"Most of 'em can't. But this kid—I kinda took a likin' to him, an' he was so hell-bent on learnin' to read that I went to the trouble of teachin' him. I took quite a bit of joshin' on account of it from Cush an' some of the boys. But you know, an' I know, it paid. Of course, if it comes right down to splittin' hairs, I might be accused of an ethical *faux pas* in readin' that letter. But bein' as readin' other folks' mail ain't a hangable offense on Halfaday, I took a chanct. Your case an' the Teton Blue's is different. Plottin' murder, especially when an overt step has be'n taken in carryin' out the plot—like you slippin' up here an' sightin' on that door with a cocked gun—constitutes skullduggery in the first degree. An' so, likewise, is saloon stealin'—both offenses bein' hangable accordin' to our code."

"I've heard how you hang folks, up here," the man blurted, his eyes wide with terror, "but, by God, you can't lynch me! I ain't murdered no one!"

"You won't be lynched. You'll get a fair trial by miners' meetin'."

"By God, I'll tell 'em I was waitin' here to git a shot at a moose!"

The big man grinned. "Well—mebbe the boys'll believe you. It's doubtful, though—especially after readin' that letter you wrote the Teton Blue."

"The Blue'll destroy that letter if he's got any sense."

"It wouldn't help your case none, if he does. I anticipated that possibility, so I took the trouble to copy it off in my notebook."

"I'll say I never wrote no sech letter. I'll claim it's a forgery."

"That'll leave it up to the boys—whether to believe you, or me an' the kid. He stood there an' watched me copy it. But come on, let's get goin'. We'd ort to make Cush's by noon, that'll give us all the afternoon fer the trial an' the hangin's. Turn around an' hold yer hands behind you till I get 'em tied. You walk on ahead. I won't bother to hobble you. An' I might add that yer free to make a break any time you feel able. In sech case the Teton Blue will be the only hangee."

WHEN THE man's hands had been secured Black John headed him down the White. They headed up Halfaday threading their way through the willow flat. As they approached Olson's old shack, the man turned and faced his captor. "Listen here," he began, "I know all about you—got all the dope in Seattle from a bunch of the boys you've run outa the country. I know you ain't no reg'lar outlaw—like pullin' robberies an' hold-ups, an' the like of that. But likewise I know that your racket is gougin' the boys that's got it. When they hit fer Halfaday every damn one of them boys fetched along the bills or the dust they'd got out of the jobs they'd pulled—an' not a damn one of 'em had a nickel when you run 'em outa the country. Knowin' this, me an' the Blue figgered on comin' up here an' takin' over—on settin' up a bunch of real outlaws. An' we'd of done it, too, if it hadn't be'n fer that damn Injun kid. But here's a play that'll be right down your alley. I've got a bunch of cash on hand—twenty-four thousan' dollars in good bills. I've got it cached where no one in God's world will ever find it. When we git to the shack, you ontie my hands an' give me ten minutes, an' I'll come back with the money. You know damn well I couldn't doublecross you an' hit out without no grub nor no blankets. You keep the twenty-four thousan' an' let me take enough grub along to git me to the big river, an' I'll hit outa the country. Is it a deal?"

Black John grinned. "Figger on splittin' fifty-fifty with me, eh?"

"What do you mean—fifty-fifty? Hell, I'll give it all to you!"

"You mean the whole forty-eight thousan' you've got in that cache under that flat rock over at the foot of the rim? Your share of the fifty-fifty split you an' the Teton Blue made of the hundred thousan' you got out of that express robbery back in Washington?"

As Black John talked the man's eyes widened, his jaw dropped, and his mouth hung open giving an imbecile expression to his face. "You—you mean—you found the cache?" he managed to ask.

"Found it! Hell, I devised it! I run acrost that nice hole in the rocks years ago, an' hunted up a flat rock that made a good tight-fittin' cover, an' tossed it down where it would be handy, an' every damn sap that comes along figures it would make a swell cache—an' it does. A man could hunt the valley from rim to rim, an' he'd never find it. Move along or we won't make Cush's by noon. I'm takin' that forty-eight thousan' along. It'll never do no one any good, where it's at. I'm assumin' you ain't got no heirs."

As the man stood by and watched Black John remove the flat rock and stow the rolls of bills in various pockets he cursed shrilly—hysterically. "Damn them guys down there in Seattle fer figgerin' me an' the Blue could outsmart you! Hell—you know everything! They got us into this! If I ever git back there, I'll knock every damn one of 'em off!"

"A laudible intention, I'm shore," the big man agreed. "But onfortunately them boys is safe. You ain't goin' back."

A mile below Cushing's Black John headed up a side gulch. "Where you goin'?" the man asked.

BLACK JOHN answered nothing, and a half hour later he called a halt, backed his man against a tree, and proceeded to bind him tightly to its trunk with a length of light, tough babiche line he had wrapped around his waist. "Always carry a length of line so if I kill a moose, I can hang up the meat I can't pack

224

with me out of reach of bears an' wolves."

"What—what are you goin' to do—shoot me?"

"Hell, no! I'm no damn murderer. You'll be tried by miners' meetin', like I told you. I'm merely leavin' you here, so I won't have two damn skunks on my hands when I get to Cush's, instead of one. It's jest barely possible that some onforseen circumstance might complicate matters, in which case I'd ruther have one man to handle than two."

"But—what if—if the Blue should knock you off when you git there! What would become of me? How the hell would he know where I'm at?"

"He wouldn't!"

"By God, I'd starve to death, without no one knowin' where I'm at!"

"'Taint likely. The bears an' the wolves would 'tend to that."

"By God, I'll holler an' yell till someone comes an' finds, me."

Black John's eyes widened. "Holler an' yell! Yer a braver man than I am, Gordon Gin. Cripes, if you'd let out a yell you'd have half a dozen bears here inside ten minutes. Them grizzlies are on the prowl this time of year. They're due to hole up fer the winter pretty quick, an' right now they're scuttlin' around eatin' every damn thing they can get holt of.

"They've got to eat enough to last 'em all winter. They eat till they're half again as big as normal. Take it in the fall, like this, we use 'em to sort of clean up the crick—like when we shoot a moose, we take whatever of the meat we can pack off, an' hang up what more of it we want out of reach, but there's always a lot of more meat on the carcass, like the neck an' legs, besides the head an' hide an' guts, which if we left it layin' around would rot an' stink up the crick—so when we're ready to go, we let out a loud yell er two, an' the bears hears it, an' figure it's somebody in trouble that they can prob'ly kill, so they come a-runnin'— sometimes as many as eight, ten of 'em. Of course, as soon as we yell, we get to hell out of there, an' when the bears find the carcass of the moose, they stop an' clean it up. It's a handy sanitary measure. But tied up like you are, if you yell you'd be in a hell of a fix. Of course, if the bears started on you from the top down, it would be over pretty quick—but if they begun on yer legs an' et up, it would take 'em quite a while to finish you off, an' you'd have to stand here an' watch 'em tear the meat off'n your legs in big mouthfuls. Prob'ly be painful, too. But you ain't got nothin' to worry about if you shet up. You won't starve to death nohow—if the bears don't get you the wolves will, come night. They'll locate you by scent, not by hearin', like the bears. An' if the Teton Blue don't get me, you'll hang—so there won't be no salvage, anyways you look at it."

VI

IT WAS THREE o'clock in the morning when Shocko arrived at Cushing's Fort to find it dark. Proceeding to One Eyed John's cabin, he pounded on the door, an when the Teton Blue opened it, six-gun in hand, he delivered the note, and vanished into the timber. Slipping into Black John's cabin, he crawled between the blankets of the spare bunk.

In the morning, he cooked and ate his breakfast and proceeded to the saloon, assuring himself before entering that Cush was alone. The man greeted him with a look of surprise. "Thought you went to work fer Shanghai, down to Olson's," he said.

"I'm queet. I'm no like dat man."

"I don't blame you none fer that. I figgered you was a fool to hire out to him in the first place. Git on in the storeroom, now, an' git out this here list of stuff fer Pot Gutted John. He left it here last night. Claimed he'd be up fer it this afternoon. Long as Black John learnt you to read, you might's well put it to some use. What you packin' yer gun fer? Stand it up in the corner yonder, an' git to work."

"Dat my gon, I'm tak' it wit' me in storeroom. Black John give me dat gon. Somewan might steal it."

"Okay. Git along now."

The lad hesitated. "De Teton Blue, she—"

"To hell with the Teton Blue!" Cush cried impatiently. "Here's the list. Take it in the storeroom an' git to work on it."

"But mebbe-so—"

"Damn yer ornery hide! Quit yer gassin'! Cripes, I git orations enough off'n Black John, without you startin' in! I told him he was a damn fool to learn you to read!"

Without a word the lad stepped over, picked up the list Cush had tossed onto the bar, and disappeared through the doorway into the storeroom.

Half an hour later, hearing footsteps in the saloon, he stepped to the peek-hole, a long slot in the log wall ingeniously placed directly beneath a shelf in the barroom upon which stood a stuffed owl, and glued his eyes to the slot. The Teton Blue crossed to the bar and ordered a drink. Cush turned to the back bar for bottle and glasses, and when he again faced the bar it was to look squarely into the muzzle of a .45 Colt.

"What—what the hell!" he cried, his glance slanting to the shelf beneath the bar upon which lay conveniently to hand his own revolver and a bung-starter.

"Don't reach fer it, Cush," the man warned in a gritty voice. "Jest put both yer hands on the bar where I kin see 'em."

"What's the idee? Is this a stick-up?"

"It's a damn sight more'n a stick-up. Me an' Shanghai has took over Halfaday Crick—lock, stock, an' bar'l. Startin' right now, we're the bosses of Halfaday."

"How about Black John? Don't be a damn fool, Teton. You can't git away with it."

"We've already got away with it. Black John's dead. Shanghai took care of him this mornin', down to Evans's cabin on the White. He'll be showin' up here 'fore long."

"How about the rest of the boys on the crick?"

"We kin count on some of 'em—Red John, an' Short John,

an' some more—they'll prob'ly all jine in, when they've found out we've took over. We'll deal with them that won't."

"How about the Mounted? How about Downey?"

"Damn the Mounted! An' as fer Downey, he'll go where Black John's gone the first time he sticks his nose on the crick—an' that goes fer any other police that horns in on us. We got it all figgered out—me an' Shanghai has. We ain't goin' off half-cocked. This here's a build-up. We tuk our time an' figgered all the angles. We'll have more tough guys in our gang than what there is police in the hull damn Yukon. From now on, me an' Shanghai won't only be runnin' Halfaday—we'll run the hull damn country!"

"You've picked out quite a chore," Cush opined. "Where do I stand in it?"

"That's up to you. We ain't got nothin' agin you, personal'. 'Course, along with everything else, the saloon an' tradin' post is ourn. If you throw in with us, you kin keep on runnin' the outfit here—an' we'll pay you damn good wages fer doin' it. You ain't the owner, no more. Yer jest a hired hand. An' now jest ease out around the end of the bar, keepin' yer hands on it. I'll step back there an' gather up whatever you've got in the way of guns an' bung-starters, an' what-not. Then you kin go back behind the bar jest like nothin' happened. After while we'll be wantin' the combination to the safe—but we'll wait till Shanghai comes fer that."

Stepping behind the bar the man picked up the revolver, the bung starter, and a couple of rifles that stood leaning against the safe, and crossed the room with them. "Okay, you kin go back, now, an' we'll have that little drink." When the glasses were filled the man raised his. "Here's lookin' at you, Cush. Hell, anyone comin' in wouldn't never know there's any change here." The man left the bar and crossed to the table upon which he had deposited the weapons, and seated himself. "Guess I'll jest set here till Shanghai shows up," he said, fingering his revolver. "An' where it'll be handy to kinda look over anyone that steps through the door. It might jest be possible that Shanghai fell down on his job of knockin' Black John off, in which case there'll only be one boss on Halfaday—an' that'll be me. 'Cause I won't fall down on it—by a damn sight! If it's Black John that steps through that door, instead of Shanghai, it'll be the last door he'll ever step through, you kin bet on that."

Neither noticed, as the man had crossed the room, that the muzzle of a carbine had been thrust through the slot under the shelf, nor did they notice the pair of beady black eyes that focused on the man in the chair.

The man was speaking again. "An' listen here, Cush, I'm watchin' you—every move an' every look. If you see someone comin' before they git to the door, an' you signal 'em by so much as a wink of the eye—out goes yer light—savvy?"

A HALF hour passed in silence, then suddenly a man stepped through the doorway, a big man—Black John. At the table the Teton Blue's hand shot out. There was a loud report. The revolver dropped from the man's hand, he jerked spasmodically to his feet, and then crashed face foremost to the floor. His legs and arms twitched for a moment, and he lay still. Both Black John and Cush were staring at the man in open-mouthed astonishment, when Shocko stepped in from the storeroom, carbine in hand. "By Gos', he no kin shoot you!" he cried, eyeing Black John. "*Me*—I'm shoot heem rat on hees head! By Gos'—no one goin' shoot you—you' teach me how to read!"

The big man's eyes shifted from the face of the boy to Cush. "How about it, now—was I a damn fool? Or wasn't I?"

Cush slowly shook his head. "I never seen the beat. Every damn thing you do works out. Who the hell could ever figger that learnin' some Siwash kid to read would save yer life?"

The big man grinned. "You never can tell. The way I figure it, a man's jest got to keep on castin' his bread upon the waters, as the Good Book says. I'll have to admit, though, that I was a mite careless, steppin' in here like I did. But when I saw you standin' there behind the bar, I figured the Teton Blue hadn't took over yet."

One Armed John stepped into the room, and stared, wide-eyed at the man on the floor with a wide pool of blood oozing from beneath him.

"What the hell!" he cried. "Did someone shoot the Teton Blue?"

"Does he look like he died of the mumps?" Black John asked. "Git busy now an' hit down the crick an' tell the boys to come on up fer a miners' meetin'. An' get Short John an' Red John, an' go up that gulch about a mile—the one that runs north from below Pot Gutted John's cabin—an' fetch Shanghai up here. We're tryin' him fer skullduggery, quick as One Armed can get a quorum."

"What's Shanghai doin' up that gulch?"

"He's standin' there tied to a tree—if he ain't scairt to death on account of the bears."

"Bears! Hell, they ain't no bears up there!"

"Shore there ain't—but Shanghai don't know it. I wanted to leave him there a while, an' I didn't want him to yell, an' mebbe get someone up there that would ontie him—an' I didn't want to gag him for fear of chokin' him to death, so I told him the bears was terrible hungry this time of year, an' they'd come a-runnin' if they heard anyone yell. Shanghai et it up, all right. He was white as a snowbank when I left him. Hustle him back here—an' the boys too."

WHEN THE man had gone, Black John turned to Cush. "Leave the Teton Blue right where he lays. He'll be good corroborative evidence of a conspiracy. I'll be back in a few minutes."

Ten minutes later he returned, and tossed roll after roll of bills onto the bar. "Shove 'em in the safe, Cush," he said. "Ninety-six thousan' divided between us. Them damn cusses didn't turn out to be honorable men, an' besides they won't have no further use fer this currency. Mix it around in the safe with them other bills, in case Downey should happen along an' want to sort of look things over. He might of got the word to be on the watch fer them express robbers. An' speakin' of Downey," he said, turning to the Indian boy, "the first time he shows up on the crick, you're goin' back with him."

The lad's eyes dropped and his lip quivered. "You mean— Co'p'l Downey make me arres' for shoot de Teton Blue?" he asked in a voice that trembled, slightly.

"Not by a damn sight I don't mean that!" the deep booming voice reassured the boy as he glanced into the big man's face. "What I mean, Downey'll take you down to Dawson, an' I'll go along. First we'll go to a lawyer an' then we'll go to the bank an' have some dealin's there, an' then you'll git on a steamboat, an' on up through the lakes, an' over the pass to Skagway. Then you'll get on a big ship an' go to Seattle, an' there'll be someone there that'll see that you get into a good school, an' into good livin' quarters. An' when you get through that school you'll go on through a college—any kind of a college you want—law, medicine, engineerin'—whatever you want to take up. An' there'll always be money fer everything you'll need. It'll come to you every month, the lawyer an' the bank will tend to that. An' when you git through college, there'll be money to get you started in whatever profession you've learnt."

"But—me, I ain't want to go away. I want to stay here—wit' you."

"No you don't. Halfaday ain't no place fer no kid—'specially a smart one. You'd learn things here that wouldn't do you no good. You wanted to learn to read an' write an' figure—well, I've taught you all I can, but you ain't even started to learn. Hell, kid—you're goin' a long ways—it's the least I kin do fer you. Don't you want to keep on learnin' more?"

The lad nodded emphatically. "Yes, I'm like I learn mooch. But w'en I learn all I kin learn, I'm com' back, an' live here wit' you."

The big man smiled, and patted the youngster's head.

"Okay, son—we'll leave it like that. But you ain't to come

back till yer through college—you've got to promise me that. You stay down there till yer through college—then if you want to, you can come back to Halfaday."

"All right. But I com' back den. You see."

THE MINERS' meeting heard the testimony of Black John, Cush, and Shocko, and the men read the letter in Shanghai's handwriting that Black John had recovered from the table in One Eyed John's cabin where the Teton Blue had evidently tossed it after reading it. When Shanghai was given the opportunity to speak in his own behalf, he realized that his case was hopeless, and launched out into a string of curses that included the men in Seattle who had told him of Halfaday, Cuter Malone, Black John, Cush, Shocko, the police, and all the men of Halfaday—a senseless tirade that was silenced only after Pot Gutted John had slipped the noose over his head, and he was drawn up half way between the floor and the ceiling.

After it was over, Cush pounded on the bar and invited all and sundry to have a drink. As the glasses were being filled, Corporal Downey stepped into the room and glancing from the man on the floor, to the suspended form, swept the others with a glance. "What the hell come off here?" he asked. "Who shot that man?"

Black John stepped forward. "I did," he said, pointing to the revolver that lay close beside the dead man's hand. "An' I done it jest in time er he'd of got me. The other one was hung after due trial by miners' meetin'." He continued, giving Downey a full account of the happenings, an account amply corroborated by Shanghai's letter. "So now, Downey, seein' that jestice has be'n done, come on up an' have a drink. Cush is buyin' one." As the officer filled his glass, Black John asked casually, "Jest on patrol, Downey, er was you lookin' fer someone in particular?"

The officer indicated the two bodies. "Those are the birds I was after. They pulled off a hundred thousan' dollar express robbery down in Washington. Those men fits the description we got to a T."

Black John shook his head slowly from side to side. "Don't it beat hell what some folks will do fer a little money! It looks like they got what was comin' to 'em all right."

"Yeah," Downey agreed. "It shore does. But—how about that hundred thousan'?"

"They prob'ly cached it somewheres," Black John opined. "An' most likely you won't never find it. There's a hell of a lot of territory between here an' Washington. They could have cached it most anywheres. But I'll give you a tip, Downey. Shanghai, there, he holed up in Olson's old shack, an' the Teton Blue in One Eyed John's. I'll be goin' back down to Dawson with you—me an' the lad, here. He saved my life by slippin' me that note that Shanghai wrote before he delivered it to the Teton Blue, an' I'm payin' him back with an education. If you think it's worth our while, we can stop in at them cabins an' sort of hunt around for a cache. It's jest a tip, Downey—you can take it fer what it's worth."

"Yeah," replied Downey dryly. "I will."

BONUS MATERIAL

WHO CAN WRITE FICTION?

JAMES B. HENDRYX is the author of numerous adventure and western novels, the most famous of which were written about Connie Morgan or Corporal Downey as central characters. Before becoming a writer, he was successively a traveling salesman, cowboy, and special writer for the *Cincinnati Enquirer.* He has also contributed short stories, novelettes, and serials to such publications as *American Boy, Adventure, Popular Magazine, Short Stories* and *West.*

HOBOS CAN AND have written very successful fiction. So have Phi Beta Kappas. And society matrons have, too.

To write salable fiction one need not be a graduate of a college, or even of a high school. Editors do not insist that a diploma shall accompany a manuscript. What they want, and will pay money for, is a story that will interest their readers.

For thirty years I have been writing and selling adventure stories—shorts, novelettes, and serials, some thirty-five of the latter having been published in book form by Putnam's, Doubleday, and Random House. And I never graduated from any school or college.

Schools and colleges deal with facts. A fiction writer deals with people—their problems, which bring out their loves, their hates, their longings, their aspirations, their disappointments, their triumphs—and their solution of these problems; or their failure to solve them. In order to handle these people convincingly the writer must know the people he is writing about. He must know what their problems are, how they go about solving them, what their reactions are to obstacles, to failures, and to successes. He must know what and how they think, how they look and act, what they say and how they say it. And the only way he can learn these things is to associate with people—the kind of people he expects to write about. But mere association is not enough. He must be interested in them.

To illustrate—after leaving the Sauk Centre high school by expulsion, rather than by graduation, I studied law for two years at the University of Minnesota. Then I was successively a traveling salesman, a tanbark buyer in the Kentucky mountains, a levelman on a projected electric traction line, a cowpuncher in Montana for five years, a prospector, an insurance salesman, a construction foreman, and a newspaper feature writer—not much certainly in the way of a formal education. But I had come into contact with many people—and many different kinds of people. Most of these jobs were just jobs. I had to eat, and wouldn't steal, so I had to work. But cowpunching and prospecting I really liked. I got into the "feel" of those occupations and of the men with whom I worked. The result is that I have, for thirty years, been writing and selling stories about cowpunchers and prospectors—but never a story about salesmen, construction men, or tanbark buyers, simply because I never took much interest in either them or their work. I have also sold logging camp yarns. While I never worked in the logging woods, I have fraternized with lumberjacks a great deal, and thus know something of their work.

Back in the days when the late George Randolph Chester was Sunday editor of the *Cincinnati Enquirer* I was doing some feature work for the paper, and George was writing fiction on the side—writing it, but at that time selling very little of it. Then he sold a story or two to the *Saturday Evening Post*, quit his job, packed eighty-five unsold manuscripts into his trunk, and hit for New York. His stuff went over big, and a year or so later he told me that he had sold every one of those eighty-five manuscripts, and most of them without any tinkering.

When George left Cincinnati all his cronies expected to see him back there. When he failed to return and apply for his old job, I suddenly realized that a living could be made by writing fiction—and no clock to punch. So I bought an Oliver typewriter and went to work. Up to that moment I had never written a word of fiction. But I went into the fiction business as deliberately as I would have gone into the green grocery business. I wrote a 30,000 word logging camp yarn and sold it to Bob Davis—and from that day to this I have made a living exclusively by writing fiction.

I started from scratch with a sketchy education and a haphazard background. Therefore, I believe that anyone else who possesses a typewriter, some paper, a lead pencil to delete about a third of what he writes with his typewriter, a knowledge of and an interest in people—any kind of people, a working knowledge of the English language—coupled with guts enough to split an occasional infinitive and end an occasional sentence with a preposition, plus a reasonable amount of imagination, should be able to turn out salable fiction.

Mind you—I don't mean literature! I don't write literature. I don't know how to write it—and wouldn't know where to sell it if I did. I know lots of people who do, though—among them my old schoolmate, Red Lewis. [Sinclair Lewis—ed.] Maybe if I had graduated from the Sauk Centre high school as he did, instead of getting fired as I did, I would be writing literature, too. But that isn't the way it is. He belongs to the literati. I don't. He dissects his characters with a scalpel; where I use an axe, or a six-gun.

I was very fortunate at the start in having the benefit of the vehemently salty criticism of that grand old man who has been step-daddy to more fiction than all the rest of 'em put together—Bob Davis. Nothing was ever passable. It was either all right, or it stank—and it stank so loudly and profanely that even the telephone girl in the outer office on the top floor of the old Flatiron Building knew that it stank. So did I.

Bob bought a great deal of my stuff up to the time he retired from the Munsey domain. He had an instinctive sense of story and plot, and I found his advice sound. But he made one bad guess. I had written and sold him several short stories, a novelette or two, and a serial having to do with a character I called Corporal Downey, of the Royal Northwest Mounted Police, now the Royal Canadian Mounted Police, and was planning another serial involving the same character. Bob vetoed the idea, saying that I had used Corporal Downey up, that I couldn't keep a sustained character going very long without causing the reader to lose interest in him. I modestly called his attention to Conan Doyle's Sherlock Holmes, and George Chester's Get Rich Quick Wallingford, whereupon Bob assured me that I was neither a Doyle nor a Chester. He maintained that he had read a lot of fiction in the course of his business, and that in his experience sustained characters petered out almost without exception. That was a good many years ago. But I am still writing Corporal Downey stories—and selling every one I write.

Then there is Connie Morgan. About that time Clarence Buddington Kelland, then editor of *The American Boy*, asked me for a story. I wrote him one about Connie Morgan, a boy who went to Alaska hunting for his dad. Kel bought it, and he bought another, and another. Then, with Bob Davis's warning against sustained characters still fresh in my mind, I killed Connie off in the next yarn. I got that one back, pronto, with a roar from Kel, "You can't do that!" So I changed the yarn—and for twenty-eight years, until the magazine folded up last summer, I wrote and sold Connie Morgan stories to a succession of its editors.

Not only that—there is Black John Smith. I have been writing Black John stories and selling them to *Short Stories Magazine* for fifteen years—and am still selling them. Also Jase Quill, "a doctor, an' a damn good blacksmith, to boot," according to his tale, has been going for several years.

So my advice to young writers is to get a character well in mind, build him up logically—and write about him. You will find such a character much easier to handle than a new one, as you become so well acquainted with him that you know exactly how he will react to any given situation, and just what he will say, and how he will say it. Also, readers will get to know the name of the character even when they do not know the name of the author. Time and again people tell me that they buy the magazines with Corporal Downey, Black John, or Connie Morgan in them—but they never did notice who wrote the yarns. It is the characters people are interested in—the characters, and to some extent, the plot. But not the author. Most of us have read the novels of Charles Dickens. Nearly all of us remember Dickens' characters. Practically none of us remember his plots.

As to the mechanics of story building I have little to offer in the way of advice, for I have no method. One or two tips, though—if you locate your story geographically be sure your geography is accurate. If it isn't, believe me—you'll hear about it! So will the editor. I recently had occasion, in a northern story to refer to a certain trading post as being on a certain bend of the Porcupine River which runs into the Yukon north of the Circle. Shortly thereafter I got a letter from a man now living in the State of Washington, who used to run a gas boat on the Yukon and its tributaries. He pointed out that Rampart House was a good eight hundred yards from where I had located it, and he enclosed a photograph to prove it! He was right. I was way off. This also goes for any historical allusion. Have it right, or leave it out. Just remember that there are people who know what George Washington ate for breakfast the day he crossed the Delaware. If it was tripe, and you mentioned pancakes, these informed ones will write the editor calling his attention to what a fool you are.

A chance word here, an incident there, a newspaper story—anything no matter how trivial, may serve as the basis for a story plot. There must be conflict of some sort—obstacles to overcome, not necessarily successfully—a problem to be met and solved. But the conflict must be such conflict as might reasonably arise in the lives of your characters; and the obstacles must be such obstacles as might reasonably present themselves; and the solution must be such solution as the people of the calibre you are writing about might reasonably be expected to work out. And they must act and talk as those people would act and talk. A cowpuncher couldn't get het up over the fact that Lord Twombly's butler served the wrong wine with the sixth course—while Lady Twombly might institute divorce proceedings over the incident.

Manifestly, the only way to learn how your characters will react to a given situation is to know them. Mix with them. Find out what they think, and do, and say—and why. Look and Listen, but don't Stop.

I can sell westerns because I worked for a cow outfit and rode the range with cowpunchers. And I can sell northerns because I have lived and worked with prospectors. The crime-police angle is essential in most adventure yarns. Thus it becomes necessary to know what and how these two opposing forces think. In Montana, at the instigation of the outfit I worked for, I homesteaded a strip of bottom land that lay right against the bad lands, so no nester could homestead it and fence off the water. Hiding out in the bad lands at that time were numerous outlaws. I got to know these men well—and most of them I liked. Since then, through certain connections, I have made the acquaintance of a number of the bad boys of two cities, and there is much about them that I like, too. Also among my friends I number several sheriffs, members of the Royal Canadian Mounted Police, Canadian Provincial Police, as well as State, and City Police, and I like them. They interest me. What they say, and do, and think interests me. I sift their reactions, gather what I can use, and sell it.

I spend a goodly portion of each year in Canada, hunting, fishing, and prowling around. I like to hunt and fish, but more than that I like to know what my friends among the Indians, the guides, and the outlanders say, and do, and think—for they are the people of my fiction. I never write stories about the people I am thrown with socially. Not because I do not like them. I do. But I can't seem to get interested in their problems, nor their solution of them—and I don't give a darn what they think or say about anything.

I spend a couple of afternoons or evenings each week playing poker or cribbage in the rear end of a billiard room—not for the money I may win or lose there—that is incidental. And not because I have any inherent predilection for the rear end of a billiard room, nor for poker or cribbage. I do this as a matter of business. I like the men who frequent this place—truck drivers, commercial fishermen, laborers, or what have you—and I can cash in on what I see and hear. Also, one night each week is my night at my home, fourteen miles from the city. On that night, these same men drive that fourteen miles, come snow, rain, or sleet, hell or high water, to play poker here. And more frequently than not they drive home by daylight. They have had a good time, and so have I. Some of them have won money, and some have lost. But, win or lose, I'm ahead. They say it; and I sell it.

My son, Harrison Hendryx, now twenty-two, quit college two years ago with my consent because the faculty would not allow him to drop certain studies and substitute others. He explained that he was writing and selling fiction, and that many specialized classes were doing him no good in his chosen field. But that made no difference—those studies he must have! He quit, and has been selling fiction successfully ever since.

So, to sum up, it is my belief that anyone with a working knowledge of English should be able to turn out salable fiction if he possesses a typewriter, a lead pencil, some paper, a knowledge of the people he intends to write about, a certain amount of diligence, a tolerant and long suffering wife who is also a good critic—and has imagination.

THE
HALFADAY CREEK
LIBRARY

JAMES B. HENDRYX

James B. Hendryx's classic series returns to print! The author of more than 50 novels and anthologies, he's best known for his characters set around the outlaw community of Halfaday Creek in the Yukon. Set during the Gold Rush of the late 1890s, Hendryx penned over a hundred stories featuring these characters over the span of 25 years for a variety of pulp magazines.

Now, Altus Press has committed to return these to print. Using the original pulp magazines as the source material, along with the illustrations from their original pulp magazine appearances, these uniform edition books will be augmented with rare material taken from the James B. Hendryx archives held by the Leelanau Historical Society in Leland, MI.

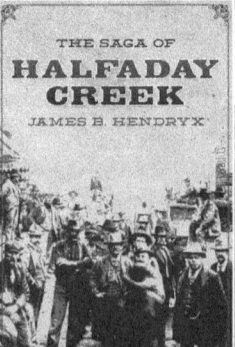

Leelanau Historical Society

Celebrating 150 Years of Leelanau History

Leelanau County was officially established in 1863 when the State of Michigan was a young 26 years old. People were attracted to the natural resources from the beginning—first as a way to earn a living and build a home, and later to enjoy recreation away from the cities. Early settlers arrived on the islands beginning in 1839, while Native Americans populated the Leelanau peninsula until pioneers began exploring the area in 1847. For the next 45 years, the villages known today—and some that are abandoned—were settled. North and South Manitou Islands and the Fox Islands officially joined the county in 1895.

The Leelanau Historical Society was launched in 1957 by a group of residents dedicated to collecting and preserving Leelanau's history. Leland, first established in 1853 and later the county seat, seemed the natural location for the Society. When the old county jail became available in 1959, the museum found its first home. Through generous donations and grants, a new museum was built in 1985 and later expanded.

Today, the collections and archives contain more than 11,000 items. Visitors to the museum learn about Leelanau life and maritime history from exhibits, educational programs and publications. The Society continues to collect, document and preserve items relating to Leelanau history.

203 East Cedar Street, Leland, MI 49654

Tel. (231) 256-7475

info@LeelanauHistory.org

http://www.leelanauhistory.org/